HIGHLAND DRAGON WARRIOR

ISABEL COOPER

D0009804

sourcebooks
casablanca

Published by Sourcebooks Casablanca, an imprint of Sourcebooks, Inc.
P.O. Box 4410, Naperville, Illinois 60567-4410
(630) 961-3900
Fax: (630) 961-2168
sourcebooks.com

Printed and bound in Canada.
MBP 10 9 8 7 6 5 4 3 2 1

ALSO BY ISABEL COOPER

Dark Powers
No Proper Lady
Lessons After Dark

Highland Dragons
Legend of the Highland Dragon
The Highland Dragon's Lady
Night of the Highland Dragon

Dawn of the Highland Dragon
Highland Dragon Warrior

ONE

1304

THE LAND DIDN'T WANT HER THERE.

That was nonsense, and she knew it was nonsense. She knew that she was one woman, unarmed and heavily burdened. She knew that there had been no disasters save the weather, and that her more native traveling companions saw nothing unusual or particularly bad in that. She didn't know whether the land had a consciousness of its own, but she'd never felt anything, whether welcome or hostility, anywhere else she'd been, and it was unlikely now. Sophia knew this.

And still she looked at the road ahead and the countryside around her—white ground, dark rocks, dead-gray sky overhead—and thought, *This place wants me gone*.

She huddled deeper into her cloak and kept walking, following the horses.

"Not much like France, is it?" asked Bayard, coming up behind her with a genially scornful laugh—whether for his soft companions on the road or the forsaken corner of Scotland they'd come to, Sophia wasn't sure. "Don't worry, my ladies. MacAlasdair's odd, but there's none can fault his tables, or his hall for warmth."

Across the back of the packhorse, Sophia exchanged a look with Alice. Neither could actually read the other's expression, given the scarves and cloaks concealing their faces, but Sophia would have wagered that Alice's blond eyebrows were lifted and she was half smiling in a *we'll-see-about-that* manner, just as Alice probably knew Sophia was looking carefully neutral. They'd known each other practically since childhood. They'd also both gotten a look at the castle ahead, the one that reached up into the sky like a vast dark hand.

Hospitable wasn't the word that came to mind. *Warm*, maybe, given everything. Sophia could see that. But welcoming? No.

Worry was pointless. It had been for days, since she and Alice had found Bayard and his company, the one group of traders who were actually going to Loch Arach so early in the year, and had paid probably too much money to join their company. The time for second thoughts might have been even earlier, before they'd sailed to Dover in the first place. Here, there was going forward or there was freezing to death, or perhaps starving. Neither she nor Alice would last long in the wild.

Sophia ran her hands quickly over the packs on her horse's back, checking for broken glass or slipped padding, a habit of such long duration that she had to fight to keep it from becoming absentminded. She straightened her spine as they approached the castle, smiled politely at the guard who came out from the gatehouse, and thought, *This isn't the first time I've been unwelcome. We live through these things.*

All the same, her stomach was small and huddled, and she felt the smile pulling on her face, too heavy for the muscles there to hold easily. She was suddenly glad of the cold, that her cloak might hide the better part of her face and that her hands might shake without anyone knowing the true reason. And when they'd crossed the drawbridge and the portcullis had descended behind them, she couldn't help stopping and looking back over her shoulder.

The sun set early in winter, earlier still in the Highlands, and there was barely any of it to begin with. She saw the light at the mountains' edge, sullen red against the gathering dark. She tried to remember that she was a scholar and a sensible woman, that she had a purpose, and that the journey would hopefully have a reward.

She tried very hard not to think about blood.

Inside was better. It shouldn't have been—now escape would be even more difficult—but the mind didn't always do the tricks one wished, responding instead to stupid cues like scent and sound. The courtyard of Castle MacAlasdair was darker, colder, and emptier than the streets of Lille or London, but it held stock and people, more of them in one place than Sophia had encountered for weeks. Even the odor of cattle and the shrieking of an angry infant sent subtle waves of reassurance to the base of her mind.

"Civilization," said Alice, echoing Sophia's thoughts. "Such as we'll get here."

"Be kind."

"Why? We're not speaking French or English, and none of them have Hebrew."

"It's certainly good I brought you along," said Sophia, shaking her head and smiling, "since you know everything."

"I know if you're not inside before I've found a place for us, I'll come drag you in by the ear."

"If anything breaks, there's not as much point in us being here," said Sophia, retreading the steps of their old and comfortable argument. "And it'll be harder getting home."

"If you freeze to death, of course, that will be much more helpful," said Alice. She followed Bayard into the great hall while Sophia went to the stables with a few of the other travelers.

Naturally, she didn't have the time or space to unpack completely, but she settled her packs as carefully as she could before handing her horse off to one of the men of the castle—like most, a dark, bearded fellow in a draped length of red-and-blue-plaid wool, who watched her with the distant curiosity she'd gotten at a dozen inns and cottages. At first, the scrutiny had made Sophia twitchy. Then she'd gotten used to it. They couldn't tell anything about her; she looked and dressed like any other woman. They just hadn't seen anyone new for months.

She got the same kind of looks as she made her way back across the courtyard. Nobody stopped to stare—they had their duties, and it was cold out—but even in the dying light, she saw a few glances back and forth, and caught unfamiliar words that nonetheless had familiar tones. *Who's that? Oh, she's with the traders. They've just come in. French, I think.*

Gossip was the same everywhere, as far as she could tell, especially gossip in winter. That was another reassurance.

Within the great hall, the smells were much better, objectively: roast meat and fresh bread, oil from the torches on the walls, and smoke from the fire in the great hearth. Humanity was in there too, but the smell was not nearly as bad as it had been on the ship coming over, or even in some of the inns. The hall was a decent size, and perhaps thirty people sat at the table within, halfway through supper from the look of it.

"Lucky girl," said Bayard, slipping up by Sophia's side as she stood and wrestled with her damp cloak. "You missed being presented."

"I thought he was hospitable." Sophia glanced up toward the high table, a place not very distinguished in this particular castle. A tall man with tawny hair sat at its head.

Between the struggle with wool and the pages serving food, she couldn't make out any more.

"Wrong MacAlasdair. Lord Dougal—Douglas…however they pronounce it—hosted us last time, and the times before, but he's not back from their damned war yet. This is Cathal, one of the sons."

"Oh." In theory, a son would work just as well for her purposes, at least if what she'd heard was correct. Bayard's voice was not promising, though. "Doesn't he—"

"Don't know. Didn't have much to do with him before. He's not in a good mood now, though. I'll swear that."

"I see."

"Ah, don't worry overmuch," said Bayard, and patted her on the shoulder. "He did say we could stay the night, and he's willing to talk with us tomorrow. I'd think he'd be in a much better mood for a prettier face than mine."

Sophia reminded herself that Bayard meant well.

The people around her seemed in decent spirits, at least. Not knowing the language—it seemed to happen far back in the throat, mostly—she couldn't tell much from the conversation, but they didn't have the faces or the manners of people who feared their lord. She took what heart she could from that and let Bayard guide her to the high table.

"He's treating us well, bad mood or no," she whispered on her way.

"None of us speak Gaelic. He knows that…or has reasoned it out."

"Ah," said Sophia, and then she was bowing before Cathal MacAlasdair.

Up close, he was… Well, he was a soldier, and it showed. When he rose out of courtesy, he was almost a foot taller than her, his chest and shoulders broad and thick with muscle. His jaw was square; his nose had been broken at least once; and beneath the blue wool tunic he wore and the blue-and-red plaid draped across his chest, one shoulder was thick with what Sophia thought were probably bandages. Good cloth and fur trim on the tunic said *knight* rather than *common soldier* but otherwise this was a man who spent his life fighting.

His eyes were bright green, almost like new grass, a shade she'd never seen in eyes before. It was the first sign Sophia had that she might have found what she was seeking—that the rumors might have truth to them.

She caught her breath.

"You're French as well?" he asked, using the language more easily than she'd expected, though with a rough burr of an accent.

"Yes," Sophia said. There would be time to explain the whole truth later, if things went well. If they didn't, it wouldn't matter. "My lord. Thank you for your hospitality."

"You're welcome to it. The roads are dangerous, especially in winter. Eat, pray, as you wish. When you tire, one of the maids will show you and your friend to beds." Cathal looked her over quickly, without heat or even the curiosity his servants had displayed. Even as she sat down, he was turning back to Bayard. "You were describing your wares."

That was that. The conversation turned to prices and supplies, leaving Sophia behind.

She didn't mind, exactly. It was enough work figuring out what she could eat—picking out onions, turnips, herring, and bread for herself, unobtrusively slipping the beef to the dogs—that she was glad not to have to put more thought into conversation, and her brain felt half frozen anyhow. Still, it wasn't a promising start.

"I'm not sure," Alice murmured, passing the wine cup

and leaning over, "whether he learned manners from a goat or a toad, but I don't envy you a bit either way."

Sophia stifled laughter. "It's not what we're used to."

"Thank goodness."

It was the *I don't envy you* that lingered. Sophia didn't mind Cathal's manners for themselves. As an omen of things to come, not quite so much.

A still-romantic part of her was surprised that she had an appetite. The rest, the scholar for fifteen years, would have expected nothing else, given the cold outside and the scarce rations they'd been on for the last few days. When she could eat from a dish, she helped herself generously— and wished she could have fooled herself about the meat.

Occasionally Bayard tried to redirect the conversation, to bring her and Alice in, but Cathal never made more than a cursory effort, and Bayard was a man of business. If his host and potential customer wanted to focus on the price of pepper, then the price of pepper would be the topic at hand. He already *had* Alice and Sophia's money, after all. Cathal's was less of a sure thing.

By the end of the meal, Alice was looking both vexed and bored, but she put a hand on Sophia's shoulder as they rose and drew her aside. "Shall I come with you?"

"No. If he'll speak at all, it'll be in private."

"I'm certain," Alice said. "And if he offers you insult or grows violent—"

"Then I'll scream." For all the good it might do. She didn't need to say that, and neither did Alice. They'd been walking into the lion's den all along, and they knew it. "But he doesn't seem the sort, and he doesn't seem interested."

In a way—a way that Sophia would never have said aloud, even to Alice—that had been a disappointment. She didn't want to put that particular pawn on the board, wanted to squirm with discomfort thinking about it, and yet…it would have been another option, although a distasteful one.

"I'll be all right," she said.

Standing at the door to his rooms, hand still raised from knocking, Sophia still wasn't sure she'd spoken the truth. Behind the door she heard footsteps. Then Cathal jerked it open and fixed her with a surprised glare. "Is something wrong?"

"No," she said, talking around the heartbeat she could feel in her throat. "I wanted to speak with you in private."

He still wore his plaid, but his fur-trimmed mantle was off, and his hair was disheveled. Sophia didn't see a woman in the room beyond, which was perhaps the only thing that saved her from death by embarrassment when Cathal spoke again. "I'm not looking for a wife, and I don't need a leman just now. You should go back to bed. I won't tell anyone you were here."

If he *had* propositioned her, if he'd even cast those emerald eyes down the length of her body before he'd spoken, Sophia would have been less humiliated. "I wasn't…*offering*!" she gasped, floundering for a few seconds for the last word. "I—"

"No? I ask your pardon then," he said, though it was clear he didn't care whether he received it or not.

Sophia had prepared a speech, a well-reasoned argument that subtly disclosed what she knew and what she was asking. It might have stuck in her mind through fear. Embarrassment and exasperation were another story.

"I heard that your family could turn into dragons," she said with enough presence of mind to lower her voice. "I have several reliable sources. And if that's true, I was hoping that you could help me."

TWO

IN FAITH, IT WAS AN UNEXPECTED TURN TO THE EVENING.

Cathal didn't ask what more Sophia had heard, or whom she'd heard it from. The MacAlasdairs didn't cry what they were from the battlements, but there were men who knew. He knew things about others too—the Welsh lords whose bloodlines were thick with sorcery, the English lady from better times who could start fires with a squint and a sigh—and so it went, in a damn web spreading the length and breadth of the world, for all he could say. Nobody had vowed silence on these matters or any other. King Edward the Longshanks and his advisors would find the knowledge no surprise.

Knowing that, Cathal didn't roar or snarl, as the lady clearly half expected from her expression, but cocked his head, settled back into his chair, and studied his new guest at more length as he beckoned her into the room.

As mortals went, she was somewhat younger than middle age, older than maidenhood. Hair: dark, pinned back beneath a sadly faded wimple. Eyes: brown, huge in her small, pointed face. Skin: golden, even in winter. Figure: short, amply curved, small-waisted. Not bad. Had she caught him five months ago, when he'd been able to see past the fog of weariness and worry, he'd have taken her up on the offer she hadn't made—and probably would have been slapped as a result. Dress: black wool gown, amber surcoat, both also the worse for wear but, he thought, of good quality originally. No jewelry. Voice: low, quiet, with a native's command of French but a slight accent.

His father or Douglas would have drawn much from her appearance. Cathal thought that she was probably decently wellborn and well-off, but any further meaning slipped away, too subtle for him to grasp.

"What kind of aid requires a dragon?" he asked and then, before she could respond, raised a hand. "I warn you now… I kill for my family and my people these days. That's all."

Wide eyes went narrow at that, but only for a moment. "Do you…" Sophia started, then sucked a breath in through her teeth and smiled with obvious effort. "I thank you for the warning. I've no need for men-at-arms. In truth, it isn't you I need precisely."

"The night's gone sore long already," he said, although he didn't entirely want her to leave him to the castle accounts, nor to the thoughts that crept in around the edges of the numbers. "Speak plainly, pray."

"I want one of your scales," she said, and although she didn't seem aware of it, her hands clasped together in front of her. "I would welcome more."

"Ah." Matters were becoming slightly clearer. Again he wished for Douglas, or perhaps Agnes, who'd always been the best of them where sorcery was concerned. "Enchantress, are ye?"

Sophia shook her head. "I wouldn't make any such claim. I study alchemy. I am…" She wet her lips. "By the standards I know, I am very good. There are experiments, properties of metals and stones, that I believe the scales of a dragon would bring out. Some of them would be most helpful to…to people."

"So I'd think." Cathal pushed his chair back and stretched his legs out in front of him, folded his arms behind his head, and asked, "Which people? There are a few men in London I'd rather not be *most helpful* to. We've had a war recently. You might have heard."

"I have," she said, and Cathal watched her eyes darken, so that the fire behind him reflected in their depths. "And believe me, I'm no fonder of the English king than you are."

If she'd been a man, she'd have spat after the title. Being a woman, she only curled her lip, either truly passionate in her loathing or a decent actress. Cathal considered her speech and her clothing, flipped back pages in his mind, and asked dubiously, "French?" She was young to be bitter about that war. Families handed grudges down, but he didn't think a secondhand grievance would be so sharp.

It took a moment, a glance over her shoulder, and a long look into his face before Sophia answered. "Jewish. And English, once, before he exiled us to serve his own greed."

"Oh," Cathal said.

English news reached even him slowly and patchily. He hadn't remembered the edict. He wasn't sure if he'd even been in England for it. There'd been a few years in Aragon about then, a blur of tournaments in the sunshine and wine in the shade. Back then, he'd asked little more of life.

Sighing, he came back from his reverie to find Sophia watching him, barely breathing. For the first time, he *thought* of the edict and of the stories that had reached him from time to time before. She'd bared her neck to the blade by telling him. While he'd reminisced, she'd waited to hear what he would do with her life.

"English stupidity," he said gruffly and shook his head.

"Common enough to most countries," she replied. Her voice never rose, and the motion of her shoulders as she shrugged was slight. "We were lucky. My mother had relatives in France. Others were less so. Only a few could take more than what they could carry. And the journey was hard.

Not everyone survived. There are more ways to kill than a sword's edge. So..." Another small shrug. Cathal got the impression that it was all she would permit herself. "You see."

"Yes." He even thought she was telling the truth, as far as he could be sure of that. "Do you want vengeance?"

Sophia laughed shortly. "I *want* vengeance, yes. I *want* justice, and a good harvest, and a fine horse to ride home on, and a bag of gold to spend when I'm there." She unclasped her hands and touched the corner of her wimple, as if to push back hair that was still covered. "*Wanting* doesn't matter except to children and lords, Sir Cathal, and I'm a great distance from either. What I *seek* is protection...and understanding. Knowledge."

"And the scales of a dragon will provide those?"

"They could. What notes I've read aren't clear, nor do they cover all they might—nothing ever does, I find—but all of alchemy is about transformation. Metal or stone, mind or body, it's all one thing changing into another." Her face lit as she talked, revealing the inner fire of the scholar on a pet subject. "The dragon has always been the symbol for the power to change."

"How apt," said Cathal.

"Yes." Sophia smiled at him, for the first time with more than politeness. "Yes, and perhaps that was because one of our early scholars knew one of your ancestors, but there might be more to it. The notes I've found suggest that the body of a dragon would have great catalytic power, could allow an alchemist to achieve great things, perhaps might even make possible experiments that otherwise could not come to fruition. And—"

"And so I should thank God you decided on scales and not my heart."

"You—" Once more she bit back a comment. "It seemed

a request even less likely to find favor with you. And I'm no murderess."

"And I would have to have one," Cathal said, and was pleased to see a blush spread over Sophia's face. He'd guessed, or at least come close to guessing, what she'd stopped herself from saying.

"I'm sure that's not for me to say."

"I'm sure."

Thinking, he looked down. The accounts were drifts of parchment and ink, as meaningless as the snow outside. His shoulder ached, a reminder that he was far from the only one with more-than-human gifts, and that the other side was amply endowed.

As always, with each complaint of slow-healing muscles and still-raw nerves, he thought, *Could have been worse*.

"What are you offering?" he asked.

The blush deepened. She was remembering how he'd opened this conversation. With such prompting, he thought of the exchange too, and of the possibilities he'd denied. Desire sparked briefly within him this time, tightening his groin for a moment—but no. He was tired, she was no serving girl to take such things lightly, and they'd both already dismissed that possibility.

"My skills," she said. "With herbs and with potions. I'm no doctor, nor even a midwife, but those in both professions have found my remedies useful at times. Perhaps you have need of such services here…and if you don't now, you may. Winter is a time for sickness."

"Any season is," said Cathal.

He stood up. Sophia caught her breath at the sudden motion, or maybe at his height, but she didn't flinch. Cathal came around the desk and stood in front of her, looking down into her face as if he could read an answer there.

As usual with augury, nothing useful came. There was only his judgment.

"We may strike a bargain," he said. "Here is my end. You carry out your experiments here. You may take the results home, but I'll not risk you traveling with anything so connected to my person. While you're here, you provide what aid the castle and the village require of you."

"Yes, gladly," she said, knowing there was more and waiting for it.

"And you go home after you accomplish one thing for me...or prove that you cannot."

Her eyes met his, wide and serious. "I would need to know the task."

"You will," said Cathal. "Come with me."

Castle MacAlasdair had never in Cathal's life lacked room. Alasdair himself had built for a legion or more of men-at-arms, not to mention the brood he'd sired on various women, and his work had lasted for generations, with occasional reinforcement when one of his descendants was in a generous mood. Now, with Cathal alone of the family at home, halls full of closed doors marked a half-dozen disused bedrooms. Playing the generous host with Sophia and her friend had been easy.

Finding the room at the end of one hall had been easy too...the only easy thing about the whole damn business.

As always, he braced himself before he opened the door, readying his muscles as he'd always done before the breastplate of his armor settled into place, telling his body it could take the weight.

On the other side, candlelight flickered in the darkness. A shadow rose within it and came to meet them. As it neared the door, it became a middle-aged woman, brown hair streaked with more gray now and face more lined than it had been a year ago. "Sir Cathal," she said and curtsied. "He's asleep."

"I would hope," he said. "I'm going to show him to our guest."

Sithaeg allowed herself no expression. Cathal wasn't cruel enough to even hint at hope, and she wasn't cruel enough to expect it. "Aye," she said and stepped out of the way. She watched Sophia, though, and Cathal knew she was as helpless not to look, and to wonder, as he had been to speculate.

Thinking not of propriety but only of darkness and the limits of mortal sight, he took Sophia's hand. It lay stiff and cold in his, but she didn't pull it back or protest, just allowed him to lead her across the small room to the large bed in the center. One candle flickered on the table beside the bed, casting feeble light over bottles and glasses and even less over the figure who lay under the blankets.

"Fergus," Cathal said under his breath. "My friend since he was little more than a boy. Close as my brother or closer, in his way." His father would have called that folly, to so value a creature who'd live perhaps a quarter of his life.

His father wasn't there.

"What ails him?"

There was sympathy in her voice, but Cathal was used to sympathy. He seized on the other thing he heard: the curiosity, the eagerness that said *here might be a job to do*.

"Look closely." Cathal picked up the candle in one hand, cupping the other around the flame. It burned almost against his skin, a friendly little creature and a relief here. "Look at his jaw. The sides of his neck."

He moved the candle closer and heard Sophia gasp.

Good eyes, he thought, *and quick reasoning.* She'd seen the translucence at the edge of Fergus's skin, how first the color left and then one could see the pillows through the faintest haze. "God's teeth!" she said, barely keeping her voice down in her shock.

"Touch him. At the edge. He won't feel it," Cathal said with a certainly he'd have given anything not to feel.

Gingerly, she did, and drew her hand back almost at once, staring back and forth between it, Fergus, and Cathal. Although her mouth had fallen open from the start, for a few minutes she got nothing out of it. Only after working her jaw did she manage, "It…my finger went through him. He's…*dissolving*?"

"You're the scholar."

Sophia caught her breath. "You wish me to cure him."

"I *wish*," he whispered with a faint twist of a smile as he remembered her speech earlier, "him cured. Our bargain would be that you try until you determine that you can't."

"And you'd believe me if I said so?"

"I'll weigh the evidence."

She took another look at Fergus, bending closer this time, sniffing the air above him, and frowning. "I've seen nothing like this in my life, nor heard of it in any accounts," she said, and then straightened and looked at Cathal. "But someone once said as much of any malady, did they not? And I did speak of discovery. I will do my best."

"Thank you," he said almost tonelessly. Like Sithaeg, he couldn't let himself hope. He took her hand to lead her back out of the room.

This time, she resisted.

"I'll need to make an examination," she said when Cathal turned to her, "and I'll need to know how this came about."

"Tomorrow," he said.

THREE

"WELL, HOW DID THINGS FALL OUT?"

Alice had always known how to pick her time. Right now, it was first thing in the morning, just when Sophia was bent over the basin splashing cold water on her face. She grunted her first response.

"I'm sorry, I thought I was asking a human being."

"Nobody human is as awake as you are at this hour," said Sophia, moving aside to let her friend wash. They'd managed to get the room to themselves—and a finer room than most people gave to travelers, with bright tapestries on the walls and thick rugs on the floor—so she spoke freely while she dressed. "He said yes. But we're staying on."

She explained the situation to Alice in a few quick sentences, struck as she talked by how little *she* knew of the details. It had been late when she and Sir Cathal had reached their agreement, and Sophia had been glad enough to put off further discussion. Now, under Alice's shrewd gaze, she wondered how much more there was to find out, and how dire the situation might truly be. Putting up her hair, she fumbled with the pins.

"Oh, come here," said Alice, holding out her hands. As she'd done a hundred times before, she dressed Sophia's hair with a quick efficiency that bordered on painful. "It's as well," she said, after an assortment of thoughtful sounds. "I didn't much like the idea of going right back again when we've just got here. Best you wait until spring before you finish up, if you ask me."

"It might well be longer," said Sophia. "And that's if I succeed at all."

"Have more faith in yourself. I don't mind anyway. This seems like a well-kept place, for all its lord's surliness. Plenty of food, decent cooking, and no fleas. I don't know how they manage *that*."

"Hmm," said Sophia. Now that she thought of it, she didn't notice even one of the itchy bites that usually accompanied a stay anywhere remotely warm, and the room was quite comfortable in that regard. A fire had been roaring away in the fireplace since before she'd woken—and she hadn't noticed anyone coming in to build it. "Magic?"

"Then more people should be sorcerers. Why don't you do this sort of thing?"

"Because there's no elixir that'll let me start fires from my bed. Not that I know of. Whatever magic Sir Cathal...or his family...knows might be different."

Alice patted Sophia on the shoulder and stepped back. "Lucky for you, I suppose, or you'd have had nothing to bargain with. Still, see if you can't get him to teach you while you're here. I'd dearly love never to scratch a flea bite again."

"I can't imagine Sir Cathal teaching anyone magic," said Sophia, remembering the blunt speech from last night and the frank-to-the-point-of-rudeness way he'd eyed her. She felt herself flush again, wondered what he'd thought when he made his...inspection...and shook her head quickly. "Or anything else."

"He didn't try anything untoward, did he?" Alice asked, reading Sophia's face carefully. "I thought you'd have told me if he had, but—"

"No. And I would have. And it wouldn't matter. He seemed to have little time for, um, *untoward*, though. He didn't seem to have much time in general."

Knowing that, Sophia half expected Cathal to put off their meeting and his explanation. Even had he been more eager to tell her the history of Fergus's condition than he obviously was, Sophia assumed that other matters would come first. She'd hardly finished her bread and ale an hour later, though, when he appeared—not the page she'd expected, but Cathal himself, walking up to her side so quietly that she didn't look up from her reading until he cleared his throat.

She flinched. She also squeaked. She was halfway off the bench, eating knife protectively in one hand, when she recognized him.

Cathal's gaze never wavered. He looked at her as if jumpy women were common facets of his day, as mayhap they were. "You'll come to no harm here," he said evenly, once Sophia'd had a chance to catch her breath.

"Of course," she said. She smiled politely all the way up into that chiseled face. "Can I be of assistance, my lord?"

"You wanted the chance to examine Fergus and receive a history of his state. I'll give you the second first. Walk with me."

"Of course." She closed her book and picked it up, tucking it under her arm. The weight of it was reassuring. "Where are we going?"

"Where I need to go. There are…" He waved an impatient hand. "Tasks. Always. I might as well explain on the way. It's no secret."

"And the examination? I'll need my supplies—"

He turned and barked a name, which sounded a bit like *Martin*, only with more rising and falling around the vowels. A dark-haired boy nearby looked up and answered in Gaelic.

"Go to—" Cathal began, switching to English and glancing at Sophia.

"The stables," she said, slipping between languages with a few seconds' thought. "The bay mare at the far end. My instruments will be in the pack on the left. They're glass, for the most part."

"Aye, so take good care. Bring them to Fergus's room," said Cathal, with a stern look at Possibly-Martin.

"And if you've a surgeon or a physician, I'll need to take blood."

"None here over the winter." Cathal flicked his hand again, dismissing the page. "Don't fret yourself. I can open a vein without killing the man it belongs to, if I must."

Already he was walking. Sophia hurried toward his side, crossing the rushes and heading through the door nearest the high table. Now, a little before midmorning, the cooking smells coming from under the door weren't as strong as the smell of burning wood. "How long has he been, er, the way he is?" she asked.

"Two months." His accent wasn't nearly so strong as that of other Scotsmen she'd met, even the others who spoke English, but the first word still came out *twa*. "Best start at the beginning. You ken the war?"

"More or less. The details..." She lifted her free hand and let it fall.

"No need of them. We were fighting the English... Aye, some ways from here," he added at her surprised look. She'd not heard that the war had reached such a remote part of the Highlands, nor had Loch Arach the look of a village that had recently seen combat. "I was at the war then, and my sister managing all of this."

"Your sister?"

"One of them, aye." He glanced down at her and flashed a grim half-smile, one that admitted no questions. "She's taken my place now, and I hers. So then. We were a ways from here on a fair desolate patch of ground, and there was a troop of the English. Not a normal part of the army, I should think. I'll give Longshanks that much. Whatever sort of devil he may be, I've heard nothing like that of him."

"Like what?"

"Ah."

She didn't immediately get an answer, because their journey through the kitchens had stopped in front of a man with red hair, a large beard, and an air of officious bad temper—probably a butler or a steward. He glanced from her to Cathal, blinked, and then asked a question in Gaelic. Cathal replied with what sounded like several of his own, and the conversation lasted an incomprehensible few minutes.

Sophia took a look around. Castle kitchens had never really been a part of her life. She couldn't quite fit the modest domain of her mother and sisters, nor even the kitchens in the grander parts of town, into the same word as this sprawling, busy maze. On one side of the room, men in bloody tunics were cutting up what looked like half a pig, while a woman almost as covered with flour kneaded bread some distance away, scolding more pages as she did so. Everyone was moving. Sophia tucked her elbows closer to her sides and took a step closer to Cathal, trying to get out of the way.

Naturally, that was when he finished talking and turned toward her. For an awkward moment, her nose practically hit his chest. There was a great deal of chest, she noticed again, and it still all looked to be solid muscle. Hurriedly, she stepped back. "My apologies."

"Think nothing of it. This way. And take a cloak." He pulled one from a peg beside the kitchen door and tossed it to her. "You chill easily."

"I do no such thing," Sophia said, though she was wrapping the cloak around herself while she spoke.

"You…humans. Mortals."

"Oh. Well." She looked down at the cloak, which smelled like onions. "Whose is this?"

Another name, this one a bit like *George*. "He'll not leave until long after we're back. Not with dinner as it is." They stepped outside, where the world was clear and blue and brittle. After what Cathal had said, Sophia forced herself not to gasp at the chill of it. "The men were vicious."

It took her a moment to realize he'd stopped talking about the cold or the cloak. "The English?"

"Aye. Past what I'd expect of men, even in war. One or two of them didna' seem quite like men at all. Their faces…shifted. There were too many shadows to them. I could say no more, not with any certainty. And their leader was a wizard. Is."

"A wizard?" For a man not entirely human, Cathal spoke very generally. *Wizard* could have meant her uncle Gento, gray-bearded and ink-stained, or Merlin Ambrosius, or Sophia herself, though it embarrassed her to even make the comparison. "How do you mean?"

Cathal shrugged. "He threw fire at us. It came from a wand…one that looked to have been a bone once, though I was never close enough to look very well. I took no hurt from it, of course. I changed shape to handle the shadow-men." He sighed, sending a cloud of steam out into the frigid air. "That impressed him."

His voice suggested that both wizards and men made of shadow were, if not usual, at least not wholly a shock to him. "Do they have many such forces?" Sophia asked. "The English?"

"Enough magic to hold us off. Nothing quite like this. Not that I've seen. A moment."

A smithy sat at the corner of the courtyard, and Cathal

swung into it. Sophia followed, glad to feel the warmth of the forge but carefully keeping both her cloak and skirts out of the way. The smith himself looked up once, spoke to Cathal, and then went on speaking even as he turned back to the horseshoe he was hammering out. His apprentice, crouched before the fire with a pair of bellows, spent more time looking at Sophia—at least until the smith himself directed a growl the boy's way.

Looking out, Sophia saw that the smithy and stables were just a few of the buildings sheltered behind the castle walls. A covered well was near the smithy itself; opposite that, another low building whose purpose she couldn't identify; and across the way she caught the gleam of stained glass and guessed that there lay the chapel. Off in a corner, snow-covered hedges marked out a square of barren earth—a garden, when the weather allowed?

It's like a tiny city, she thought, and the idea was unsettling. She'd known the idea of a keep, of course, but walking through the reality brought it home. If Cathal and his people had so much behind the castle walls, it was probably because they could get it nowhere else so quickly, nor be assured of their safety in the process. Out here, the castle was a lone flame in the darkness.

She shivered, which she could have told herself was the cold, and then swallowed, which she couldn't, and fortunately Cathal chose that moment to start walking again.

"What did he do? The…magician?"

"Made me an offer." Cathal's jaw tightened. "Not a bad one, by his standards. Not…" He shook his head, golden-brown hair shifting in the cold breeze. "He said they could use a creature like me. Pointed out the benefits. Then I cut his arm off."

"That would be an answer, yes?"

"It was."

Passing the stables, they headed for a door near the gatehouse. Cathal went a few yards without speaking, and Sophia was nerving herself to ask another question when he began again.

"The arm…crawled. It must have. But the word sounds slow, and it was quick. It'd flown some ways when I struck—they do betimes, aye, if your blow's strong enough, and I was sore angered—and it wrapped its fingers around Fergus's leg. The stump of the arm was still bleeding."

Sophia put a hand over her mouth, stopping the small sound of revolted surprise that she couldn't suppress any other way.

"The magician said something. I didn't know the language—and I've Latin and Arabic both. Fergus fell down screaming. The magician said he'd melt like the snow in spring, did I not come and join him. His name, he said, was Valerius."

"I doubt it," Sophia said without thinking. Cathal turned toward her, eyes sharp, and she shrugged. "At least, I doubt that his mother or her priest would know it. At least it wasn't *Maximus*. Or *Rex*, though I suppose Edward the Longshanks would have had a few things to say about *that*."

Mirth stole onto Cathal's face, not softening its lines but warming it from within. His smile was wide, and his teeth surprisingly white for a man in this country, though perhaps not for one of his blood. "I hadna' considered that view of it."

"I could be wrong. He *could* be a very well-preserved Roman. Or have a very pretentious family," Sophia said, unable to resist a smile as she spoke.

"Aye, well, they'd have to have *something* amiss with them," Cathal said, and then the warmth faded from his expression. "As it may be. I went for his head. One of his shades went for me. Gave me this." He patted his shoulder, over the bandage. "And by the time I'd dealt with that wee bastard, his leader was gone. Vanished into the shadows, my men said."

"And since then…" Sophia let the sentence trail off.

Cathal nodded. "As you saw."

He opened the door and held it so she could go through. Passing him was like walking by a fire. Sophia resisted the urge to hold out her hands. Beyond, a short hall led to a winding stone staircase, just broad enough for one person to climb at a time. She followed Cathal, glad of the chance to think without speaking for a time.

Directing her thoughts required a greater effort than she was accustomed to. With Cathal walking just before her, she spent some time noticing the shift of muscles beneath plaid and tunic while he walked, the straightness of his shoulders, and the lift of his tawny head. In the dimness of the castle stairs, he stood out like a flame.

By the time they came to a landing and he opened another door, she'd collected her thoughts as much as she thought she was likely to manage. "I've never tried to counter a spell before," she began in the interest of honesty. "I *have* read one or two passages about it, and some more notes, but I can't say I ever paid as much attention to that as I did to other things. I'll see what I can remember, and I have a few books with me. Does the castle have a library?"

"Aye. I can't swear to all its contents."

"If you'll permit it, I'll see if anything there can aid me." The MacAlasdairs were a family of dragons, and at least parts of the castle seemed to run on magic. Somebody might have bothered studying it, or even writing it down. "You would have told me if the village had a magician… even a cunning man, or a witch nobody talks about?"

She hadn't gotten her hopes up and therefore was not too disappointed when Cathal shook his head. "We've a midwife who knows a bit of herbs."

"She might be helpful. I'll need to talk with her, though that'll be later. And I'll need a room…not to sleep, but where I can experiment."

"We've rooms enough. Especially now. The one by Fergus is empty."

Sophia hesitated, uncertain about asking for too much, but then practicality stepped in. "A more isolated chamber would work better. There are explosions from time to time."

"Naturally," Cathal said. "I'll find you a place. For the present…here," he said and opened the door from the previous night.

Now the room was light enough for Sophia to see her bags on a table by the hearth. She could see Fergus's face too, in more detail than she'd been able to before. He didn't look unusual: brown hair, square jaw, pale skin. He would have blended in very well with the rest of the men in the castle, if he'd been awake and moving. Stillness, even more so than his growing dissolution, distinguished him.

"He's young," she said, unthinking.

"They're all young," said Cathal.

With nothing to say in response, Sophia turned from Fergus to the table where her supplies lay. Already she was making lists in her head: the necessary tests, the herbs she had and those she might even be able to get in the Scottish winter, and the small vials of ground metal or stone. She'd have to be careful of her resources, she thought, remembering the sense of isolation in the courtyard.

She'd have to be careful of many things.

FOUR

Cathal had bled men before. Such times had been rare and unskilled: he'd spent his manhood as a knight, not a physician. Yet war was war. The aftermath of battle left more wounded men than hands to heal them, and the days and weeks after led to fever as often as not. He'd cut arrows out of flesh a time or two; he'd opened veins when that was necessary. The process was faintly familiar. He also was covering no new ground. Bleeding had been their first thought for a cure, and the cut on Fergus's arm was only half healed.

It was still hard, and Cathal was glad of it. In the work of remembering which veins were minor, of tying them off and passing the blade of his knife through the candle flame, of making sure not to overlook any step, he could almost forget the man on whom he was working.

Conscious, Fergus had never been stoic. His profanity when injured had made priests shake their heads and brought pages and squires to listen and further their education. Later he'd go to confession and truly repent, but that never had stopped him the next time he'd taken a wound during battle or had a tooth pulled. Profanity in English, Gaelic, and French had blended, coming from his mouth at a speed and volume that would have been a miracle if not for the subject matter.

Now he lay soundlessly compliant. Picking up Fergus's wrist, Cathal felt it as boneless as wax, even where the flesh was still solid. He swore himself before making the cut, but only inside his head.

Sophia knelt and held a small vessel—blue pottery, incongruously domestic-looking—under Fergus's arm, catching the blood. Her hands stayed steady, her eyes focused, and her face showed no sign of distress, only concentration and thought. Men might have been surprised, had they not grown up with Cathal's sisters—or not seen the field after a battle, when the women who followed an army often did as much to save its men as any of the physicians.

Cathal was not surprised, but still watched her: the brown-wimpled top of her bent head, the faint lines on her forehead, and the way her dark eyebrows slanted inward, then the straightness of her shoulders and her spine, one unbent line down to the floor where she knelt. Although far from angular of body, she still spoke to him of right angles and clear paths, order and calm—the opposite of the way Fergus was fading at the edges.

"Enough," she said finally, and the sound was almost surprising.

Cathal turned to binding up the wound. He'd send word to Sithaeg that it would need further attention, but the woman should have a chance to eat first, and to sleep as much as she'd ever seemed to since the curse had taken her son. "Will we need to do this again?"

"I fear it's likely," Sophia said. She rose to her feet, holding the bowl carefully. "This is only a start. I'll test it with the metals, see if he lacks any elements, and then..." She shook her head. "But I doubt you want the details. Let me then say that this is for investigation. I may yet need more blood for the healing itself, *if* I find a way to carry that out."

"Very well," Cathal said. "And I know that this is chancy. You don't have to keep warning me."

She had set the bowl down on the table with the rest of her things while Cathal was speaking, and she turned then to look at him, brown eyes wide and grave. "As my lord wishes," she said, "but I think it worth remembering."

"Be assured. My memory is very good."

"I'm glad to hear it," she said, and dropped a curtsy.

Polite, Cathal thought, *careful, and still very dubious.* It probably wasn't worth pressing her. "I'll find you a laboratory," he said. "I'll send word. Go wherever you wish. You might even find an escort to the village if you enjoy the cold."

He left her with those words. Suddenly, he needed to be in that room no longer, nor torn between watching Fergus decline and looking for reassurance from a woman so clearly reluctant to give it. He sought the western tower instead.

Up there, before Cathal had been born, his father had built a turret that rose some little way above the rest of the stone, opening into a small, round chamber. In bygone days, Cathal and his siblings had played there on rainy days, seeing the world spread out below them in a taste of what flying would be like when they grew old enough to change shape. Now the furnishings were old and dusty, and little light came through the shuttered windows. All of that would be easy enough to change.

For the most part, the turret was also isolated, as Sophia had desired for her laboratory. Aside from a few guards on the battlements, most of the castle's residents avoided the western wing since it held nothing for them. The vast majority of the time, that was also true for Cathal himself. It hadn't been the case for his father or his siblings, but they were far away now.

When he'd been a stripling, a few years after those when he'd played in the turret, he had, like his siblings, spent days in the largest room of all those in the western wing.

There strong walls and stronger magic had kept him—and the rest of Loch Arach—safe while he'd learned to master shape-shifting and to keep a mostly human mind while in the dragon's form.

Nearby were other rooms, smaller but no less potent in their own way. Cathal had no doubt of that, yet he'd only had reason to enter two, and one only in times of peril. He'd done so after his encounter with "Valerius." He didn't think that Sophia's presence merited a visit now. He could use slower methods.

Hope never really merited urgency, after all.

Even in summer, messengers rarely reached Loch Arach. Sophia's companions had brought general news with their spices and cloth, but even that news was, at its freshest, weeks out of date. Likewise, the messages Cathal had written for the traders to pass on would perhaps reach their destinations in a month or two.

Pigeons were quicker. Pigeons also needed a permanent target and, like all other animals the MacAlasdairs didn't breed themselves, were unreliable around them at best and often ungovernable. As her children had reached maturity and gone out into the world, Cathal's mother had called on her knowledge and the inhuman side of her own bloodline and had established an alternate method.

On the very top of the western tower, in the middle of a ring of silver-etched runes, Cathal knelt and lit three blue candles. He watched as the flame on each expanded and melded with the candle itself, until three creatures stood before him, each a half-solid blue manikin the height of his ankle. Blank white eyes opened and featureless faces turned toward him, ready for his command.

Cathal drew three letters from the pouch at his belt and handed the first to one of the spirits. "Douglas MacAlasdair."

Douglas would be with Robert the Bruce most likely, far away, discussing a surrender that still made Cathal's lip curl when he thought of it. Last time they'd spoken, Douglas had thought the Bruce was playing a deeper game than he showed, and Cathal had often had reason to trust his older brother's judgment. Better Douglas as an ally in such matters than him; even the thought made his skin itch.

"Moiread MacAlasdair, wherever she is." If William Wallace and John De Soules were still at large, as Bayard had said they were the night before, then Moiread would not be returning soon. She'd been eager to fight. Cathal had joked that she'd have stabbed him herself, had she waited too many months longer. She'd also believed far more strongly than Cathal had and hoped a great deal more.

In the fall of Stirling Castle, Cathal himself had seen only the last convulsion of a slow death, a final blind struggle against a wound that allowed for no more recovery than a slit throat or an opened gut. Before Falkirk, when Philip of France had turned his back, winning had begun to look to Cathal like a child's dream.

He had been wrong before. That didn't look like the case this time.

One spirit waited, the other two having vanished to whatever road they walked. The spirits didn't reach their destinations instantly: sending messages this way took a few days most of the time, weeks when Cathal had been in the Holy Land, and it didn't work at all if one party was on the water. ("Probably something to do with the elements," Agnes had said. "They're creatures of air. Fire or earth would likely stop them too, but why would we spend a week there?")

Cathal passed the remaining letter over. "Artair MacAlasdair."

His father was likely preparing his own forces to come back, perhaps negotiating with Longshanks and the Bruce, always with a set face and a shrug when anyone pressed him, though they might do so in a manner which would have had Cathal drawing his sword long since. *Endurance* was Artair's watchword—it showed in the castle he'd rebuilt, in the wives he'd outlived and the various children he'd sired—and *patience* another.

Rome wasn't built in a day, he'd said often as Cathal had raged against a slight or confinement when young. In the days of the war, when he and Moiread had raged against the English or despaired at setbacks, his father had added to the saying: *and neither did it so fall*.

Perhaps that was easier to say when one had almost seen it. Still, Cathal had remembered the words bitterly over the last few months, thinking of them over and over as he watched Fergus decline.

Rejecting Valerius's offer had been a matter of honor—and probably of wisdom, as sorcerers who waved thighbones around probably made poor allies and worse employers—and Cathal didn't regret it. Nor would he have regretted trying to kill Valerius if he'd done so. He'd killed scores of men through the years, with practicality heated by the passion of battle, nothing more or less.

He'd struck out of rage and offended pride. He knew that. He'd known it in the instant he'd swung his sword. His first thought had been that the wizard would pay for making such an offer, and more for even thinking he'd accept.

Cathal thought he'd meant to kill the man quickly, just

the same. He prayed that he had, in the stunted and half-formed prayers of which he remained capable. And he wondered every day if he was deceiving himself on that score. He was glad he hadn't seen his father's face when he'd told Artair about the curse, even if it had held as little emotion as his voice had. Cathal wondered often enough about *that*, too.

Straightening up, walking to the edge of the battlements, he found a new element introducing itself into his speculation: what Artair would think of his newest guests.

Guest, really.

Alice was a pleasant lass—in a sharp-tongued way wherein she clearly neither liked nor trusted Cathal, and which was really rather to her credit—but she didn't enter his thoughts the way Sophia did, nor did her presence lighten them.

In Fergus's room, doing nothing more yet than a surgeon's everyday work, Sophia had made him think of figures on stained-glass windows. She was gold and darkness in his mind, the shades of fire on a winter's night.

Be wary, he told himself. *Don't justify her warnings; expect no miracles*.

He grew tired of not expecting.

The western tower was sturdy, the sky blue and inviting, and his day's immediate duties were behind him. Cathal straightened his spine, gulped in clear, cold air, and leapt off the tower.

Even now, the moment of free falling was exhilaration and terror, the back of his mind insisting that he could die here even as the rest of him knew otherwise. Then the transformation took over. Suddenly there were wings unfolding from his shoulders—much larger, scaled shoulders now— and air beneath them, bearing him up and taking him away.

FIVE

AFTER FIVE DAYS, SOPHIA HAD MADE MORE PROGRESS than she'd expected at first. She could find her way around the castle by herself.

Fergus's blood was coming along nicely too. She'd set half of what she'd taken aside in a tightly stoppered glass jar—no point in cutting the poor boy open more than she had to—and the calcination stage had gone well. Now seven smaller vessels stood in the room off the western tower, each over heat appropriate to the metal it contained, and she carefully watched as the fluid within bubbled gently.

Colors had not appeared yet, but—she glanced down at the hourglass—it wasn't time.

She had no doubts about her technique, at least. She'd taken more care than she ever had with an experiment before, and nobody could ever have called her haphazard or flighty to begin with. The laboratory helped as well. The room was spacious and well lit, and the heat steadier and more reliable than she would have expected, particularly on short notice. As dearly as she would have loved to work with any of the furnaces she had back home, she'd known she'd have to do without them. The castle's hearth and the various braziers were better than she'd hoped for.

She'd mentioned as much to Cathal the day before. They sat together for meals, as befit the castle's current lord and an apparent gentlewoman, and Sophia was glad of the opportunity to speak a friendly word. For a woman out in the world, her uncle had said, kindness would be better armor than steel, and plain words were their own sort of magic.

Also, she'd wanted to see Cathal smile again, the way he had when she joked about Valerius. The memory made him loom a touch less when Sophia encountered him about the castle. If she was going to stay as long as she might, she'd need more such perspective.

Alas, she'd chosen a poor moment to speak. She hadn't seen the man-at-arms approaching the high table—even in her time there, that happened often—and looking, Alice said later, like a stormy day. Cathal had heard her thanks, but whatever he might have replied had been lost in the storm of Gaelic that came next, and the moment to repeat herself had never come around again.

If that was her greatest disappointment at Loch Arach, Sophia would count herself far luckier than she deserved. She had reminded herself of that later.

Meals often went in such a fashion—or Cathal was simply absent. There was no reason for Sophia to be sorry when that happened, perfunctory and distracted as his conversation often was, and yet she felt the absence, noticed the empty place on the bench, and from time to time wondered where—or what—he was.

Once, she'd paused in her unpacking and gone to look out the tower window, thinking to stretch her back and ease her eyes. In that moment, she'd thought she'd seen a great winged shape far away, and perhaps a glint of blue in the sunlight. She'd leaned her elbows on the windowsill and peered through the hazy, greenish glass, but the shape had vanished, and she hadn't yet gotten up the courage to ask Cathal about it.

If thanking him for the room and its comforts hadn't gotten his attention, maybe *I thought I saw you flying the other day* would. On the other hand, what she'd had of his attention hadn't been entirely comfortable.

On the *other* other hand, if she'd sought comfort, she wouldn't have been spending the winter on a mountain in Scotland.

Sophia eyed the bubbling vials closely, checked the flames under each, and went still when she heard a knock at the door.

"Will anything explode if I come in?" Alice called from the other side.

"I think not."

"You're not quite a comfort in times of uncertainty, you know." When Alice pushed the door open, Sophia saw that she was carrying a small tray with bread, cheese, what looked like eel pie, and a small flask of wine. "You also missed the noon meal."

"I did?" Sophia glanced toward the window, but afternoon light in Scotland wasn't what it had been in Paris, and the glass didn't help. "I'm sorry. You didn't have to bring me anything."

"No. I'm a very generous woman and will doubtless receive a just reward one of these days. But it wasn't my idea. Is this all right," Alice asked, jerking her chin at a clear space on one of the tables lining the room, "or will you turn into a rat?"

"I'll be no more likely to than usual. Not your idea?"

Alice pulled one of the two stools up and broke off a piece of cheese. "Whatever else I can say about Sir Cathal, he's not a blind man. He asked me where you were. I said you came and went without leave from me, but if I knew you, you were probably up in this tower messing about with fire and silver and turning your hair green—"

"My hair's never turned green."

"—and he had one of the pages fetch this. He was going to take it up himself, but I thought there was less chance of disaster if I did it, since I'd remember to knock first and not go about poking the fire or drinking potions to see what they do."

"I doubt he'd do that," said Sophia, a chunk of bread and cheese halfway to her mouth. "Any of that."

Alice shrugged. "Well, I'll let him come next time, then." She nibbled the cheese, looked up, and grinned. "I hope you're not too disappointed."

"Don't be silly," said Sophia, and she truly *wasn't* disappointed, or not mostly. She was too surprised. Pleased too: the thought had been a kind one, and it was flattering to know that she'd been on his mind at all. "I'm no good to him if I starve," she said, as much to herself as to Alice, "and I'm sure he knows that hunger clouds judgment. Besides, he was probably looking for a chance to see how the experiment was coming along."

"He doesn't seem like the sort who'd need an excuse for that," said Alice. "How *is* this going? You still have your eyebrows, I note, which is a pleasant change."

"I've only lost them *once*."

"Yet."

"And I was sixteen, and the crucible was faulty." This was an old dance, and Sophia quickly moved on, breaking the bread and cheese into smaller portions as she talked. "I think… I *think*…it's going well, but this is only the first part. Finding out what's wrong."

"Other than 'extremely sinister evil magic,' you mean. Ugh." Alice shuddered. "Perhaps we did well to spend a dozen years away from England, if this is the sort of thing they get up to."

"I don't get the impression that it's common."

"A little goes a long way."

"Well, *that's* true," Sophia said. Despite the fatigue of the journey, she'd taken long enough to get to sleep the night after Cathal had told her his story. "But you know there could have been such men in France, and we just never crossed their paths."

"Oh yes," said Alice, rolling her eyes, "you're *very* comforting." She sighed and shook her head. "I did want to see the world, didn't I?"

"So you said back home." Sophia chewed a bite of pie and studied the face before her: light where hers was dark, angular where hers was heart-shaped, and more familiar than her own, especially since their months of travel when mirrors had not figured heavily in their lives. "Though I admit you cannot have had this in mind. If you do want to leave—"

"Do not," said Alice, blue eyes narrowing, "be foolish."

"I'll not lose sleep trying to figure out a way then," Sophia said and smiled.

"Don't. You kick when you're restless." Alice picked up the flask of wine, took a drink, and passed it back to Sophia. "Besides, I'd never find anywhere nearly as pleasant to stay the winter. I've just about fit myself into the kitchens, and one of the girls here knows a little French. We're swapping songs. You know we've not heard most of those here."

"I do," Sophia said, although in truth, the minstrel's songs had all blended together into pleasant incomprehensibility for her. Without words, music had never quite caught her attention, but she knew what it meant to Alice. "By spring, we might even speak some of the local language ourselves."

"Oh, if we can make our throats work with it," said

Alice, shaking her head good-naturedly. "Maybe you can brew a potion for that while you're up here. Or we could just put small rocks under our tongues. Speaking of which—brewing potions, not rocks—have you had any word about this midwife? The one who knows her herbs?"

"No," said Sophia, "but she wouldn't be very useful just now. Everything I've been able to find says that the first step with a spell is determining which planetary influence it primarily falls under. Herbs won't be of any use until I can do that."

"I'll believe you," said Alice, "since I really have very little idea what you're talking about. Finish your pie."

Sophia did as she was told. Eating the bread and cheese had reminded her body of its physical nature, and her hunger was greater than she'd thought. Such was often the case; it was why many magicians had apprentices. Alice wasn't her apprentice, nor did Sophia travel with her for those reasons, and yet Alice filled that place, a role which, Sophia was discovering, was rather essential.

"Thank you," she said, when the mouthful of pie was gone and she could speak.

"You'd be dead without me, I know," Alice said. "Or in a horrible mood all the time. Stalking the halls and trying to gnaw on people's shoulders when you forgot to eat."

"I think I'd try the kitchens first, even in that state."

"I'd advise it. Nobody here looks the sort who'd tamely submit to you biting hunks out of their arms. I do, of course, but then I'm not nearly as mild and proper as you might think, so I wouldn't try that either." Alice rose from the stool, brushed her skirts into place, and reached for the tray, which now held only crumbs and the empty flask of wine.

Laughing, Sophia waved Alice's hand away. "Leave it. I'll bring it back."

"The aura of cheese won't contaminate your experiments?"

"I shouldn't think so." When Alice still looked dubious, Sophia added, "It truly is the least I can do, since you climbed all this way."

"And you'll remember it?"

"I swear"—Sophia put a hand over her heart—"I'll bring it with me when I come down. Which I also swear to do, and in good time for the evening meal."

"Do," Alice said, "or I'll have one of the men-at-arms come and carry you down. Not in any dignified fashion either, but over one shoulder. Like a sack of grain or a recalcitrant pig."

"Hark at the lady. You don't even know their language, and you'd command them to start carrying off strange women?"

Alice shrugged. "Very well… I'll get Sir Cathal to do it," she said and was out the door before Sophia could take the last word from her.

No magician, Alice had nonetheless conjured up a very vivid image. Even under tunic and surcoat, the lines of Cathal's body were clear, and clearly strong. Sophia doubted he would have any trouble throwing her over a shoulder, or in keeping her there.

After another glance at the flasks, she rose quickly and went to the window, pressing her hands against the cold glass. The fires, she thought, were working a little *too* well.

SIX

Mornings for Cathal, since he returned from the war, meant a trip to the western tower. He went before the rest of the household was at mass, before anyone had thought to light a fire in the castle, and while his blood let him shrug off the cold easily enough, he often had a harder time with the hunger. In a hall below Sophia's turret, he opened a door to a square room without windows, lit only by the first rays of the rising sun through the cracks in the stone. He could have taken flint and steel to the torches on the walls—his mother and a few of his siblings could have lit them with a thought or a muttered word—but most days he didn't bother. He wasn't human, and dim light offered him no hardship.

At the center of the room was a five-sided table: part of his mother's dowry, carved from a single block of ash. A map of Loch Arach and its borderlands covered the surface, burned into the wood in deep black lines.

There were no chairs around the table, or anywhere else. In this room, you stayed on your feet.

The dawn's light bathed the map in red-gold, but it remained only sunlight when it touched the wood, not turning to the darker red that would have meant battle, nor the yellow of plague. The first signs of the day were clear.

Cathal crossed the room to a dark corner, where a small well descended into the earth below the castle. Lowering the bucket—made of ash as well—was routine now, his hands as trained to the motion as they were to drawing his sword or mending his gear. His mind, not yet fully awake, wandered, making lists of the tasks ahead, bringing up the memory of the last song the night before, and reminding him that he was only a short staircase below the room where Sophia spent most of her days.

Might she be up there already? She wouldn't be one for mass, that was certain, and she might be wary enough to retire to the turret before the rest of the castle went to the chapel. Later, he could go up and see for himself. It would be wise to check her progress on occasion and to see what use she was making of the room he'd given her.

It would be pleasant to see her face in the rosy light of dawn, to stand alone with her in a warm room and talk as he never seemed quite able to do at meals. Everything about the great hall spoke to him too much of his role and his duties, and he could never quite break free of them long enough to think of conversation. Odd that his days had been longer on campaign, and physically as hard or worse, but he'd always been able to charm a pretty lass when he'd wanted to.

Mayhap that was the difference. He was trying to be a good host to this one, not win himself a tumble in his tent.

The succession of images that thought called to mind— women in his arms, now with Sophia's face to accompany their full breasts and sleek thighs—made him nearly drop the rising bucket. Water slopped over his hand. Even though the water here was warmer than normal, and Cathal didn't mind most cold, it was an unpleasant shock.

Mind to your tasks, boy, he scolded himself, in the voice of a long-dead man whose squire he'd once been. *Or do you need that water poured over your head?*

No, sixteen was a long time past, and even if his burdens had felt a touch lighter over the last few days, Cathal knew they were still there, a long list of tasks that didn't leave much room for pleasure of any sort. His body was still disposed to argue the point, but he pushed those urges to the back of his mind, picked up the bucket, and brought it over to the table.

On most days, the water ran smoothly into the channels of the map, then vanished. When drought was forthcoming, it disappeared midair. Cathal had seen that happen in his boyhood. This time, the water hit the first of the carved boundaries and froze instantly.

Blizzard.

He began to swear steadily. By the time he'd emptied the rest of the bucket, he'd exhausted Gaelic and switched to English. When he reached the staircase, he'd worked his way over toward French, and he'd just started on Arabic when he heard a quiet inhalation from above.

Turning, he already knew he'd see Sophia on the stairs above him.

One hand covered her mouth, but above it, her eyes crinkled up at the edges, evidence of a hidden smile. Unbound and uncovered, her hair fell about her shoulders in a dark cloud. She'd tied it loosely back with a scrap of blue ribbon, but a great deal had escaped. Preoccupied as he was, Cathal was struck by the urge to step forward and brush the loose hair back from her face, to feel the silk of it against his fingers and then the warmth of her skin.

In his mind, he went on cursing for a few seconds.

"Trouble?" she asked.

"Blizzard," he said, and then the only other thing that came to him. "Didn't think you were awake."

"I wish I wasn't," she said. She reached up to touch her hair, as if realizing its condition belatedly, and dropped her eyes for a moment. "Some operations must take place at dawn. I thought I'd perform them and then go back to sleep. I didn't think I'd be seen, really…"

Now he saw that she wore a cloak, though she'd pushed the hood back onto her shoulders, making it useless for concealment.

"My good fortune, then," he said and smiled at her.

The flush that spread across her cheeks reminded him of the dawn itself. Her lips parted slightly. "Oh," she said, half breathing the word. For an instant, the very stairs and walls felt insubstantial, and he and Sophia might have been the only solid things in the universe.

Then she cleared her throat. "Your friend—Fergus—his cure will have to do with the sun and with Saturn. Solidity. The translation of spirit into matter. The spell's impeding that. There are elements missing in him or deficient...an amputation, if you will."

"Poetic enough," said Cathal, grimacing. Once again he wished "Valerius" near enough at hand to throttle. "You can restore such things?"

"*Someone* can," she said, straightening her back as she spoke, "and I'm the one who's here. I have a few notions about how to begin."

"Good." And it was, though the change of subject had been a fairly effective cold bath—and that, in turn, reminded him of the map's prediction. Tasks settled back on his shoulders like hawks made of lead. "I must go. I beg your pardon."

Part of the difficulty was that the weather *then* suggested no such thing as a blizzard. The sky was clear, that bright and almost brittle blue that happened in high places during the winter; the air was still and, for February in Scotland, warm. If Cathal hadn't seen the map, he wouldn't have thought Loch Arach in any danger of calamity.

Nobody else in the castle *had* seen the map, or indeed the room where it lay. Prophecy didn't figure largely in their lives—except for some of the guards, most of them had little to do with magic in general—and although his father must have warned the folk of the castle and village about similar peril, Cathal was damned if he could remember how. He wasn't sure he'd paid enough attention to learn the process in the first place.

Approaching Niall, his steward, he therefore felt like an utter fool.

"There's a blizzard coming," he said, having always preferred to jump the fence rather than go around. "Likely a bad one. How are the stores?"

Then he waited for questions or disagreement, watched the old man—*half my age*, he always had to remind himself now, his brain as likely as any mortal's to be swayed by gray hair and a bent back—for skepticism, and got none. What Niall actually did was make a clicking sound with his tongue, expressing general disapproval to the universe regarding this sort of messing about, and then start in on his usual list: so many cords of wood, less grain than he'd have liked, and so on.

Cathal listened carefully, forcing the figures into a mind still unused to remembering such things or relating them to the lives in his care, but all the time slightly amazed, even though he realized he shouldn't be. Niall had been his father's steward for forty years, and his predecessors had doubtless passed on certain bits of knowledge along with the books of accounts, little tidbits like *Oh, and the lord knows the future now and again*. Prophecy firsthand wasn't part of Niall's life. Secondhand, it was just another fact of Loch Arach, like keeping horses away from the MacAlasdairs.

Such a calm reaction should have been reassuring, and yet—

—and yet there was a whole world here that Cathal barely knew, and his experience was almost all from outside.

"I'll go hunting today," he said when he'd forced a picture from the tallies: not as much food or fuel as he'd have liked, particularly if the storm lasted, and he'd no notion of how long that would be. "And I'll bring back wood as well. Send messengers to the village. Tell the folk they're welcome up here and to prepare if they'll stay in their homes."

"Aye," said Niall. "Three days hence?"

"Aye," said Cathal, a startled echo. Yes, the map had always showed three days in the future, never more and rarely fewer. He knew that. He hadn't expected that knowledge from Niall.

He didn't, it seemed, expect half of the things he should.

As the day progressed, Cathal found that feeling growing stronger and stronger. The stable hands and smiths, the folk of the castle, even his guards reacted much as Niall had. Some showed their displeasure more, some were surprised, and a few even looked doubtful for a second or two, but everyone accepted the news. Even Father Lachlann, whose place in the Church would have let him voice doubts to Loch Arach's temporary lord, spoke no word of contradiction or even question.

They all assumed Cathal knew whereof he spoke. He did, so that trust should have been at worst a pleasant surprise, but it merely bore down on him like the walls themselves until he could escape into the air and then the forest.

Hunting offered relief, as it always did. The cold air streaking past him cleared his mind; the challenge of sighting and diving occupied him; and the dragon's shape was largely a creature of instinct and impulse. The human side of him remained, but it was easy to let it lie dormant for a time, to give over doubts and let the ever-turning wheel of thought give way to a creature at once of the moment and of centuries. All would settle itself in enough time. Meanwhile, there were clear skies above and prey below.

As usual when he wasn't hunting for himself, he touched the stag as lightly as possible, breaking its neck with one swift blow and keeping claws and teeth out of the matter. The folk of the castle all knew what Cathal was. Still, none but the men who'd fought with him had been close when he was in dragon form. Most pretended not to see. Artair had believed in making that easy for them, and Cathal agreed with his father on that score.

For similar reasons, he always landed, on his return from the hunt, in a small clearing just outside the castle walls. From there he would transform and carry in his quarry if it was manageable, or send out some of the men if he'd brought down an elk or a boar. Nobody asked how it had happened, and he always looked human by the time he saw anyone.

He was human, barely, when Sophia stepped out from between the trees.

SEVEN

SHE WAS TOO LATE TO SEE ANYTHING—A PITY, EVEN though she hadn't come out with that intent. Spotting the dragon in flight, Sophia had caught her breath and stared at the vast greenish-blue form, taking in the outstretched wings and the lashing tail, unable to believe that anything so immense and so far from human could spend most days as a man. Then, seeing the creature descend, she'd followed. Who wouldn't have?

What she'd found was Cathal standing above a dead stag. He looked just as he had that morning, clothes all in place, sword hanging at his side, and even his hair only slightly disheveled, but when Sophia walked out into his view, he drew his head and chest back in surprise, not a motion she'd seen from him or from any human being. Snakes acted so, startled and ready to strike. She stopped in her tracks.

"Satisfying your curiosity?" he asked, watching her with narrowed eyes.

His voice sounded deeper than usual, though Sophia wasn't sure whether to credit that to transformation or anger. Now was not the time to ask.

Now might have been the time to lie, but she couldn't think of anything plausible. "Yes, but no." She raised a hand. "I saw you land and came over to watch…but I'd come out to go to the village and then realized that I'd no hope of making my way there without a guide. I hadn't known you were…out. Hunting."

Cathal regarded her silently. One hand went to the fastening of his cloak, which Sophia now noticed was a silver dragon's head. His was a family powerful enough to hint at their true nature. She would do well to remember that.

She would also, said her conscience, do well to remember that Cathal was not a salamander nor a griffin nor a two-headed calf, but a man and her host.

"I'm sorry," she said, dropping her eyes. "I shouldn't have intruded. I saw nothing. I give you my word on it."

Honestly meaning apology and reassurance, she realized too late how suggestive the last sentence sounded. The winter air wasn't nearly frigid enough to chill her blush in that moment, and she couldn't make herself look up at Cathal.

Not until she heard him laugh.

"Well," he said, and she lifted her eyes to discover his face open with mirth and his hair ruffling in the slight breeze as if it shared the joke. "I'll cherish my modesty yet, then. And I'll not faint just now."

"Please don't," she said, measuring the length and breadth of him with her eyes. "I could no more carry you back than I could that deer."

"Come now, lass," Cathal chided her, shaking his head. "If I'm more than half its weight, I'm either the worst glutton in the world or a far worse hunter than I'd thought."

"And you both weigh less than the mountain. After a certain point…" Sophia spread her gloved hands, illustrating helplessness. She glanced back to the stag. "It is a very large animal. Especially for winter, I think?"

"Aye, it'll do. I hope." Cathal followed her gaze, then looked back to her, studying her face. It was a gentler kind of assessment than the sort he'd given her in his solar, Sophia thought. "Will you be able to eat it?"

Instinct and travel through England made her glance behind her before she responded, and she lowered her voice as well. "No. It's... We would have trapped it and then cut its throat. There are other restrictions too." Seeing concern enter his face, even if it was just the worry of a host for a guest, Sophia smiled and fought back the urge to step forward and touch his cheek in reassurance. "If my life is in the balance, that will no longer matter. And until then, I do very well. You set a good table."

"I sit at one," he said, shrugging, "and I nod at the right times when the cooks and the steward talk to me. Forgive me. I know that the Mussulmen hunt and eat their game. I'd thought it might be the same for your people."

"It was a kind hope." The reference made her remember the profanity she'd overheard that morning and that his statement that he spoke Arabic. "Were you on Crusade?"

"A few."

She had always been good at figures. The ones she did now showed a picture almost as staggering as his flight overhead had been. "How old are you?"

Sandy eyebrows came together as he thought. "A century and a quarter? Maybe less. Remembering each year gets difficult. I'm the youngest. I know *that*," he added with a wry tone that she recognized well.

"You and my brothers," she teased in return. "Never will any of you forget it, and heaven forbid the rest of us should."

"Oh aye," Cathal said, "I expect we'll let it go the moment our elders forget to remind us of *their* place in things."

Sophia laughed and held up her hands. "I can't argue that point with you either... I've an older sister myself. And she knows it. I can *still* remember every word of her last lecture."

"And how long ago was that?"

"When I boarded the ship for England. She was worse than our parents. They resigned themselves to my peculiarities years ago, but Rachel…" She shrugged. "Her eldest daughter should be getting married soon, so that might take her mind off me."

"Peculiarities?" Cathal asked, cocking his head slightly.

Sophia couldn't make out whether he was teasing or honestly curious. She wrinkled her nose at him. "Alchemy. Scholarship. Being a Catherinette—" Cathal's puzzled look reminded her that not everyone had spent the last ten years or so in France. "Over twenty-five and unwed. I never worshipped the saint, of course, but…you understand. You must know that none of these are usual in a gentlewoman."

"Oh," he said, like one reminded of long-forgotten things, and smiled ruefully. "Aye. That. I haven't spent much time with…gentlewomen…these past few years."

"I'd imagine there weren't many on Crusade."

"A few. Wives. Daughters. A handful who themselves fought."

"What was it like over there?"

"Hot. Dry. Old, and it's me saying that." Cathal smiled again, then sobered. "Or do you mean the fighting? It was war. War is verra much the same, one time to another. The English, the Saracens…" He spread his hands, and Sophia saw again how large they were. A scar, long faded but still visible, crossed one palm. "We all bleed the same. Even my clan. Everything I've faced, anyhow."

The restriction caught her interest. "Are there things that don't?" she asked, because curiosity was stronger than dread and *not* knowing had never helped anything.

"So I've heard. Ghosts. Shadows. Demons, mayhap. But I've only ever fought men."

"Oh."

Sophia glanced down, looking at ground where the snow had disappeared in patches. The earth revealed was muddy and dismal looking.

Lost in thought, she didn't see or hear Cathal move, only felt the sudden warmth of a hand under her chin—warmth that spread down her neck the way heat from a normal touch never would have. She wanted to blame his nature, but she didn't think she could.

He tilted her chin up, his touch unexpectedly gentle. "Whatever you're thinking of," he said, "you may as well ask. I'll take no offense from it."

"Oh," she said again, this time because she couldn't initially remember where her thoughts had been going. She took a breath. "You don't sound like... There are those who talk about glory. High purpose. In war, I mean."

"There may be those who find it." He slid his hand away and stepped back. Sophia fought off the impulse to follow him. At least his distance was clearing her head, and his expression was less playful—although, as he'd claimed, he didn't look offended, simply matter-of-fact. "The glory fades by the second war, I find. Perhaps the third."

"But you keep going."

"Aye, well, there's little enough glory in most tasks most days. They've still got to be done...here for my people and there for the rest of us. Wars are better for all when skilled men are fighting. I'm skilled. At that," he added, and sighed. "And it was a damned sight simpler out there."

She looked up, past the square line of his jaw, and saw the shadows under his eyes. MacAlasdairs, it seemed, were no more immune to sleepless nights than any other men. As much as the words Cathal said, as much even as the resignation in his voice, those shadows illuminated her experience of him from a different angle. Beneath distance and curtness, she now saw weariness and uncertainty, a man struggling to fit himself to an unfamiliar role.

"Anything is simpler when you're used to it," she said. "I don't think your steward would fare so well on campaign, any more than he would in my laboratory. I know I wouldn't."

As soon as she'd spoken, she thought, *Well, of course, idiot. You're a woman*, and expected Cathal to say likewise, either laughing at her or taking offense at the comparison. When he didn't, Sophia remembered his sister, the one he'd said had taken his place fighting the English, and then that he'd spoken of women fighting in the Crusades. It was easy to forget facts in expectation; she'd never liked that about her mind.

"And you've had many more years than most," Sophia continued, because the silence had taken on weight and she didn't know what that would end up meaning if she let it go unchecked. "Centuries. Well, a century."

The word felt strange in her mouth. It didn't quite want to attach itself to Cathal, particularly when he smiled. "That's a way of seeing it, perchance," he said, speaking as if he was turning the idea over in his mind, inspecting the shine and the facets of it. "It's *been* centuries since Loch Arach had a new hand at the reins. Those here tell me everything they think to, but…they'll not know everything *I* don't know, aye? No more than I do."

"That's always what catches me," Sophia said. "I learned from a few teachers, and that was all right as long as I could just imitate them every step. But then, when my situation was different from the ones we'd practiced, I didn't know to ask, and they hadn't thought to tell me. And then with experiments, there's so *much* not to know, especially at first. You have to…to"—she gestured, trying to grasp the words—"hunt down ignorance before you can address it."

Cathal nodded. Sophia realized that she perhaps hadn't said the most helpful thing she could have and was about to apologize when he asked, "And what happens when you don't catch your prey in time?"

"Well, I lost my eyebrows once."

He stared at her, then laughed—quickly, but deep in his chest—and the laughter shook some tension from him. "They grew back bonny enough. Shall I take that as an omen, sorceress?"

"I've never been very good at divination," Sophia said, shaking her head and smiling. Then, more soberly, "But it's always been my principle that…that you do the best you can, you *secure* what you can, and then you do the work you're called to do, and you can't fret about more than that. I do fret, too much, but I try not to."

"And then you end up in Scotland, looking for dragon scales."

"Essentially, yes," Sophia said, and turned her hands outward. "I don't know if the principle is the same for what you're doing. I've never been nobility, obviously, and I've never been in charge of anyone, let alone a castle. I don't know how widely the theory applies. But war can't be a very certain thing, can it?"

"No. It's just over more quickly," said Cathal, again in the thoughtful manner he'd had before, his voice distant even as his eyes met hers with a focus that made the ground feel slightly unstable beneath her feet. It wasn't lust this time; she wasn't sure what it was. Then it was gone. "You should go in," he said. "You're mortal. It's cold."

"I… Yes, it is," Sophia said.

She hadn't noticed that for a while.

EIGHT

FOR THREE DAYS, CATHAL HAD LITTLE TIME TO THINK. He hunted, or he helped to butcher and salt his prey. He met with Niall to go over lists of supplies, or he approved his chamberlain's notion of what rooms in the castle they might open for any villagers who wished shelter. It occurred to Cathal that such duties sat more lightly on him since he'd talked to Sophia, and that the lift to his spirits after their conversation was longer than hunting usually gave him. He noted it, had neither leisure nor energy to worry about what it might mean, and so was simply glad of the benefits.

The world was full of things he didn't understand. When they worked to his advantage, he rarely found it helped to question them.

He didn't see Sophia herself very much. She kept to her turret, emerging once in a while for meals. As Cathal mostly grabbed bread and meat while on the way to one appointment or another, it was rare that he even met her eyes across the table. The one evening when they dined together for any length of time, words did come more easily between them than in the past. They talked trivially about preparations and the weather in France, then touched briefly on Cathal's time in Spain.

As with his mood, he noticed that he spoke more freely with her, marked the fact, and put it aside. He would have time to consider it later.

But when the villagers began to arrive, he was glad

to see Donnag among them. Middle-aged, nearly as tall as Cathal himself, and little more than skin over bones, Donnag had served Loch Arach as midwife and herbalist for forty years, or so Cathal's father had said. Any plant she didn't know didn't exist for about fifty miles.

Of course, she didn't speak French or even much English, certainly not the sort that Sophia would understand. They'd need a translator. Out of everyone in the castle or the village, Cathal knew the most languages. Father Lachlann might have been able to interpret under other circumstances, but given both Sophia and the task at hand, he seemed a bad choice.

It would have to be Cathal translating. He'd make time in his duties because Fergus's condition demanded it. Far from being another imposition, the thought of interpreting for the women made him smile. Dwelling on that, like the translation itself, would have to wait.

Waiting came to an end almost precisely three days from the morning when Cathal had first seen the blizzard approaching. The snow was already falling from a lead-colored sky as he performed the morning rites. By the time he entered the great hall, the wind outside was beginning to moan; by noon, it was howling. The shutters held firm, though, and fires blazed in the hall and the kitchen, adding their warmth to the heat of many people in a room.

Now, he thought, there was nothing for it but waiting and response. A crisis would arise, or not, and he'd know the shape of it then and how to act accordingly. As Sophia had hinted, the feeling was not unlike battle.

He saw Sophia in the hall, seated in a corner with Alice by her side and a book on her lap. Cathal thought that he recognized the book as one his mother had brought with her many years ago. Magic, and indeed reading, had never called to him like they had to Agnes. He'd looked through the library as best he could after the incident with Valerius, but he'd found nothing that seemed useful.

Perhaps it'd be different for Sophia.

He crossed the room as, off in another corner, a man began to play a lyre. The instrument was old but well-tended, and the bard was skilled enough, for all that he doubtless lived by farming. It was an old tune, one that even Cathal remembered from his childhood. His mother had never been musical, but his father—his father had hummed whenever he walked.

By the time Cathal reached Sophia, he was smiling in reminiscence, and perhaps that was why Alice gave him a less-wary curtsy than usual.

"Your pardon, ladies," he said and bowed. "The midwife's about. I'll make the introductions...unless you've met already."

Sophia shook her head. "No, she was busy when we made it to the village," she said and began to rise, tucking the book under her arm. "Alice?"

"Duty calls, I know. I'll find you later," the blond woman replied and drifted over toward the music.

They found Donnag seated in front of the fire, one of the privileges of her age. She cast a quick look between Sophia and Cathal, lifted her eyebrows—*I hope she's not breeding, my lord*—and only then gave them the usual polite greeting.

To Cathal's mild surprise, Sophia managed a very passable Gaelic response.

"Can I aid you in aught?" Donnag asked. At that, Sophia looked blank.

"She wants to know what we want," Cathal said in English. "I don't know how much you've picked up."

"Not very much...*hello* and *goodbye*, *please* and *thank you*, that sort of thing. *Bread* and *cup* too, or so I believe, and *stairs*." She smiled ruefully. "Mostly we point and gesture."

"Aye," he said. "I'll teach you later. Donnag"—he switched back to Gaelic—"this is Sophia, a scholar from France. An alchemist. She's trying to help with Fergus. Might need herbs."

"Ah?" Donnag had tried her own skills on Fergus when Cathal and his men had first returned. That failure had stung, he knew, but she showed no resentment now. "If she can manage it, I'll be glad to help. What does she need?"

The hour that followed was both fascinating and confusing. He'd heard scraps about plants and the celestial bodies before, but he'd never been either interested enough or obligated to pay attention. Now he listened as Sophia talked about needing plants that corresponded to the Sun and to Saturn, and found himself startled when Donnag, as often as not, nodded in all apparent comprehension.

"She says she gathers ash leaves at dawn on Sundays" was the sort of thing Cathal found himself saying, careful of his translation as he'd rarely been before. So much depended on him getting the details right, particularly when he understood very little of the whole picture. "Marigolds too. Not that you'll find either fresh just now, but she has some dried back in her cottage."

At such information, Sophia would look sober and thoughtful, and slowly nod, prompting a similar expression from Donnag. Language aside, they clearly understood each other very well.

"She came at a bad time. This *happened* at an ill time." Donnag shook her head, her brow wrinkled, and Cathal didn't think he needed to bother with translation. Long fingers, stained with herbs and soot but still straight, plucked idly at the gray wool of her gown. "There's more of

Saturday's plants around, I suppose. Yew, here and there, and holly."

"I've seen them both," Cathal said, and they both stared at him: Sophia, though she couldn't understand the words, because he no longer sounded like a dutiful translator, and Donnag, who could understand him, obviously wondering why he'd felt he had to speak up, yet too mindful of his rank to ask. He coughed and changed to French. "She says yew and holly for the...correspondence to Saturn? I couldn't pick yew out of the rest of the evergreens around here, but I've seen clumps of holly here and there in the forest. I can take you. When the weather clears off."

"Would you?" Sophia gave him a quick, brilliant smile, her dark eyes meeting his and almost glowing in the firelight. "That would be lovely. Very helpful. And—"

As quickly, she was back to using him as an interpreter, discussing plans with Donnag and asking about the virtue of dried herbs as opposed to those pickled or preserved in alcohol. When the conversation ended, Cathal felt as if he'd just spent an hour with his boyhood tutors—but his youthful self would have been shocked and faintly revolted by how much he'd enjoyed the education this time.

The storm raged for five days. Even more than was usual, Castle MacAlasdair became its own world, shrinking in space around those inside its walls even as it grew in their perspective, those walls marking the boundaries of everything known and safe. Outside, the wind shrieked day and night, and the snow fell sideways half the time, spitting into the face of anyone daring to put their head out of a window.

Cathal called the guards off the battlements after the first few hours. No human enemy would attack under such conditions, and against any supernatural enough to strike, men with swords would be little use. He posted a few guards inside each of the towers, and nobody came in to slit all their throats and set fire to the castle.

Besides, he turned out to need guards more indoors. Close quarters heated tempers as well as bodies. The limited amount of plain food didn't help, and the constant wailing from outside set everyone's nerves on edge. Villagers whose small feuds had been gentled by distance now faced each other across their bread and ale in the morning, and many of them didn't like it. Cathal and his men-at-arms separated brawlers tactfully when they could, pulled them apart forcefully when they couldn't, and found in many cases that years of killing men hadn't prepared them for trying to keep people from killing each other.

He used his voice and his rank most of the time, and left physical intervention to others. In man's shape, he couldn't shatter oak doors or snap the necks of half-ton beasts, but he was still stronger than human sinew would explain and his own temper thin enough. When the soldiers themselves fought, as proved not uncommon as the storm wore on, Cathal took a more direct hand. There he knew the measure of his strength and the need for control.

Control was the word to remember. He tried. His world had too little space and too many people, the sounds of constant talking and the smells of food and sweat at best. He'd lived in cities, but cities had been outside. He went to the battlements as often as he could. Even he couldn't fly in the storm, but he walked the lengths of stone, stared out into the swirling whiteness, and forced his mind to some semblance of calm.

Tiredness was an unexpected ally. Had he been able to summon the energy for real anger from the first, his patience might have been far shorter. If he'd had more strength for transformation, the results might have been emphatic and bloody. That happened from time to time. He'd heard stories. He hadn't been conscious of thinking about them during his days of effort before the storm, but he wondered, now that he had time to think, if they hadn't been in his mind regardless.

He did have time to think—and after the third day, there was little he could do to exhaust himself. From nights of dreamless sleep and dragging himself out of bed, Cathal found himself waking earlier with more heart for the day ahead, even though he knew it would likely contain little to please him. The body took its recovery where and when it could. The mind had almost nothing to say about it.

Sophia's presence did help, though. He had to look that truth in the face—that seeing her through the crowd made the mob in the great hall less overwhelming. Although his duties and the sheer number of people made conversation hard, simply knowing she was there added to his new vigor. Knowing she was working to help Fergus was some of it; some was her calm, and her ability to pull her own world around her at need, blocking out chaos and noise; some was that seeing her reminded Cathal of the wider world, and that the castle and the fifty-odd people inside were really only a small part of it.

And she was a damned good-looking woman, of course. Cathal couldn't deny that element—but he'd wanted women before, had them before, and any improvement to his mood had been temporary at best.

Still, when he had a moment of quiet in the midst of the tempest, he watched the play of firelight on her gold skin or noticed the smooth curves of her body beneath her dress, and the next crisis was often easier to get through

than he'd expected. Whatever the cause, he wasn't about
to look a gift horse in the mouth—much as Sophia's mouth
was worth looking at.

On the fourth day of the blizzard, the water in the oracle
chamber poured without freezing. The sky spat on them
unabated, so Cathal kept the knowledge to himself. Even
he didn't entirely trust prophecy, particularly when it was
hopeful. The snow fell steadily, and the wind kept up,
but on the morning of the fifth day, both seemed lighter,
blows at the end of a long fight. By the evening, the snow
had stopped.

Wary yet, Cathal waited until the morning to send
word, but the sky was clear at dawn, and when the map
showed no trouble coming, he let the villagers know that
they could return to their houses, providing some of his
men for escort. Sophia and Alice went too, he saw—
Sophia with Donnag, Alice watchful by her side. They
returned that evening with windblown hair and many
small, cloth-wrapped bundles, which Sophia took directly
up to her turret.

Noise dwindled to normal. Thirty people in the castle
had been irksomely loud when Cathal had first arrived,
but now seemed blessedly quiet. He slept, stretched, and
began to go about the normal course of things—only to
find himself with another guest at noon on the second day
after the blizzard.

This one was an Irishman, short and lean, with a flute
at his side and trinkets in a pack: good news for the ladies,
but nothing that concerned Cathal at first. But the man
motioned Cathal to one side, dug around in that pack, and
removed a letter with a dark, unfamiliar seal. "A man at the

border sent this from his lord," the peddler said, holding up a hand to fend off any displeasure. "He paid well, but he also didn't seem the sort to refuse, my lord."

"No," said Cathal. He knew already whom the letter would be from, and the messenger dwindled into a vague shape and a vaguer sound. Cathal walked away and climbed the stairs to his solar, only opening the seal once he was alone. If Valerius had included any magic with his message, it would be well for Cathal not to be around people.

There was no magic. There was very little: only a few words.

Have you reconsidered yet? Time grows. Your friend shrinks.

V.

NINE

SOPHIA DIDN'T HEAR ANYTHING UNTIL THE DOOR OPENED.

Looking back, she wasn't surprised. True, Cathal was a large man and had no reason to walk quietly, but she'd always been able to shut out the world. It had been a source of Words in her youth, when she'd immersed herself in a book and let stew boil over, or stared out the window contemplating a new theory while seven-year-old Aaron spread blue dye liberally over his hands and clothing. She'd grown into the habit rather than out of it.

The last of her ingredients was just achieving coagulation. She could watch the faintly orange liquid in the beaker become solid, but she *had* to be standing by with the rest of the assembled mixture, now dark and murky in its golden chalice. The final step wouldn't be a split-second matter, but a minute one way or another could flaw the whole experiment.

And so, when the door creaked open behind her, she didn't take her eyes from her apparatus. "I'm fine, Alice. I'll come and eat after this," she said, her voice edged. She'd *told* Alice that morning of her likely schedule. Her friend usually had a better memory for such things, and more consideration when they were happening.

"What's 'this'?" Cathal asked, sounding far from calm himself. "And how much longer will you take at it?"

She did turn then—just her head and just long enough to see him standing in the doorway with his arms over his chest and glaring at her, the apparatus, or both.

A second later, she spun back to look at the beakers. The break in her concentration had done no harm, but the demand rankled—and she disliked how quickly she'd turned to see him. She hissed through her teeth. "Not an hour more, if it goes well. My attention will be vital to ensuring that it does."

"Oh aye," he said, a bit meeker now. "And what part of the process will that be?"

"The end of this experiment, I should *hope*," she said. "Ash is the devil itself to distill, you might be interested to know, and all the worse when I'm working with dried leaves rather than fresh ones."

"Don't you need holly? Or yew?"

"I might, in time. Saturn is tricky. Best to restore the solar forces first, if I can, and then proceed from there as needed." She dared a glance back over one shoulder. "Would you like me to draw up a plan for your perusal, my lord? I can, though it may well change dramatically. I'm very much in unknown waters here, as I believe I mentioned at the first."

"No," he said and cleared his throat. "Won't be necessary. I just…" He glanced down at his hands. One was a fist with something in it. Cathal stuffed whatever it was into the pouch at his belt. "I wished to know. Not unreasonable, is it?"

"Wishes have very little to do with reason," Sophia said sharply, turning back to the apparatus. Then, thinking better of herself, she added, "But it's a compassionate thing to fear for your friend, and I've no objection to telling you. I'd have answered your questions at dinner just as well, if you'd asked them then."

"I hadn't thought to ask before," he admitted.

"And now you have," she said. Had she been able to

face Cathal for any length of time, she'd have given him a quizzical look. "I won't pry..." She of all people could understand the desire for knowledge, and he'd forgiven her own trespasses, or however the Christian prayer had it. "And perhaps I should have told you to begin with, but it's not safe just to walk in without notice."

"No?"

"I meditate before I start each phase of an experiment. If my mind's impure or my concentration insufficient"— she gestured outward—"then the process may fail. All beginnings require clarity, particularly in a matter that's spiritual in itself. Fergus's cure, if it exists, will involve more than boiled herbs. I must make *some* contact with greater forces."

"What sort of contact?"

Now Sophia could feel his gaze, startled and maybe a shade uneasy, on the back of her neck. He was a fine one to talk, considering his bloodline. She didn't point that out, but merely shrugged. "Nothing as blatant as your saints claim. There exists a feeling, a state of mind... *Connection* is perhaps the simplest way to put it. If I can achieve that before I begin, my work is much more likely to succeed."

Cathal was silent. She could hear his breathing, low and regular. Despite the task before her, not to mention her exasperation, her whole body prickled in response to the sound.

"There are also practical considerations," she said, breaking the silence. "And those are more dangerous. I work with open flame here, you notice, and at times with volatile substances. I did, I believe, mention the occasional catastrophe. The timing is... *There*."

The substance in the beaker shivered into its final form, turning from orange to the golden-red of the sunrise, clear enough to see through, yet as motionless as the glass surrounding it. Losing track of all else, Sophia seized the tongs, grasped the beaker, and pulled it off the flame. Only then did she let out her breath.

"We have a minute," she said, conscious again of Cathal standing behind her. "It must cool slightly first… but only slightly."

She set the beaker on the table, put down the tongs, and held her right hand an inch from the glass, feeling the heat pressing against her palm.

"What is that?" Cathal asked.

"Powdered topaz, originally. The most difficult of the ingredients, as you might imagine, for it's most reluctant to give up its form. Indeed, only with the proper state of mind and the right alignment of the planets will any of the stages work on it. It took years before I had either the money or the confidence to handle it at all." She smiled, remembering how proud she'd been that first successful time, and then realized she was rambling. "Yet its virtue is most potent, and it will heal most merely physical ailments, when its power is applicable."

"Oh." He sounded surprised by the flow of information, but also…amused or admiring. She couldn't decide which—perhaps both. So many elements made up a human being, and perhaps there were even more in Cathal, blend as he was of human and not.

The heat had abated. She moved her hand to rest against the beaker and found that she could leave it there for the count of ten seconds. "It's ready."

Pouring the topaz into the rest of the mixture required steady, slow care, so she grasped the beaker with the tongs once more and took a long breath to keep her hands still. Smoothly she brought the glass vessel up over the golden goblet, and smoothly she turned it, letting the contents begin to pour out.

Bright touched dark. Sophia heard a sound like a low bell. Then a tongue of golden fire sprang up from the goblet, as wide as the cup itself and half again as high. The top of it wavered just below her hand holding the beaker. She could feel the heat, just as she had earlier, but now it was greater, and far from comfortable. She pressed her lips together and went on.

At the first appearance of the flame, she'd heard Cathal catch his breath. He was breathing again as Sophia kept still and tilted the beaker further toward the goblet, but his breaths were quicker. He might have stepped closer too, though he was holding still from all she could tell. She didn't have the leisure to look at him.

The purified topaz kept flowing into the rest of the mixture. Sophia watched it but couldn't see how it was blending because the flame obscured the surface of the goblet. *It* grew and changed, shifting from deep, almost brassy gold to a clearer, paler shade, like midday light in spring. The heat increased too—and then the flame stretched upward, licking at her skin.

It hurt. She yelped. Dignity had never been of much concern to her. She'd done most of her experiments alone, with none to impress and few to hear. She'd learned to hold herself still and cry out at the same time, and now her hands never moved, even as her voice ascended to a lark-like height and shaped a very unbirdlike "*Yeow!*"

Boots moved on stone.

She felt Cathal's body, inches from her own, and in the same voice cried out, "No!"

For a mercy, that stopped him in his tracks. Sophia clenched her free hand in the folds of her skirt, breathed twice through her nose, and finally said in a low but steady voice, "I can't move yet."

"You're hurt," he said, though he made no further move toward her.

"I'll heal. It's almost done."

Indeed it was. The beaker was almost empty, only a last few drops remaining. Sophia tilted the tongs once more and watched through blurry eyes as they fell in. Pain ran sharp and insistent from the side of her hand up through her arm; tears ran down her cheeks with it. She ran her tongue around her lips and tasted them, mingled with her own sweat.

And then it *was* done, the beaker empty. Slowly, wanting to be fast and therefore deliberately taking her time, she pulled her hand away, out of the flame. Slowly she set both beaker and tongs down on the table. With her other arm, she wiped her eyes on her sleeve and looked back at the goblet.

The flames were dying down, now barely dancing along the rim. Inside, the substance had turned to red-gold, translucent and almost glowing.

She breathed out a prayer in Hebrew: thanks and praise.

"I don't know precisely what effect it will have," she said, turning to Cathal. He was standing rigid, a soldier on parade or a knight at vigil, staring at her. "But I am convinced it will do *something*. There are bandages in that trunk in the corner and also salve, if you would be so kind."

The base of her hand, from the tip of her little finger to the bracelet of tiny lines between palm and wrist, was bright red. Odds were it would blister, and it was a truly awkward place for a burn. Still, it could have been far worse, and she had succeeded. Sophia leaned against the table and let herself grin.

"That must hurt like the very devil," said Cathal, coming back with the items she'd requested. He peered from her hand to her face and shook his head.

Sophia laughed, giddy in the aftermath of both injury and success. "It's pain. It exists. Then it doesn't. On this scale, I can exist alongside it; it doesn't consume me. Surely you've felt the same."

"Aye, *I* have," he said, "but you're… Nae, never mind. Hold out your hand, please."

She did, but couldn't resist asking, "A woman? A mortal?"

"And a civilian."

"Such heavy weights for me to bear."

The salve was cool and instantly soothing; she'd been making it for a long time. The sharp smell of barberry wafted to her nose, reminding Sophia of August days back home, the late-summer sun and the sounds of people passing outside the garden wall. She closed her eyes for a second, and then felt Cathal's fingers stroking down her wrist past the end of the burn, far more vivid than memory, spreading warmth in their wake that was as pleasant as the flame had been painful.

Before she thought about what she was doing, she leaned toward him, her body alive to his presence and, as if of its own accord, seeking more warmth and contact. Cathal's hand on her wrist went still in response, and she heard him make a sound low in his throat, not quite a hum but not yet a growl.

When he let go of her hand, she opened her eyes. Cathal hadn't drawn back. He stood a few inches from her still, and she was staring at the hollow of his neck, where his collar parted to show pale skin. Sophia couldn't make herself lift her eyes to his face. Her own cheeks were already starting to flame, both with embarrassment and with the desire that she could neither deny nor banish. She didn't want to read rejection in his eyes, and God forbid she see kindness there.

When he took her hand again, this time to wrap it in bandages, Sophia made herself stand very still and think about formulas. That didn't work entirely, but it kept her from doing anything else foolish, even if she was far too aware of every brush of his skin against hers. As he knotted the bandage, she tried to think of a single dignified thing to say—and couldn't.

Then she realized that Cathal still held her hand, his fingers light around hers. He did step back as she watched, but only so that he could bow low over it, then brush his lips over her knuckles. It was only a second, but the feeling ran through Sophia like flame itself, taking the breath from her lungs.

"I don't ask that you injure yourself in my service," he said, "but you have my deepest gratitude, lady."

The words were polite—more courtly, even, than she would have expected. His voice was rough, though, and his eyes blazed green into hers.

Don't assume, Sophia told herself. *If you're wrong, you're embarrassed—and if you're right, you're in far over your head.*

She cleared her throat. "Be grateful once we've seen the results," she said.

TEN

AT THE BEST OF TIMES, LOCH ARACH WAS A LARGE PLACE.
Now the halls and stairs stretched themselves out, almost
infinitely long, taunting Cathal with their distance. Given
what he'd just seen, he knew the sense of Sophia's request
that her laboratory be far from anyone's lodging. All the
same, as he strode through the corridors, he wished for a
minute that he'd denied it and quartered her in one of the
rooms next to Fergus, explosions be damned.

Sophia herself kept up better than Cathal would have
thought. Potion covered, wrapped, and held firmly in
both hands, she was only a foot or two behind every time
he glanced back toward her. She didn't complain or ask
him to slow down either, though he did the first time he
noticed that her speed came with a price. She was taking
two or three steps to every one of his, and by the time
they'd descended the staircase, she was showing it. Black
curls were emerging from the sides of her wimple, her
cheeks were flushed red-bronze, and her breasts rose and
fell rapidly.

Even hurrying, even with two layers of wool and some
pretense at courtesy in the way of his view, Cathal noticed
these things. The lust that had started in the laboratory, at
the nearness of her body and the feel of her small hand
in his, still sent its tendrils outward through his body. He
could ignore them better when he was walking. When
Sophia had leaned toward his touch, eyes closed and lips
parted in relief, his body had come to full wakefulness after

the winter's sleep. With an urgent errand before him and the castle full of people around him, he was still half hard from looking at her, still conscious of every breath of hers that reached his ears.

Triumph fed desire. He'd known that for years.

Had he forgotten the feel of it? He didn't remember the aftermath of battle ever being quite so heated, or quite so intoxicating. There had been joy, yes, and lust when the women were willing and comely, but the temptation of Cathal's memories had never been quite as intense as what filled him on the way to Fergus's chambers.

Then again, he'd always been able to satisfy those urges quickly. The women he wanted had always been available. Since leaving youth for manhood, he'd taken care to ensure that. He'd been careful where he set his eyes and where he let his thoughts stray; he never stood too close or talked too long to a woman whose affections weren't for sale in some way. Poets could talk all they wanted of courtly love, but pining after the moon was a silly modern notion. It would never last, and it, by God's eyes, wasn't for Cathal.

Now, perhaps, life had forced him into the situation he'd tried to avoid. That wouldn't be new. At least there were advantages to this particular unlooked-for complication. If Sophia wasn't for him, still she was pleasant to look at, and temptation was as enjoyable as satisfaction from time to time. If the potion worked, she would be gone before desire became torment.

In his right mind, Cathal told himself, he would find that an unmixed blessing.

Less mixed, at any rate. He wasn't a saint or even a monk, had never had any aspirations along that line, and a strictly practical life would have been boring.

He grabbed the reins of his thoughts and pulled them

away from his groin just before he and Sophia reached the doorway to Fergus's room.

Either a helpful friend or her own exhaustion had sent Sithaeg elsewhere. The girl beside Fergus was Janet, one of the kitchen wenches. She gave Cathal and Sophia a startled look but spoke no word, only rose, bowed, and got out of the way.

"You should likely leave," Sophia said with an apologetic smile, "just in case."

Neither did Janet ask *in case of what*? If she was a smart girl, she probably didn't want to know. With another bow, she was out the door before Sophia and Cathal made it to the side of Fergus's bed.

Duty, weariness, and his own aversion to watching futility had kept Cathal from visiting more than once in the last few days, and that had only been a swift look in. He'd felt guilty about that. Now he thought it had been wise. In the aftermath of Sophia's cool annoyance, not to mention the proof of how dangerous her task could be, he saw that Valerius's note had clouded his judgment, as the sorcerer might have intended. Had Cathal spent more time watching his friend's decline, cloud might have become full eclipse.

In the afternoon light, even dimmed and scattered by the windows, he could see through Fergus's skin. The shapes of muscle and tendon in his hands were milky and vague; his bones were more solid, like tiny chips of pearl caught in ice. The flesh of his arms was more translucent yet.

Fergus's face was a skull, only faintly veiled, and his closed eyes were pools of milky water.

Cathal swore in Gaelic. Beside him he heard Sophia gasp, as she'd done the night she'd first seen Fergus, but her voice was less startled and more appalled when she spoke. "God's *wounds*!"

"You don't believe in those," Cathal said, unsure whether it was joke or accusation, only reaching for anything that wasn't the man before him.

"Belief has nothing to do with profanity," she replied, and Cathal could hear her controlling her voice, going from ragged to clipped with every word. "I'll need you to hold him up, since I sent the maid away."

"Aye," Cathal said and knelt. The floor was hard and cold on his knees. He welcomed the solidity, even the pain; he cursed the contrast between it and the body he took hold of. Putting an arm around Fergus's back was still possible, but the flesh itself had a wispy feel, and while Cathal's hand didn't go through his old friend's shoulder, it felt as if it might at any moment.

Only the barest movement, the faintest sound, indicated that Fergus still breathed.

Have you reconsidered yet?

His whole body clenched, chest and throat and guts, a feeling he knew well from the heart of battle.

Fighting would do no good now. He wished, bitterly, that the situation were otherwise, that this was a problem he could solve with fist in face, sword in chest, teeth in throat. Remembering where he was, keeping his hands and arms gentle was all he could manage.

Physically, propping Fergus's head up was no effort at all. Sophia could have managed it. A child might have been equal to the task. For Cathal, it was a joke. He had only to kneel, and wait, and keep still. Unable to look at Fergus's face for very long, he watched Sophia instead. Also kneeling, across the bed from him, she unwrapped the potion with deliberate care.

This was not the time or place to get slipshod. Haste wouldn't help anyone.

Telling himself these things helped a little. Cathal took a slow breath in and let it out, on impulse letting it power a series of quick words in Latin, phrases that he'd learned in youth and used rarely. The world shifted around him: magic overlay familiar objects in washes of color and light. Magic was no weapon of his and didn't come easily to his hand, but he knew enough to let it provide warning in case the potion flamed up again, or exploded, or attracted unwelcome attention. Glancing at Sophia's bandaged hand, he wished he'd thought to do as much earlier.

The shades around her were dawn-pink, he noticed, but the goblet was more dramatic by far. It, or the substance inside it, or both, glowed as if Sophia held the sun itself in her hand. When she set it to Fergus's mouth, gentle as she was, Cathal went absolutely still, every muscle tense.

Enough mind, or perhaps just reflex, remained that Fergus opened his mouth at the touch of the metal. Sophia tipped the goblet forward, as slowly as she'd done everything since they'd entered the room, and the potion flowed bit by bit down Fergus's throat. His flesh, sparse and translucent as it was, hid the glowing liquid from view, and for a short time there was no sign that anything had happened at all.

Sophia righted the goblet and stood, her face set in the blank expression of one determined not to let disappointment show.

Beneath Cathal's hand, Fergus's shoulder felt suddenly warmer than it had a moment before. Even as he flexed his fingers, testing whether the sensation was real or his own imagining, the heat grew. A glow, subtler than the potion's, spread out from Fergus's throat, banishing the pallor of his skin and turning his flesh substantial where the light touched.

Not daring to speak, Cathal felt an incredulous smile

widen across his face, moving, it felt, with the shining effects of the potion. He heard the sound of a single harp string, faint at first and then growing. The glow reached Fergus's chin and his shoulders, then passed upward over his cheeks and outward to his arms.

In an instant, it stilled. The sound cut off. A wind from nowhere brought a chill and the smell of grave dust, and the light of the potion went out.

Fergus's eyes opened, a washed-out version of the merry brown ones Cathal had known: washed-out and now wide with terror and urgency. "Hhhh..." His voice came dusty from a disused throat.

Cathal crossed himself. Sophia stood with her hands at her sides, struck dumb and motionless. Fergus's throat worked, his lips writhed, and finally he managed speech.

"He. Wizard. He has me. In his grasp. Grip is...tight." Those pale eyes found Cathal's face and focused. "Captain."

"I'm here," Cathal said, and his hand tightened. The flesh beneath it was still more solid than it had been, but what comfort was that next to the horror in his friend's expression? "We're..."

We're *what*? He could in truth promise nothing—no rescue, no salvation, not even a quick death, for Cathal knew not what happened to the soul of a man killed under such a spell, and what he imagined was all hideous. He could but promise effort, and what earthly good was that?

And so he would lie. He'd done that before. *You'll be fine, lad. We turned the bastards. We're safe. We won.* The phrases came to his lips more easily than the paternoster. This time, the words would just be more complicated and not entirely false. They wouldn't give up; they were working on the problem. All he had to do was leave out a few details.

Cathal opened his mouth and saw that there was no need

to say anything. Fergus's eyes were closed again, and his jaw hung limp. He still breathed, and he still had the measure of solidity that the potion had given him back, but no more. His hands were yet half fog, his closed eyes pallid wisps in an otherwise solid face, and the spirit that had briefly animated him had vanished once again.

Now Cathal knew where it had gone or—he feared, more accurately—where it had been dragged.

ELEVEN

In the aftermath, Sophia sagged against the stone wall. The cup hung empty from one hand, droplets of the potion falling onto the floor by her feet. It was far heavier than it had been. Her very bones were heavier than they'd been a few minutes ago, and her head was a boulder, far too large for the neck that was supposed to support it. Sophia let it drop forward and let her eyes drift shut.

She'd take up her duties again in a moment. Once she regained…she couldn't say what. Breath? Strength? Life itself, or at least vital energy? She just needed a minute to summon any of those things, and then she knew she'd make herself go on. She'd need to think; Cathal was waiting for an explanation.

No, he wasn't.

His hand clasped her shoulder: a friendly touch, warm and stabilizing, and the sensuality that it sent curling through her, even in her depression, was secondary to the feeling of support. "It was well done," he said, quiet but fierce, pausing before each word so that it landed in her weary ears and sank in. "It would have worked. It did, some."

She let herself rest a moment against his hand; she clung to his words. "It did," she said. Fergus's flesh had changed—was changed yet, for when she opened her eyes, he looked even better than the man she'd first seen, and nothing like the half-wraith that had met her eyes on entering the room.

And he'd come back. Horrifying as he'd been in his

desperation—his *desiccation*—he'd been able to inhabit his body again for those few moments.

She gathered knowledge like a cloak around her.

No experiment fails if it tells you why *it fails*. That had been Roger the Mad, her second teacher, glaring at her across the ruins of an alembic and preparing an avalanche of questions. Her father, a fine merchant and passable poet but no great scholar, had put it more simply: *Walking is learning not to fall*.

"So," she said and stepped forward into the room, raising a finger. "The flaw was not in the potion itself, yes? At least there was no flaw that I saw, nor you? The flaw, if we can call it such, was interference."

Not really addressing Cathal, she turned toward him nonetheless. He'd hooked his thumbs into his belt and was watching her, his brow furrowed but a hint of a smile on his lips. "Aye," he said slowly.

"Or"—she raised her hand again—"conversely, the flaw was incomplete knowledge of the situation. Restoring the balance of a man's elements can heal his body and his soul both, *but* only if both are intact. Had 'Valerius' severed your friend's leg, for instance, no potion nor salve could grow him a new one. None that I know of, at least. Alchemy cannot turn a man into a lizard. Um, begging your pardon," she added, abruptly remembering her audience and what he was.

"No need," he said, still smiling. "There's no alchemy in that, lass."

"Can…" For a second she thought to ask if he *did* resemble a lizard in that respect, and how injury in dragon form affected his human shape, but this was no abstract lecture. "No. Forgive me. So. In like manner, this sorcerer has captured a portion of Fergus's soul—his astral, or spiritual form—and keeps hold of it. I'm yet uncertain, and perhaps I cannot be certain, whether the wizard uses this aspect to wound the physical body or whether the absence of that portion of the animating spirit innately causes the body to become less…physical. There may be an element of compensation, or an attempt at such. Regardless."

"Regardless?"

Sophia nodded. "The exact mechanism is immaterial. Fascinating, yes—in a horrible way, of course—but the problem for us, and for Fergus, remains the same whether the deterioration is innate or willed. I cannot replace what's gone…" She remembered a few passages she'd read, and grimaced. "Not in any sense but those which are abominable, and nothing that would suit your goals besides. You want your friend alive, not…"

"Not," he agreed, putting into that word all that she was searching for a way to explain. He'd stopped smiling. "What now?"

"I'm not yet certain." She walked back to take a closer look at Fergus's body before she spoke again, and the sight did confirm her hopes. "Let us then discuss what we do know. First, the potion I made is capable of halting and to some degree reversing the physical transformation. I don't know how long that will last; it would be well for me to make additional supplies. Second, Fergus's soul is still in the world. Valerius's prisoner."

"A hostage," Cathal muttered, shaking his head. "He's demanding *ransom*, the whoreson… Sorry."

She flicked away offense and apology both with a wave of her hand. "Quite probably. That implies, though it doesn't guarantee, that Valerius won't try to harm or destroy the spirit."

"Could he?"

"It's implied, in places. I know not what that would mean, or how it would be done, but…it is perhaps possible. I—" Sophia caught herself mid-sentence, before she could digress into lore and theology. Fergus lay behind her on the bed, breathing steadily and shallowly, a young man with at least a mother living and a friend in front of her.

"I'm sorry," she said, reaching a hand out toward Cathal and then letting it fall to her side. "I…have a way of running through knowledge when I try to puzzle out a problem. I meant no disrespect."

"No," he said. "I want to hear truth without silk over it, and Fergus…he was fond of a puzzle. Is." He shook his head again quickly, and the smile returned to his face, though now Sophia saw the effort that it cost him. "Besides, I like to hear you talk. You sound as though you should be in front of students at a university—"

"They'd not even let me through the doors," she said, but pleasure at the compliment bent her head.

"Fools. You're more useful, at that. Perhaps you sound like a general instead, with a map and a table of sand."

Sophia laughed. "Fighting ignorance? I like that. Fighting Valerius in this case…and I might wish for better scouts than my memory or better troops than my hands, but I suppose most commanders think so of their forces, yes?"

"Aye," he said, and silence fell between them for a long, taut minute. It was almost a disappointment when he spoke again, though his voice was, as always, low and rich and pleasing to the ear. "We're to get Fergus's spirit back, then?"

"Yes. And keep his body in a condition to receive it until we do. We can… That's part of the good news. The other part is that, well, souls do differ from bodies in some ways. I don't think I could reattach a leg, not if enough time had gone by, but from what I've seen today, I believe that Fergus's spirit can…reinhabit his body. Once we get it back, that is."

"Killing Valerius would have pleased me as it was," Cathal said. "It would bring me much more joy now. But I'll need to find him first. Or Moiread will," he corrected himself, and had the self-control not to sigh or scowl.

"Perhaps. But there might be other ways. How much do you know about magic?"

"Some. Not so much as my sister or my father. Not so much as you, I'd wager."

Sophia shook her head. "Practically…well, it's hard to tell. Alchemy, if it is magic, is of a very specific sort, and I've not practiced any other kind, nor read very much. There are a few general principles, though, and one of them is that of linkage."

"What happens on one side of a connection hits the other, even at a distance, aye. Do you mean Valerius is using that, or that we can, or both?"

"Possibly the last," Sophia said, "and hopefully the second." Channels opened before her, and encouraged by Cathal's praise, she let her mind race down them. "Alchemy is, in many respects, the art of translating the mind—or the spirit—into matter, of using physical substances as catalysts for the expression of both human and divine will. It should in theory—and does in practice, although the cases are more minor—work in the opposite direction."

"Heal Fergus's body, and we make his spirit stronger?"

"It's my hope, yes. That in itself would not, I think, solve the problem, or Valerius wouldn't have been able to cast his spell in the first place. But it is, maybe, possible that if we strengthen or otherwise empower the body—perhaps in a manner with more of a spiritual connection than that which I tried earlier—or if I find a different manner to connect it to the other planes of existence, a less obvious one, Fergus might be able to extract himself more easily and quite possibly to escape for longer periods of time and tell us more when he does."

Cathal started, torn between hope and horror. "God's teeth, I'd not even thought… He *knows*. He knows at least a bit of what's happened to him. What goes on happening." He rubbed his mouth. "Where is he, do you think? And how much of this world does he still see?"

"I don't know," Sophia said, fighting back her own revulsion at the thought. The possibilities—from those she'd vaguely heard about to those she could only imagine—curdled at the back of her mind. "I *believe* that a spirit so abducted becomes in some way a part of its captor. I think…I hope…that my source on that was only referring to how the…the forces of the universe might act on it, and not to the spirit's experience itself."

"I see," Cathal said heavily.

She wished for better news to give him and could only find plans—and more objections. "As for killing Valerius, that might work, but it may only make the situation worse. Fergus said that the wizard has him in his grasp, and a dying man may break what he clutches."

"Or take it with him."

"Or that, yes. I would like to think otherwise, that there's some provision at that final extremity—the world would seem so unjust, if a bad man could take a good one away even from the eternal—but I know nothing in that regard. I would ask your sister or your father, in your shoes, though I know you must have done so already."

"Yes," Cathal said, "but now I've more to tell them. They may see a shape now where there were only stars before."

Liking the metaphor, she smiled. "Indeed. And I, for my part, shall see what my notes and experiments can bring forth. Practically"—she raised a hand—"and I swear this is no ruse, a stronger catalyst may even be able to improve the potion I just tried. Dragon scales, for instance."

"That could be." Cathal nodded slowly, while Sophia watched his expression for suspicion or offense. She saw none. That didn't mean none existed, but she didn't think Cathal would bother to conceal either, not from her, and so she relaxed a little. "Would you need them now?"

"No, nor yet tomorrow… I'll need to work out the rest of it. Adding a new substance, especially one as powerful as I believe this to be, requires a very careful balance."

"Explosions again?" he asked with a quick grin that lightened the air in the room.

"Quite possibly," she said, teased into mirth for a second and then subsiding, "or a substance whose effects are more bane than balm, at least as far as you and Fergus are concerned. I doubt either of you would wish him to…grow scales himself, perhaps, or start breathing fire. If you do that."

"I can," said Cathal, "and I wouldn't wish that, no." He stepped toward her, stopped himself after that one movement, but held her still as firmly with his gaze and the solemn question on his face as he could have done with his hands. "Do you truly think this can succeed, madam? Knowing what we know now?"

Sophia considered it: turned the question over to look at its other sides, prodded the soft spots of her own doubts and fears, and finally nodded. "I told you before that I make no promises, and I hold to that. But I'm not a woman for blind hope. Valerius has your friend in his grasp, yes…but men and kingdoms have slipped away before or broken free. We may yet find Fergus a way around the hold."

"Or make him strong enough to break some fingers?"

Cathal's smile was wolfish this time. In theory, it might have been frightening; in reality, Sophia found herself smiling back and felt a sympathetic heat in her chest. "Or that," she agreed.

TWELVE

MORE MESSAGES; MORE TIME ON THE ROOF OF THE TOWER, talking to spirits of the air; and little enough in reply. Douglas spoke of waiting and intrigue, and expressed regret but couldn't help. Moiread didn't write at all. Cathal could only hope that was carelessness on her part, not inability.

Some of the men have heard tales of an English necromancer. I'll find what more I can, said the letter from Artair, but Cathal didn't expect very much, nor a quick arrival. His father was dealing in the fates of lords and nations, not of one man, and even his time was limited.

A letter to Agnes got a response as well, though she was busy with her own home and affairs. *All the same*, she wrote, *I am loath to think of a loyal retainer like Fergus suffering such a fate, or of this man having the presumption to dictate to you. Souls and their capture are unfamiliar to me, but I shall look to the library here and to my contacts elsewhere. It does sound*, she added, *as though your alchemist has the right idea of it.*

Even as Cathal read to the end of the letter, he kept looking back to those two words, *your alchemist*, and glaring at the paper. He couldn't have said why, save that he could hear Agnes's voice as it had been in their childhood when she would frequently imply that he, if he made an effort, might not be *completely* and hopelessly stupid. Over the years, she'd stopped doing so maliciously, just as Cathal had stopped pushing her into the horse trough when she was wearing her best gown, but the echoes still lingered.

She has a name, he thought, and then, *And you're but five years older than me. Our* sire *doesn't speak of mortals as pets, not often. Stop showing off.*

And yet he was certain she meant no harm.

Family: they never quite stopped needling you, even by accident. It had been a while since Agnes's affectations had bothered him—but then, Cathal knew, he'd grown touchy enough over the past few months. Doubtless it was only that.

Yet, when Sophia asked him to show her the holly he'd mentioned, he felt a certain incipient smugness toward Agnes and a hope that whatever Sophia discovered would work on its own, that this human scholar was good enough to solve the problem herself, without any assistance from a condescending quasi-mortal sorceress. She didn't have as many years as Agnes had, and she had not the bloodline of Cathal's mother's side, but all the same, he was beginning to suspect Sophia could hold her own in argument with any of them.

She could certainly surpass any of them for enthusiasm, he thought when he met her and Alice by the castle gate. Sophia was talking, explaining some principle that Cathal couldn't overhear. Her gloved hands were flying about as they'd done in Fergus's room, and he could see her dark eyes sparkling even in the depths of her fur hood.

Alice, in the way of friends, listened with a combination of interest and tolerant amusement. The two of them had clearly been down this road a few times before. When Cathal approached and Sophia stopped talking, Alice turned and gave him a long look, one not as sharp as her gaze had been at first but still extensive and thoughtful.

"Madam," said Cathal, tempted to ask what she was searching for and if she'd found it.

Adding to the impulse, he received a few more of

the same glances as the three of them left the castle, and Alice's gaze returned to Sophia after each. Whatever message passed between them was foreign to Cathal. He had the vague feeling that he *might* have come up to some obscure measure, in Alice's eyes, but only just.

In truth, he couldn't fault her. With Fergus up in the tower, he could have nothing but admiration for a friend's concern. And, like Sophia, she made her way through the snow without complaint, both of the women following in his tracks along the path he made. It was hard work for them, hindered by skirts as well as weaker frames, and the journey between the castle and the forest was a quiet one. The crunch of feet in snow and their quick breaths fell into the empty air, and made in time a rather companionable rhythm.

Once they reached the forest, the going was easier in some ways. The trees had kept down the worst of the snow-drifts, and fallen pine needles made for an easier foothold. Cathal forged ahead still, finding buried logs and boulders before they could become a hazard, but simply walking took less effort than it had done on the way.

"It'll be your Lent soon, will it not?" Sophia asked.

Cathal had to count the days, tapping his fingers against his thigh, before he nodded. "Aye, I suppose. Hardship for you?"

"No, not generally," said Sophia. "If nobody's eating meat at all, you see, I'm far less conspicuous. Toward the end, of course, there's Passover, but..." She spread her hands, long fingers in black gloves opening as if to let go. "That's toward the end. Time enough to think about it."

"I always liked the day before Lent, back home," said Alice. "They'll parade an ox down the street, and children go from door to door for crepes."

Sophia laughed. "You only liked not having to cook as much for yours."

"If you'd ever had to feed a man and two huge boys every evening, you'd be just as happy," said Alice.

"Where are they now?" Cathal asked, turning back to glance at her in surprise.

"Yaakov's dead...a fever, five years back. The boys are apprenticed."

"And I gave her big eyes," said Sophia, shaking her head in pretended remorse, "and begged her until she said she'd come with me to strange, cold lands, so that I would have company and my family could sleep nights."

"I wanted to *see* the strange, cold lands," said Alice. "At the time, at least. I wanted to hear new songs and new stories, and see castles and cities in this part of the world. And I wouldn't have let you go alone in any case, you who forget to sleep when you've got your head in a book."

"That... Well, yes," Sophia said, surrendering the point. "Oh! Is this the place?"

They'd come into a small clearing where the trees were largely evergreen and the shrubs around them grew thickly, many still green even in early February. "If I remember right," Cathal said and then nodded as he spotted the bright-red berries of a holly bush under one of the trees. "Aye."

"Why, I think I can find a number of useful plants here. If there's time, of course—and if you don't mind. Ordinarily I'd say that you could return to the castle, but I doubt either of us could find the way back from here."

"I don't mind," said Cathal. "Glad to be outside the walls."

"All the same," said Alice, "there's little sense us staying out here until our fingers fall off. We may as well split up. I think I know enough of what you'd want, Sophia, and Sir Cathal—"

"Holly, at least. Do I have to do anything when I pick it?" he asked.

Sophia shook her head. "Some plants *do* require special care in their harvesting...mistletoe, mandrake, a few roses...but I shouldn't think we'd find any here and now, and I can't foresee needing any such soon."

"Good. Stay within sight of the clearing. I think there's naught out here now to hurt you." There were wolves enough, largely a threat to the dead, and in the winter a few might be desperate enough to attack a living human, but none would come within a good distance of Cathal even in human form, and he would hear anything approaching. "Scream if you need to."

"Be sure that we will," said Sophia.

At first, they split the clearing equally, but when Cathal moved from one tree to another, he caught Sophia's scent: herbs, strong soap, and ink, overlaying human female, particularly *her* in a way that humans didn't have words for. He looked sideways and saw her no more than an arm's length away, carefully breaking small branches off one of the evergreen trees.

"Yew?" he asked, remembering her earlier conversation with Donnag.

"Pine." Sophia didn't turn her head, and her hands never left off their motion, just as they hadn't in the laboratory. But her voice was friendly now, and she went on. "It's not specific to either of the experiments I'm doing at the moment, but it's good for cleansing, and that's necessary enough. I'll need to purify the room a few times as I go along. Also, if there are women in the village or the castle who want to have children, I can make a potion with the cones or the nuts, or show Donnag how, but perhaps she knows already."

"I wouldn't have any idea," said Cathal. "Our rites use

pine, though I never looked very closely at it. Father or Agnes would hand me what was needed, and I'd take their word. But I doubt Donnag knows about those. I didn't know it was the same for mortals."

"I'd imagine some variation…that you're better innately at translating will or divine power through your flesh." Sophia broke off a final branch and straightened up. "Or that it's easier for you, rather. Regardless, the same principles would apply, I'd think. You are also things of the world, made by the same creator, yes?"

"Yes," said Cathal. The work had disarranged Sophia's cloak, and when she straightened, a breeze blew her gown and kirtle against her body, clearly outlining her full breasts and the flare of slim waist to rounded hip. He felt very much a thing of the world just then. "At least I think so."

"You think so?"

He shrugged. "The oldest ones belonged everywhere or nowhere. So they say." The stories were old ones, but new to Sophia, and as long as she was watching him with wide eyes and parted lips, Cathal was glad to keep talking. "Gods, if not your god…or Father Lachlann's. Or the Fair Folk, maybe, as they call them around here. They could be in this world or others, as they chose. Not so solid."

Unshocked, wondering, Sophia stepped forward, looking at him as if for some evidence of divine glow. "You look quite solid to me," she said, smiling a little.

Right now, my lady, parts of me are extremely *solid.*

Cathal bit back the reply and cleared his throat. "It's been generations. We get more mortal with each. And I'm young," he said.

"So you mentioned," she said, and then shook her head a little. "But you're…both, you mean to say. Beings of this world and not."

"Aye. It also varies among us. Some think of themselves differently. Mostly, I'm a man."

"Yes," she said, too quickly, and then caught her breath. "I mean…" If she'd had anything further to say, it vanished. Her lips moved as she stared up at him, but words died before they could emerge.

There were only a few inches between them now. Her lips were full and dark red, her eyes shining, and Cathal *was* mostly a man. Kissing her took no more thought— *allowed* no more thought—than drawing his next breath.

Sophia didn't so much step into his arms as flow there, smooth, sure, and quiet. As her hands settled on his shoulders, her lips parted under his and she tilted her face upward, not merely yielding but eager. She was warmth, she was softness, and Cathal hadn't realized until that moment just how strongly he'd craved both. Heedless of the snow, the possible spectators, or anything else in the world, he wrapped his arms around Sophia and pulled her against him, thinking only of the moment and of making it last.

THIRTEEN

SOPHIA HADN'T BEEN EXPECTING THE KISS, NOT consciously, yet from the first brush of Cathal's lips against hers, it had felt inevitable. There was momentum here, borne from weeks of awareness. It rose within her body and mind alike, blissful heat even in the midst of winter. When Cathal's tongue slid past her lips, she sighed into his mouth. When his hand splayed out against her back, his fingers brushing the upper swell of her buttocks, she yielded to the gentle pressure and tilted her hips forward.

He *was* being gentle. Even through his urgency, Sophia could tell that much. This was a man used to sword and armor, capable of deadly strength even in human form, but the arms around her, though firm, didn't crush her, and neither the hand at her back nor the one cupping her head pressed too hard. His touch was a suggestion, an urging, but there was no force in it, and he kissed her slowly and surely, lips and tongue coaxing her response.

It didn't take much. Sensation spread out from his hands and mouth, delicious ripples in a pond, and an overpowering wave at the front of her body, where she arched against him with only their clothing in the way. His chest was just as broad and solid as it'd looked, and every breath they took together rubbed her breasts against it, until her nipples were stiff and pushing at her gown. If not for her cloak, she realized, Cathal could have seen them clearly. The thought sent a dizzy wave through her body, even as she blushed. She wanted him to see—to know the effect he was having, even if she suspected she was making it obvious already, panting and clinging to him as she was.

His own response was obvious: the ridge that nudged at her stomach, hard against her even through their layers of clothing. The cloth concealed size and shape to a degree, and Sophia's reading had only revealed so much. Now a certain curiosity mingled with her desire—not one she could gratify, though even approaching the thought sent that giddy feeling through her stomach again and made her sex pulse.

Settling for a more minor experiment, she ran her fingertips up the back of Cathal's neck, tracing the line of his backbone up under his hair, then around to the spot behind his ear. Confirmation came in the involuntary flex of his arms around her, the clenching of his hands, and a sudden depth and hunger to his kiss, catching her by surprise but raising no objections. She couldn't imagine objecting to anything. She couldn't imagine anything but *wanting*.

"Sophia!"

The voice, usually welcome, fell on her ears like the yowl of a starving cat.

Sophia had time to step back, even if she nearly tripped over her gown in the process, and time to spot Alice, coming around from behind a tree with a small collection of plants in her hands. She even had a moment to pat at her wimple, as if that would help matters, and to answer in a voice that sounded vaguely normal. "Right here... Are you well?"

"Of course. But I found these, and I didn't know whether they were the sort of thing you were looking for." Approaching, Alice held out a selection of short branches, their leaves shiny and green despite the cold. "You should have brought a book for me. With illustrations."

"There were plenty of books back home with

illustrations, or where do you think I learned from?" Sophia headed quickly to her friend, putting distance between herself and Cathal without looking back. It was a relief to have the excuse and to have a reason for a flippant response.

Even so, Alice didn't speak for a moment. Sophia felt those sharp blue eyes on her face, where she suspected her cheeks were still flushed, and where her lips still felt the memory of Cathal's. Her eyes might have yet been glassy with desire too, so she kept her gaze carefully on the plants that Alice was holding out. She might have frozen to death, had she stood there naked, but she was certain she wouldn't have felt more exposed.

Just at the moment, the cold was itself welcome. The heat in her body was subsiding, flame returning to embers, but it was still very much present. Sophia took a long breath of chilly air.

"Well?"

She blinked at Alice. "Um…"

Alice shook the handful of stems. "Are these useful, or do we leave them for…well, not wolves, I'd imagine. Deer?"

"I don't know." Scholarship, like the cold, was a handy path back to calm, a return to the world she knew. Sophia took the plants and was glad that her hands didn't tremble. "These are unfamiliar to me as well, and yet I think worth at least bringing them back. I can consult my books or ask Donnag, and in any case, a thing that retains life in adversity is almost certain to be of use in our current matter."

"If you say so," Alice said and took the plants back. "Not that I'll say anything against tenacity. It's served us well so far."

"Endurance," said Cathal, and his voice sent a shiver through Sophia's body. "Patience. My father would approve."

"Well, and as he was the man we came to see," Alice

said, "that's an excellent recommendation. I'm sure those qualities come much more easily to him—and to you— than they do to us, for all I was praising them earlier."

"To him, perhaps. You both strike me as ladies of strong will," said Cathal.

Sophia busied herself arranging what she'd picked, still not trusting herself to look into his face. He was the opposite of a gorgon, and she a very odd Perseus, and yet the effect was the same. She did see Alice tilt her head, though, before she replied.

"For humans, perhaps," her friend said, polite and not openly unfriendly. "But to creatures like your family, I'm sure we're very impulsive. And very…brief."

"I think," Sophia said, raising her head at last because she couldn't kick Alice in the ankle without being obvious about it, "that perhaps we should go back. We have what we came for."

"We do indeed," said Alice. "And it doesn't do to exhaust ourselves."

"Was that completely necessary?"

Sophia had to walk back, making polite conversation the whole time, and then pull Alice into the corner beside the fireplace before she could actually ask. After so much time, a lesser woman might have found the question confusing. A different woman might have pretended to.

"If I hadn't thought so, do you think I'd have said it?" Alice replied unflinchingly and almost immediately.

"I know what you thought. I asked in the hope that you'd think twice, vain though that hope may be."

"Ah, well, if we're on the subject of thinking twice… or even once…"

Heat swept over Sophia's face, completely unrelated to the fire near at hand. She couldn't even protest that Alice was unjust. She *hadn't* thought very much when she'd been in Cathal's arms, and certainly not of anything beyond the two of them. In truth, that had been part of the allure. "I know," she interrupted. "And nothing happened, not truly."

Had she been younger, or Christian, or heaven forbid, a lady, that might not have been true, even out in this near-wilderness. Looked at from a distance, what had passed between her and Cathal had been only a kiss, such as any lord might steal from a dairymaid or a farmer's daughter— not quite the best of behavior, but easy enough to let slip past. She had no high relations to take offense, and she doubted he had enough chivalry to feel he had to make any gestures, but thought he did have enough to keep from trying for anything more.

If she let herself feel disappointed about that, Alice would *certainly* have a few words on the subject.

As it was, her friend sighed and shook her head. "I'd say you should have been more thoughtless at home—or at least in France—rather than spending so much time in your books. Not that you should have been *truly* improper, mind, but...at least you'd have a few callouses built up, yes? Useful around men like Sir Cathal."

"You sound like I'm thirteen or fresh from a convent. You know that isn't so."

"I know that smiling at a few boys down the street and then going back to your studies doesn't count for much." Alice put a hand on Sophia's arm. "I know that you've got freedom out here, and time to use it. And I'm not saying that I wouldn't be tempted either, if I were in your shoes. But I also know that *he's not human*. If he

were human, he'd still be Sir Cathal MacAlasdair, and
you'd be Sophia Metzger, and you know very well what
I'm getting at."

"I know." Sophia wrapped her arms around herself,
but managed a smile and a little laugh. "Alice, it's not as
though I think I'm going to marry the man. I don't dwell in
books all the time."

"No," said Alice slowly, "no, I don't think that. You
neglect yourself, but you've never been *sentimental* before."

"And I have no intention of starting now, or with him."

"I believe you. Does he know that?"

"I…" Sophia considered the question as best she could,
though it came with disconcerting memories of the look on
Cathal's face just before he kissed her, and of being warm
and wanted in his arms. Sophia shook her head quickly. "I
very much doubt he thinks I'm mad," she said acerbically,
"and I'm certain he knows I'd *have* to be to imagine that
there'd ever be anything…significant between us."

Alice nodded. "Just as long as he considers what's…
significant"—her arched eyebrows and pursed mouth
gave the word an unmistakable meaning—"to you. He's
a man, remember?"

"You think we'd be here if that had slipped my mind?"

"And he doesn't seem the forceful sort, I'll give him
that…not that they always do." Memory thinned Alice's
lips and drew a sympathetic noise from Sophia. Being
unmarried, she hadn't heard as much of the gossip back
home, but she knew enough. Alice went on. "But he's lord
of this place—in fact right now, if not in title—and he's got
plenty of opportunities to be persuasive…and he might not
really think anything of the risks you'd be taking. I thought
it was worth reminding him. I still do."

"Not so many risks," Sophia said, her voice falling as

she looked into the fire. She'd made her choices long ago. Few men wanted a scholarly wife, and her studies had left little time for courtship. In the right frame of mind, she counted herself lucky that she'd *had* the choice to make, that with one daughter married and two sons, her family had been both able and inclined to allow for an unwed scholar. But on some nights, and on a certain sort of gray afternoon, she couldn't keep her mind from wondering about the untrodden path. "It isn't as though the rabbi will have a list of men for my father when I go back, is it? And at my age, it's hardly likely that—"

The hand on her forearm gave it a gentle slap. "'Hardly likely' is still possible, and you know it *almost* as well as I do. Remember Madame Laurent? Forty-five and *twins*."

"I remember," said Sophia, who'd gone in with salves and potions to help the midwife. It had been a long night, but the yelling of healthy babes—and the look on Madame Laurent's face—had been reward enough.

"So. And you never know—if you were at home, you might change your mind. You're not a hag, you know, and this isn't so scandalous that a man might not overlook it… maybe a widower, one who had his own life too."

"The world does contain many things," said Sophia, the nearest she could come to equaling her friend's probably forced optimism and the closest she *would* get to admitting, either to Alice or herself, how little the prospect appealed to her.

"Well, then."

"You don't have to try to convince me. I'm not going to go throwing myself at the lord of the castle out of…of despair or recklessness. It was a moment. I don't plan to repeat it, and I don't think I'll even have the chance." Sophia managed another smile. "But it is good of you to worry."

"No, it's just *worried* of me to worry." Alice slipped an arm around her friend's shoulders.

This time, smiling was easier, and Sophia leaned into the embrace easily. Concern was good, and perhaps the reminder *had* been necessary. Her own resistance was evidence enough of that.

FOURTEEN

Sophia fell.

She couldn't remember what or where she fell from; she couldn't see what or where she fell *to*. She knew only falling, the headfirst plummet that left her stomach far behind. She gasped for breath and clutched at nothing. The landing would be painful. The landing might well be fatal. She could do nothing about that.

At first, there was only darkness around her. Sophia stared into it with wide eyes, looking for anything to grasp, any possibility of aid, but there was only black void. She'd been screaming from the first, but when she realized that the fall was taking longer than it possibly could have, she stopped and realized that there was nothing else around her to hear. The world might have ended.

Then she began to see shapes in the blackness. They didn't look like the products of strained vision—she knew those well—but all the same, she shut her eyes for a second. On opening them, the shapes were still hanging in the void. Now a few of them were moving. They didn't move like earthly things. They didn't look like earthly things either, not in shape or color, but Sophia couldn't have said precisely what they *did* look like. The mind shied away from specifics.

Through her fear, that inability irritated her. Details had always come easily to her. One pinned down the universe with knowledge. One looked, described, researched, experimented. Sophia's mind had always served her well in that regard, and to have it fail her, even under such circumstances as these, vexed her all out of proportion. She glowered, braced herself, and then focused on one of the shapes.

It was almost blue, except where it was more almost pink. It was a circular sort of square. It moved sideways and diagonally at the same time. Sophia closed her eyes again and shook her head—a head now shot through with pain, as if she'd tried to look directly at the sun.

A very deep part of her mind, one that barely managed words, said *things beyond*. It wasn't knowledge exactly; it was more instinct, like recognizing the smell of blood or the sound of thunder. Given time, she might have been able to translate the feeling into words, to pin it down in its turn and make it concrete, but the fall *wasn't* endless. Sophia couldn't see land when she looked down, but she felt the end approaching.

The shapes changed. Without looking too closely again—and even Sophia's curiosity quailed at the prospect—she couldn't have said how, exactly. It was like they became grayer or greener, more twisted or sharper. The first ones hadn't felt bad, only impossible to look at. These others…

…she couldn't say. She didn't know if she wanted to say. Sophia knew only that their presence was a shudder down her spine and a twist in her gut. She shouldn't have been able to fear anything more than falling rapidly toward an unknown destination, but looking at them was worse than that.

Ground hit her, rather than the reverse. On one breath she was falling, trying not to look at the shapes around her. With the next, she was flat on her stomach, her face in dirt, jarred and probably bruised. She still breathed, though, and she felt no broken bones, which was a minor miracle.

She pulled herself to her feet. It took surprisingly little time; she almost rose as soon as she thought it. Having ground beneath her feet was a new sensation, and one that should have reassured her more than it did, but this ground felt unpleasant, squashy, and unstable. When Sophia looked around, she didn't like her surroundings much better than the non-place she'd fallen through, even though they made more sense.

The ground below her was part of a tiny path, no wider than her shoulders and perhaps narrower in places. As far as Sophia could see, it wound forward and back through an immense forest of dark trees. They weren't the trees around Loch Arach—or not in any place she'd seen. For one thing, they all had leaves. Noticing that, Sophia realized that there was no snow on the ground either, nor did she feel cold.

What was she wearing? Strange that she couldn't remember that. She looked down to check and, in doing so, glimpsed movement from behind her.

Forgetting about her clothes—a shapeless gray dress, which would have struck her as odd, had she had time to think about it—Sophia spun around. Better to know, always better to know, even though it would likely only be a squirrel or a deer and she'd feel silly.

It was a face.

It was a face made out of shadow, one without eyes. It rested atop a shadow-body like a man's, save that it was too tall and too thin. There were three of them, and they were coming toward her.

Rationality and civilization asserted themselves for a second, letting Sophia stand her ground and open her mouth, even while she shuddered inwardly at the way the things looked and moved. "Hello?" she tried, holding up a hand. "Can I aid you?"

None of them answered. None of them seemed to take any notice of her, except that she felt their not-eyes focusing on her, and the paths they each took on their stretched, spindly legs would converge on the spot where she stood.

Then rationality failed and civilization surrendered to far older and stranger forces. Sophia spun around, though turning her back on the shadow-things was the hardest thing she'd ever had to do, and bolted down the path, not knowing where it led and in that frantic moment not caring at all.

Whatever they were, they wanted nothing good.

While the shadow-things moved silently, Sophia's flight wasn't. The ground squelched with every step, wet and sucking like quicksand, and the smell that rose up from it was not that of earth after rain but stronger and meatier. She became rapidly grateful for the sound of her own panting breath in her ears as a distraction, and grateful as well that she was wearing sturdy boots.

She hadn't known until that thought that she *was* wearing sturdy boots. Her dress came to mind again when she realized that, and the combination nagged at her, like the nature of the forest. Where was she? Where had she been before she'd started falling?

The path narrowed even further. Branches scraped at her arms and pulled her hair, and Sophia began to feel a malice to it, that the trees were deliberately reaching out to wound her. That was irrational; this place didn't make much sense, and these were not normal trees.

And she cried out in dismay when the path ended at one.

There was no way through. The underbrush was thick on either side, the leaves almost blending together into a solid gray-green mass. Sophia looked back over one shoulder.

The shadow-things were still there, and they were gaining. Even as she paused to look, they darted forward, the

movement more like fish than anything that walked on
land, or should.

With the strength of panic, she leapt, grabbed a low-
hanging branch, and pulled herself up. The wood was slick
and half rotten itself. She actually felt her hands sink into
it. Slime surrounded her fingers, and the few solid bits of
bark that remained scratched her palms.

Sophia looked down. The shadow-things were standing
around the base of the tree, near-featureless faces tipped
upward to watch her. Neither hunger nor hatred could show
themselves on any of those faces. Still Sophia felt them,
and she shuddered as the creatures stretched their long
arms upward, the tips of tendril-fingers brushing through
the air just an inch or two below her branch.

The rotten wood gave way beneath her.

Only a few seconds passed between the initial break and
the moment when the branch split, just enough warning
for Sophia to lunge frantically, blindly upward. Her hands
found a higher, thicker branch and scrabbled for purchase,
her fingernails sinking into the damp bark. She dangled
there as the branch below her tumbled to the ground, her
arms already starting to ache.

One of the shadow-things wrapped a hand around her
ankle. Sophia felt the cold of its grip burning through her
boot. It pulled with a strength that belied its insubstantial
form, and the branch to which she was clinging started to
give under the pressure.

"*NO!*"

She shrieked the word, not in cosmic denial but with all the
frustrated willpower she'd ever used on balky horses, disobe-
dient dogs, and troublesome younger brothers: *This is* enough,
and if you keep acting up, you're going to be so very *sorry*.

And under her hands, the branch became solid again.

Analysis would have to wait. Sophia kicked out at the shadow-thing, hitting it squarely in the face, and yanked herself upward with all the force that fear and anger could give her. This time she didn't stop, nor did she look down, but found another branch and kept climbing, calling on dimly remembered skills from her childhood and finding them surprisingly near to hand.

The bark even felt drier now. She pulled herself upward over five feet, then ten, and no hand found her ankle again. When she did let herself glance down, she didn't see any shadow-things pursuing her. Perhaps they couldn't climb.

That did leave the question of how she'd get down, but she climbed as she thought. It could be that the shadow-things would get tired and leave, or that, like wolves, they'd find other, easier prey.

Then again, perhaps Cathal would be in flight nearby and would see her. Sophia would have put him up against a pack of shadow-things any day. He would have to find her first, of course, and she didn't get the feeling that she was anywhere near Loch Arach.

So how did you get *here?*

As she asked herself the question, she broke through the top of the forest.

Treetops stretched away around her. A few reached above her head, but even those, so high, were easy to look around. The view wasn't reassuring. All the leaves were dark, and the sky itself was a muddy reddish-gray shade that Sophia could *perhaps* put down to clouds over a sunset, but that struck the deeper part of herself as more significant and less natural. If there was life in the forest, even as little as a squirrel in a tree or a spider on a branch, it hid itself well. As far as she could make out, the only beings nearby were her and the shadow-men.

More like shadows than men. Cathal had said that. He'd been speaking of the creatures he'd fought, the less-human minions of Valerius. They'd sounded different, the way he'd described them, but still…men who looked a bit like shadows, shadows that took the vague shape of men. Was a connection so unlikely?

The forest was on a hilltop, it seemed, so Sophia could look down over the dark sea of treetops and into the valley below. A castle squatted there, comparatively low and wide, vainly clutching at the sky with stumpy towers. She could see that the forest ended a little way from it, revealing bare earth and a dark river. Human habitation: it should have been an immense relief, but nothing in her wanted to take a step in that direction, even if it were a practical option.

She shifted her weight, wrapping one arm around the tree trunk and freeing her other, and looked down. The shadows around the tree were thick. There was no way of knowing whether they were natural or animate. If she'd had flint and steel, Sophia thought, she could have lit one of the smaller branches and thrown it down, perhaps even injured one of the things in the process.

A small shape settled itself into the palm of her free hand for a second, long enough for her to recognize it as a tinderbox, and then, as she looked down in surprise, it shimmered and vanished.

"What—"

"Sophia." Disembodied, a voice filled the air around her: Alice, sharp and no-nonsense, with an edge of alarm. Sophia looked around for her, seeing nothing. "Sophia. Wake up. *Now*."

And a short, hard shake of her shoulders knocked her out of the tree and the forest alike, back into the world of her now-familiar bedroom at Castle MacAlasdair, back to candlelight and Alice's narrow eyes.

"I…" Now relief came, and oh, it was blessed. This was her room, her bed, with stone walls around her and no shadow shapes chasing her beneath a rotting sky. "Thank you. How did you know?"

She put out a hand to grasp Alice's shoulder, thinking both to thank her and to confirm her solidity. Pain jabbed into her palm at the first contact—not much, not really, but enough to draw a yelp from her and to startle her into dropping her hand. Then she stared at Alice's shoulder and at the bloodstain on her chemise.

"That," Alice said grimly, "is how I knew."

Sophia turned her hand up. Three scratches ran across the palm. Now she felt the others, the ones on her shoulders and neck, and a cold pain in her leg. "The trees… In my dream there were trees…"

"Dream trees must be fearsome. Look at your ankle."

Alice stepped back, far enough to pull up the hem of Sophia's chemise. At her ankle, just above the bone, a ring of purple-red skin encircled her leg.

FIFTEEN

"This…" Cathal began, and then couldn't say anything else.

Sophia's hand, palm upturned, rested in his. In his grasp, her hand was tiny, the small bones delicate as glass ornaments, and Cathal kept his hand perfectly still. He knew his strength too well. More than that, he knew the rage that was building within him, tightening the muscles of his shoulders and neck. Perfect control was more important when imperfect control could mean disaster. Artair had told him that many times.

Let himself go, even slightly, and the rest would give way like an avalanche. The time would come, shortly, when he would be dangerous to be around. He had no wish to hasten the moment, or to threaten Sophia further. Bad enough that he couldn't keep her safe.

None of the welts on her palm were truly bad. He'd had worse just about every day he'd been a squire, between training and chores. Any kitchen boy would pick up greater wounds peeling turnips. Yet the scratches blazed bright across her dark palm, dried blood an accusation like letters of fire.

She left her hand in his and made no attempt to move it. Her skin was warm and smooth against his palm, though on her fingers themselves he could see calluses, and ink stains, and a few small red marks that looked like burns.

"Let me see your ankle," he said, curt and low in his chest.

Really, he hadn't expected protest from Sophia, nor even truly from Alice, but the lack was almost as painful, as was the quick grace with which she sat down and raised her skirt. "You'll have to come around," she said, "for I don't think it would help matters were I to sit on your desk."

She spoke with mild, friendly tones and smiled wryly, just as she might have done in any other mildly troublesome situation, as if Cathal hadn't put her in danger, as if he hadn't failed in the most basic duty of a host. When he extracted himself from his chair and came over to her, he studied her face, looking for anger or accusation, and found none.

Kneeling in front of her felt like homage, and he minded not at all.

That moment passed swiftly, though, shattered by the sight of the ring of discolored skin around her ankle.

He didn't think either of the women knew enough Gaelic to translate the oath he swore, but his voice probably made the meaning quite clear. Alice's eyes narrowed. "You've seen this before? I thought you might have."

"Yes. No." He left his hands cupping Sophia's leg, letting its weight and solidity, the heat of life and the firm muscle of an active woman, be a reminder to him. She was still here; she was still well; the wound would heal. "The shades I fought were more human. They used weapons. Mostly. But enough of their nature came through even there. And it was cold."

"One of them stabbed you, yes?" Sophia asked. "You mentioned that, I believe, and your shoulder—"

"Aye. Had it been only a man and a knife, I'd have been back in battle in two days, mayhap a week." He rolled his shoulder back and forth, remembering. "And it was cold, the knife. Not like winter. Like…deep places, or darkness."

Without words, he stopped.

"Darkness, yes," said Sophia. She looked away for

a moment, and a shiver passed through her body. "There wasn't much life to them, nor to anything else in that dream."

In the pause between words, slightly too long, and the way her hands now clasped each other, Cathal saw the effort her calm words took, and the work behind each smile. He wished he'd had the right to put an arm around her, or even to take her hands in his. Even without the right, he wished Alice weren't watching, so that he might have done it regardless.

He didn't. She was. The world turned on facts, not desire.

Facts, then, were where he turned, continuing the story. "Two of my men did touch the shades. Skin to skin. There comes a time for fists even in battle, more than once in a while. Baithin's fist looked as your leg does, after. Tralin's neck was worse. Darker."

"Did it heal?" Alice asked.

"In time. He'll bear the scar the rest of his days." He looked down at Sophia's leg again, sternly locking away any reaction he might have had as a man, ignoring the shapely outline and the golden-brown color and peering with an attempt at detachment at the wound the shade had left. "I said it wasn't like winter, their cold, but the marks it leaves are."

"I've heard of that a little," said Sophia, leaning forward to investigate, "though I've never seen it before…but then, I never would have. Even London was warmer than here."

"By some measure. This'll be unpleasant. I'm sorry," said Cathal, and he brushed a thumb over the red-and-purple skin. Muscles tensed beneath his hand, and Sophia hissed. "That's good," he said, "even if you don't believe me."

"No," said Sophia, visibly making herself relax. "I do. I've read, you know, that if it hurts, that means I can still feel, yes? That the…injury…isn't too deep?"

"Aye. It hadn't looked that bad, but it's best to be sure."

"I had boots on, in the dream," she said, her face taking on the look of contemplation that Cathal was coming to know well. "It's a strange thing to think that what I was wearing in the dream could have spared me pain in the waking world."

"These things were in the dream, and they *caused* you pain in the waking world," Alice pointed out.

"Oh, yes. But they weren't human, and I had assumed that. But then, not all my injuries came from them, did they?" Sophia turned her injured palm upward, her eyes lighting up in a way that Cathal would never have thought to see on anyone contemplating scratches on her own body. "So the question is, is it not, whether the shades were only parts of the dream, or different beings in it, as I was? And why the dream could hurt me, and where it came from."

"Valerius. I've no proof, no," Cathal said when Sophia started to object. "But who else would want to, who could manage it?"

"That's certainly most likely. I'd suppose that my first attempt to cure Fergus established a connection between the two of us. The shades are another strong argument in that direction, unless they're more common than I think." She gave him a small smile. "I've an idea who my enemy is. Isn't that the first step in winning a war?"

Slowly, reluctantly, Cathal released her leg and stood up. "He doesn't have to be your enemy," he said. His heart ached with every word he spoke and with each one he knew would follow, ached with regret for Fergus and thwarted vengeance, but Sophia had struck her bargain without knowing she'd be making herself a target thereby. Honor, even his battered version of it, demanded he rethink the terms now. "You can go home. I'll give you the scales. You've done all I could ask of you."

Color flooded Sophia's face. "By God, sir…" A look between him and Alice, and she bit her lip, though she still stared up at him with blazing eyes. "I know you mean it kindly, but do you think I'd leave a man with his soul in the grasp of…of that *creature*? Especially after what I've seen? I may not go to war, but I try to have courage, and honor too, and if I have skills that can save a life or a spirit, I know my duty is to use them. What would I be if I turned and ran now?"

"Alive," said Cathal. He wanted to kiss her again, to pull her close and know that bold spirit more fully. He wanted to shake her and tell her to be sensible and leave now. As with comfort, he had no right to do either, and he couldn't deny her argument.

"Yes, but for what kind of life?"

"Not necessarily even that," Alice put in, her own voice dry and detached. "Though it's a good piece of oratory, Sophia, very inspirational. But if this wizard has a tie to you, why would he find it harder to come at your mind in France than he would here?"

"The sea might be a barrier," Cathal said.

For that piece of speculation, he received an interested look from Sophia and a flat one from Alice. "But it might not," she said, "and then we'd be well away from anyone who knows the man or his methods. *Not* a good idea. We'd also have to find our way down out of the mountains, and the roads are still half frozen."

"I could carry you both. Easily."

"Wonderful. Then, assuming we didn't fall off a mile in the air, we'd just have to find a ship that could take us across the channel and hope it didn't sink. Or you could take us personally and leave everyone here undefended and leaderless for a few days." Alice shook her head. "Anything could be fatal. I hate to say it, but so far, all Valerius has done is give her bad dreams and a few minor injuries. If that doesn't get worse, it's better than risking travel, and if it does, we don't want to be on the road when it happens."

"And it doesn't matter, regardless," Sophia said, and then added more gently, "unless you want to go, Alice. You can."

"No, nor do I want to. Everything you said applies to me, you know…unless you mean to suggest I can't be of any help." Alice made a face at Sophia, affectionate and determined at the same time. "And this place is still more interesting than home."

"Be certain," Cathal said, bending forward. "You might not have boots in the next dream. You might not get away in time."

Sophia shuddered, and for a moment Cathal hated himself, but then her eyes cleared and she held up a hand. "Wait. I *did* have boots. Why would he let me…unless he only intended a warning…but… And then he clearly can't… Not all of it…and—"

"Finish a sentence, pray," said Alice. "Before I pour a basin over your head to bring your senses back."

The face Sophia made at her was practiced but also absent, halfhearted at best. "He can't control all of the dream. I *think* the shades are separate, his creatures but still themselves, and I think that he had to pull me there, through a place that isn't entirely his. And I *was* shaping things in the end. Not very well, but I managed it."

"That's a relief. Obvious, since you're *here*, but we'll take any good news just now," said Alice.

"No, but this could be an advantage," Sophia said, leaning forward. "I mentioned connections. If the dream is his sending, he must put something of himself into it…and if

I can shape it, then that much of him is in my power, or it could be."

"Like a fight," said Cathal, trying both to understand and to ignore the way Sophia's breasts pressed against her gown in her new position. The former helped with the latter, though not as much as would have been genteel or knightly. "Hard to strike without getting in the other fellow's range."

Sophia nodded slowly, chewing on her lip some more as she thought the metaphor through. "Yes. And if I can, oh, grab his arm and pull him even more forward, then he's in *my* power. I can't fight him directly with magic, any more than I could fight you with a sword…but it's possible that I could make him fight himself."

Cathal actually smiled. "How can we better the odds?"

"Well, a part of him would be best. A part can change the whole," she recited, almost singsong, "and a likeness can change what it's like. If you'd saved the arm, we'd probably be doing very well," she added with a wry smile of her own.

"I'll bear that in mind for the next time."

"It's always better to prepare. A lock of hair, a drop of blood, a true name, all of those have great power…which is, I'd imagine, one of the reasons he goes by that ridiculous alias. To a lesser extent, anything you can find out about him might be an aid. And I'll contemplate the problem." She got to her feet. If the ankle gave her any trouble, Cathal didn't see it. "The world is the divine cloaked in matter. Dreams, which have only will and no matter, should be a midpoint. If I can bring my will into greater harmony… Well, I shall have to see."

"See right," said Alice, gripping her friend's shoulder, "and study hard. I don't think this will be the last dream he sends."

SIXTEEN

For the next few nights, Sophia slept without trouble. She was nervous enough the first night to consider drinking wine before bed, but decided that she'd need unclouded judgment if Valerius *did* send another nightmare, and spent a good long time staring into the darkness, making herself breathe regularly in and out, before she relaxed enough to doze off.

Her undisturbed nights after that were not entirely reassuring. Whether Valerius needed to gather strength again or could only send the dreams when the stars were right, every night that progressed without a nightmare was one closer to the next occurrence. Sophia had been granted time to prepare. Knowing that weighed on her, keeping her always conscious that she should be working, and that she could be doing more.

Then there came an afternoon when she couldn't.

The laboratory was full of work. Near the window, the burned remains of the holly, blended with powdered jet and the skin of a snake, sat in a clear glass beaker and caught what sunlight the winter day was able to provide. A little solar energy to go with the saturnine would harm nothing, Sophia had thought, and it was almost always essential to the fermentation phase.

Where more blatantly solar forces were concerned, she'd nursed a small amount of her precious stock of cloves through the calcination process once more, had transferred it to a blue glass bowl and carefully added water to start the dissolution phase. The topaz was powdered and ready for calcination itself, but there would be several hours before the planets aligned properly for that, or for Sophia to begin any of the other processes that she could manage just then.

As she always did, and as she had done more often in the days since the first dream, Sophia had turned from action to contemplation, seeking both to strengthen her own will and to bring it into harmony with that of the Most High. Barred by her age, sex, and unmarried state from studying the *Sefer Bahir*, the book that explained greater secrets of the universe, she'd nonetheless picked up bits from books and teachers, as birds picked up crumbs in the street. She bent her mind to understanding what she could and prayed in all ways she felt might be acceptable.

At times, as she shaped her lips around the words, she felt her will almost like a hand, capable of reaching out, of grasping or of striking, if she only knew what to do with it. At other times she felt that her mind opened and she saw a light that was only *light* because she could think of no other word for it, a light that was in reality everything.

Such moments were few. They were brief. They almost always left her weary, as though she'd been running uphill or lifting heavy loads rather than just standing and focusing on words. Pushing herself too far in contemplation, as with anything else, could be disastrous. She knew that from both teaching and instinct.

Besides, there were hours for contemplation too, and once she'd added water to the topaz, the timing would be wrong.

One wanted to become part of the right harmony, after all. She'd heard a few stories about what could happen otherwise. Opening those doors under the wrong circumstances could let in beings Sophia hoped never to encounter.

So she found herself standing in a room where she could

do nothing, with the afternoon ahead of her, and feeling more alert and restless than she would have expected. It might have been the approaching spring—it was hard to tell with the snow, but the days were getting longer, the air a shade less frigid.

At home, the snow would have melted weeks before. By now, at least the first tightly furled crocuses would have come up. There might be grass and the earliest buds on the rosebushes and in the trees. Mother would sit outside on the first day of real sun and risk scandal by uncovering her hair. *I'm an old woman*, she said, *and God made the spring breeze. He'll understand.*

Memory hit Sophia in the pit of her stomach.

It was spring, and the remembrance of other springs. It was Alice saying, *Someone should tell your parents*. It was Passover approaching. She'd accommodate, if she was still here, doing what she could and trusting that her work would justify her failures in the end, but she didn't *want* to adjust, to make do or leave out. She wanted the preparation, her father's voice at the table, all the small rituals that marked the greater one, that marked off the passage of time and the smooth turning of the world.

Alice had always liked watching the city celebrate Lent around them, observing the same way she listened to songs out here: *This is not mine, but that doesn't matter*. The celebrations in the street had always made Sophia feel a touch left out, but back home that had been a minor, momentary pang. She'd had her family, her friends, her own part of the world.

Here, there were just her and Alice, and a good fifty people who, kind as they were, might turn much less so if they knew precisely what kind of women lived under their roof. But then again, the Scots weren't necessarily the English.

Everything was cold here, and alien.

Sophia looked down at her skirt and found her fists clenched in the black wool. *Foolishness*, she told herself, *sentimental foolishness, and you're too old for that*. She'd left home knowing that her absence was apt to be long, and that she was going among strangers. Her mother had wept, and her father had cleared his throat more than necessary, but every child leaves eventually. She might have married and moved to Holland, as one girl they'd known had done. As it was, if she didn't die, she'd at least return in a year or so.

Uncurling her fingers, she told herself that Cathal knew her and was still kind. (*More* than kind, and that memory wisped across her body with a tingling pleasure, but that was not the point.) His people had been kind too, and friendly enough, given that she was still clumsy with the language, and perhaps inclined to accept anyone Edward of England had wronged. She didn't know. She didn't have to find out.

She was here with a task, and she was here to learn. Once those goals were complete, she'd go home, and Loch Arach's inhabitants could think as they wished. Standing about moping wouldn't help.

Out of both habit and caution, Sophia made a last inspection of her vessels, made sure that progress was steady and that neither instability nor contamination was a danger. Then she descended the staircase, walking briskly and not giving herself time to think very much.

The hall was crowded as always: benches pushed back against the walls between meals, servants cleaning or changing tapers or simply going hither and yon on various errands, and a few people with more leisure sitting by the fire. Sophia spotted Alice's blond curls among the last crowd. She sat listening to an old man play the harp. The tune was one that Sophia recognized by now, and she found, as she heard Alice's voice mingle with both the old man's and the sound of the harp itself, that she could even pick out a few of the words: *eat* and *I*, *know*, and *lady*.

She didn't know enough to follow the song, not as quickly as they were singing it, and she had no taste just then for standing by and watching, but she smiled as she passed by, glad to see the intent look on Alice's face. At least her friend was gaining something from the journey, other than freezing and worrying about Sophia; she'd always claimed to, but it was good to see impartial evidence.

Out of the great hall, Sophia descended into the kitchen, welcoming the heat that almost immediately surrounded her. When her experiments demanded flame, the tower was warm enough, but otherwise it became quite chilly—the small hearth that could fit into the room didn't quite make up for the height of the place and the age—and Sophia stretched out her hands in pleasure.

"Lady," said Matain, the dark-haired page she'd slightly met on her first morning in the castle. He came toward her quickly, smiling. He was a helpful one, or well trained, or just eager for a change in routine. He also might have been glad for an excuse to stop turning the spit—there was sweat running down his face. "Are you hungry?"

It was one of the sentences she knew, but he still spoke slowly and as clearly as he could, given the noise of the kitchen: a considerate lad.

"If you have anything," Sophia said, and for a moment she could tell herself that it was because she didn't want to waste his time, and that mayhap a good meal would put her in a better mood, even if she felt not at all like eating just then.

"Half a meat pie," he said. "From dinner. But—"

His hesitation told her what she'd already guessed would happen: a few of the servants, at least, had realized that she ate no flesh. "No, that will be good," said Sophia.

If she'd wanted to, she could have kept deceiving herself a little while longer. She could have told herself that she'd only accepted to try to keep suspicion down, and that any subsequent ideas had sprung into her head only later, when she didn't want to throw good food to the dogs. She could have lied inside her head, but she didn't.

Strengthening her willpower—putting all of that force toward contemplation, experiments, and resisting Valerius's subsequent dreams—hadn't left her very much for daily life, it seemed, and tearing herself away from melancholy had used a great deal of what remained. As soon as Matain brought the pie back, wrapped in a white cloth, she headed not to the kennels, nor to the hall, but to the staircase that she'd walked her first night, the one that led to Cathal's solar.

The door was closed when she arrived, but she knocked—she'd come too far to waste the effort—and gruff as his "Come!" was, it relieved her. She would have felt foolish indeed if she'd faced an empty room.

Cathal was leaning back in his chair, booted feet on his desk. A bottle of wine was open in front of him, but he didn't look drunk. Indeed, he was carving into a block of wood, which argued either that he was sober or that he could regrow fingers. When he saw her, his hands stopped moving.

"Are you well?" he asked, giving her face and body each a quick look that was nonetheless hot with intensity.

"Yes," she said, and it wasn't an untruth, just a wholly inadequate description. "I... My work doesn't require me at this moment."

"I can say the same. That I'm not needed," he added as he got to his feet with a smile that might have been apologetic.

His mouth looked very firm. It had been when he kissed her—but not hard, not brutal, though she thought he could have been, and the idea wasn't entirely unpleasant either. He'd simply known what he wanted and guessed very well what she did. But then, he wouldn't lack experience, really, even less than most men of the world.

She dropped her gaze from his lips to his hands, which didn't help, and tried to ignore the warmth between her legs. "I came with a bribe," she said and held out the pie, an inadequate and not entirely welcome shield. Then, because it was the first thing that came to mind that *wasn't* his body pressed against hers, she asked, "What's the song that sounds like this?" and hummed a few lines.

Briefly Cathal frowned, puzzled, and then his face cleared. "Ah. 'Twa Corbies' I think is the title. It's two crows, talking over a dead knight." He lifted his voice, a pleasant baritone if nothing that would have impressed Alice, and sang:

> *His hound is tae the huntin gane,*
> *His hawk tae fetch the wild fowl hame.*
> *His lady's ta'en anither mate-o*
> *Sae we may mak oor dinner swate-o.*

"It is," he added, with a shrug of his broad shoulders, "a wee bit grim for some. My brother never liked it."

"No? But it's not untrue... It's almost comforting in its way. Life going on, even after us, and our mortal remains being useful at the end. Though I suppose nobody really wants to think of the world going on, even if we should."

"We should?" Cathal asked, not disagreeing, just interested to see what she'd say.

Sophia shrugged in her turn. "It would be *good* of us to want the ones we love to be happy, even without us, yes? To keep on with their lives and their work? But I don't think very many do."

"I'm no' sure hawks and hounds are truly loved ones, at that," Cathal said, his eyes glinting a little with good humor, "but aye. It's one of the reasons not many mortals know who we are, or get close to us when they do...or so I've heard, not being one myself. But you wouldn't have come with a bribe just to hear the meaning of a song, I think."

Recalled to her purpose, such as it was, Sophia shook her head. "No. I have questions about you...and your people."

"I might answer. You did bring me food."

SEVENTEEN

THE WAY SOPHIA WAS STANDING IN THE DOORWAY, holding out her bribe with both hands even as she kept one foot tucked behind the other, reminded Cathal of statues he'd seen: clay maidens on sunny fountains or rising from the midst of gardens. None of them had been famous art, and they'd appealed more for it, stayed longer in his mind than works of more renown.

Always she called to mind places other than icy Loch Arach, and by doing so made the castle itself easier to bear. If he'd been a philosopher, Cathal would have found a text or two in that paradox. None would have been as interesting as simply watching Sophia while she placed the pie on his desk and found her seat.

She moved purposefully, with no apparent thought of performance or allure. It shouldn't have been intriguing, and yet Cathal felt his blood quicken—only slightly, but surely—at every step she took to close the distance between them.

When she'd settled into her chair, her wimple brushing lightly against the back of her slim neck, she turned her dark eyes to his face, and a small smile lifted her lips at the corners. "And now, naturally, I cannot think where I wish to begin."

"Would wine help?" he asked, remembering and offering the bottle.

Sophia regarded it, tilting her head in momentary thought, and then spread her hands in an airy motion of concession. "It could hardly hurt," she said.

She took a sip without asking about vessels, her mouth closing around the neck of the bottle in a way that made Cathal glad he'd seated himself again. He surreptitiously shifted his weight, relieving some of the pressure at his groin, as she put the wine down, shaking her head. "Unwatered. I should have expected. But…is your head for it greater because of your blood or your profession?"

"I'd wager the first. I've known many a knight or soldier undone by little ale, but it's taken a great deal to put any of us"—Cathal gestured around the castle, referring to the MacAlasdairs—"in our cups."

"That could be useful."

"Often. Other times, no." In the aftermath of his first battle, the seasoned men had given him the traditional remedy: wine and a woman. The former had taken off enough of the edge that he could lose himself in the lady—a Spaniard in her forties, with a comfortable disposition and red hair that owed much to ochre—and he'd rarely found it worth the trouble to go deeper down the bottle.

"It does depend on the goal, it's true, but perhaps I should say it would almost always be fortunate from a mortal perspective."

"Aye. Mostly. If you're a reputable sort, there's no need to get a man drunk."

Her eyes widened a little, but she smiled. "And if you're not, I'd imagine you might receive a nasty surprise if you managed it."

"Like as not. They keep an eye on us when we're striplings—the older ones—and that's one of the reasons why. Youth and drink is bad enough in mortals."

"Oh," said Sophia, fastening on this new line of thought. "Are you always gifted? Stronger, that is, and faster than most humans? And can you always change?"

"No and yes, I think." Cathal allowed himself a moment to watch her try to work that out, enjoying the way her lips pursed while she thought, and then explained. "Likely we're always a bit ahead of mortals physically. The difference isn't so vast as all that—a sturdy village boy could put up a decent fight when I was young enough for that sort of thing—but I don't remember ever being quite the same. But we don't take the dragon form until later. I think I was thirteen. My voice had changed already, I know that."

She laughed. "It's difficult to imagine you that young or that awkward. But that would have been generations ago, yes?"

"A few. We age as men do for the first twenty years or so, thank God."

"Your mothers do, I would suspect. The thought of raising a two-year-old for ten years…" She shrank back in her chair, holding her hands up in front of her face. "I doubt there'd be any survivors."

"You know it well?"

"My brothers. And Alice's sons. Her mother died on the passage over, you see, and her sisters had their own families to think of, so I helped with what I could. They're good boys, all of them, although none of them would want me to say *that* these days." Sophia laughed again, but it was quieter than a moment before, and there was a brief wistful look in her eyes.

Normally Cathal wouldn't have thought of her in connection with children, or of any woman whose acquaintance with him had been similar. With him, mortals generally slotted into categories. He inwardly stripped them down to the roles they filled—*soldier* or *shepherd* or *whore*—and such family and other complications as they might have were of passing interest at best. In his life, he'd only encountered a few exceptions.

Evidently Sophia was going to be one of them. He could picture her with children, could see how she'd be good with them—not the Madonna, nor the village women with their babies, but turning her interest and her patience in that direction.

She must have cared a great deal for the boys she was talking about, he thought as he looked at her, and cared still.

"They're apprentices now?" he asked.

"Alice's, yes. Samuel—my oldest younger brother—is a baker now, in his own right, though he's still working with his master. He was eight when she had Matti. Her first."

"You can't have been very old yourselves. You or her," Cathal said.

"Seventeen," said Sophia. "It's not unusual, I think. Lucky, but then, she was a very pretty girl, and her father was very respectable."

He remembered that she'd talked about unmarried women over twenty-five as a class apart from the norm in France. Now that he considered it, he supposed it might be the case everywhere; he'd never paid much attention. "My father had two centuries and more when he wed," he said, "and my mother fifty years."

"You swim in time," she said with no bitterness and only a trace of envy. "We...we ration it, and if we don't count each drop, that's only because we can't."

"But you do more with it. We've no Alexanders, to my knowledge. No Charlemagnes. One or another of us may carve out a domain enough for himself and his offspring, the way Roman Alec did here, but there's none of us gone further that I know of."

"Is that so unfortunate a thing? You don't want to bleed

a country and its men so that you can put your name on a map... I see no ill in that lack," said Sophia. "You yourself said there's no glory in war."

"Not glory, and not war. But building a nation—"

"On the backs of those in your way?" she asked, arching dark eyebrows.

"Were the Franks the worse for being Romans?"

"Would..." Sophia began, and then stopped. Small teeth caught the corner of her lip, and for the first time she looked away from him.

Thus did Cathal know what she was thinking, and he smiled, though not entirely with good cheer. "Would we be the worse for being English, you're wondering? I think so. From what I hear—from what I know of Longshanks, and most especially of the men he employs—I think it, and a pity it is, for I also think it's what's to be. But..." He sighed. "I'm no prophet. Mayhap we'll be better for all this, a generation to come."

"But you fought. You'll keep fighting."

"Aye. And Edward's not much of a Charlemagne, nor even Caesar, but that's not the whole of it." Cathal reached for the wine again. He wouldn't have predicted the words that came out of his mouth, but they weren't surprising: scraps of thought he'd had in the middle of the night or on cloudy afternoons now finding shape and pattern as he spoke. "If we fight, we might keep enough of us afterward. We'll be more likely to hold on. They might let us, might grant us more concessions if they think we're likely to be trouble otherwise."

"Like haggling at the market," she said, "only with lives."

"It's the craft of kings. And the nature of men—to find a line grown blurred and squabble over the place where it was. Or to try to make their names in such fights."

"Not your nature?" she asked.

"A bit of it. I'm not quite human. For the rest, we're a more hidden people. We don't need the world to know us. We blend well when it seems convenient. By the time I knew him, my grandfather went to mass as often as I do. But when he was my age, he gave a sheep to Jupiter Capitolinus on all the old holidays. Did both for a while."

"He must have lived a long time."

"The old ones do," Cathal said. "I couldn't even swear he's dead. He went away, told my father that Loch Arach was his now, and vanished. But if he knew about the war and lived, I think he'd have come back for us. Perhaps."

Sophia frowned. "Perhaps?"

"He has many descendants. If a few of us can't save ourselves now, he may not worry himself about our fate."

"Oh," she said, and didn't look any happier for hearing the answer. They sat silently for a little while, the sunlit table between them and the bottle of wine shining cloudy green and red. "You said you'd have been able to fight within a few days, if the man who'd stabbed you had been normal," Sophia finally said.

The change of subject was as welcome to Cathal as she'd clearly thought it would be. "That's true. There's not much that can do us lasting harm. If you took my head off or dropped the roof on me, it'd kill me outright, and *my* arm wouldn't grow back, but anything else heals clean, and it's only ever taken me a month at worst. Scars linger for ten years or so."

"That's extraordinary." She breathed the word out, leaning forward. "If we could isolate that principle—"

"Then I'd have all the physicians in the world after my blood. And I'd be willing to share some, at that, but I've never known it to work, lass," he said, sorry to see the light in her eyes dwindle. "I tried when I was younger. With a friend of mine, another squire. We swore blood brotherhood, cut our arms, and bound them together, but when he broke his leg, it healed as crooked as any man's."

Sophia nodded. "Blood is always a chancy substance. Too many planets govern it, and they vary so greatly by the person. I wouldn't venture on that experiment until all my others were done... That is, even if you were amenable," she added with another embarrassed smile. "Even so, the potential is exciting. Do you become ill?"

"It's rare. Never been the dangerous sort, not that I know of. But it happens. The dragon shape doesn't feel it," he added, remembering winters in his youth, "so we'll often shift form to get away from the unpleasantness. I spent nearly a week that way one spring."

"I do envy that," she said, making a face, "but then, I think there would be much to envy about your people in general. Even without the long life or the healing. To be another sort of being for a little while, to have that view of the world and not always have to be yourself... Oh, but do you look at all like yourself? I can't imagine the likeness is very great, but are there similarities?"

It might have been the wine or the conversation. It might have been her proximity or the knowledge of what waited outside. It might have been that Cathal was just tired of being responsible. He caught her wrist in one hand, not holding tight but feeling every motion as she froze in surprise, then relaxed, and never tried to pull away.

"Come with me," he said. "I'll show you."

EIGHTEEN

CATHAL WAS ALWAYS LEADING HER PLACES, SOPHIA thought—down corridors and out into forests. Of course, the castle *was* his, or his family's, but still it would have bordered on embarrassing to be following him yet again, had excitement not overwhelmed most other feelings. She barely remembered to pick her cloak up before they left the castle itself.

Putting it on was the first time she freed her wrist from Cathal's hand, and she did so with reluctance, still feeling his touch on her skin as they walked out the door and reminded of it with every step. The path through the snow was narrow. Two could walk abreast, but it was close. Her arm brushed against his side frequently, and his against hers, and each moment of contact was its own thrill.

There were many sources of excitement, she was discovering, and many forms of curiosity. She was glad of the chance to gratify one. It didn't stop her from feeling another.

Then too, their destination was the forest again. The path wasn't the same, but seeing the line of trees coming closer stirred memories, and those memories stirred her body, so that she was almost glad of the chilly air around her and of the exercise, so that she could excuse her voice when she spoke. "Is this always where you change?"

"No," he said, looking down at her. His voice was slightly hoarse too, Sophia noticed, and she doubted that was exertion. A tingling flush swept over her skin. She made herself concentrate on the words, not on his voice or eyes or lips. They were interesting enough in their own right. "I often jump from the tower and transform on the way down. You couldn't follow that way."

She shook her head. Even the thought was dizzying. "It must be exciting, at least for one who can do it and survive."

Cathal laughed, eyes glinting leaf-green with the afternoon sunlight. "My brother still thinks I'm out of my wits. And Moiread—the younger of my sisters—waits longer than I do before she changes. Almost hits the ground at times. Daft girl," he added affectionately, and then a thought made him frown.

"Oh...she's the one fighting now, is she not?"

"She is. Not as reckless with men's lives, I don't think." He sighed. "We didn't talk of war much until it happened. Not the practical side. And I wasn't here often."

"But she'd been to war before?" Sophia asked, turning to questions when she could think of nothing comforting to say.

"Raids, at least. Skirmishes. Not like me."

"But then, perhaps she'll know the countryside better."

"That could be," Cathal said and turned back toward the path.

They were approaching a clearing now, smaller than the one where they'd gathered herbs and kissed, but still of decent size. The trees that ringed it were larger than the others she'd seen, and there was less snow on their trunks than those of their fellows. The snow on the ground was shallower too, and Sophia could actually spot patches of dirt and brown grass. As they got closer, those patches shaped themselves into patterns: too smudged at the edges to be very clear, but definitely the marks of something large.

"Stand there," Cathal said and left her side to walk into

the middle of the grove. "I'll not hurt you. You've my word on that. I'll ask yours now, that you won't scream or run."

"I swear it," Sophia said, raising a hand and not quite holding her breath.

She did her best to keep looking at Cathal while he changed. Only a handful of people in any generation likely saw the transformation, if that many. She would probably never have the chance to do so again in her life, and she wanted to etch every detail into her brain. Sophia clasped her hands and watched, intending not even to blink if she could help it, and not to look away no matter how grisly the process.

Watching was harder than she'd expected, and without a drop of blood or a glimpse of bone. Cathal shifting wasn't revolting, it was simply…difficult to watch. Part of the hardship was speed, for his form changed very quickly. The rest was that the human eye didn't want to follow what happened. She remembered the *things beyond* in the beginning of her nightmare. The change of form was a lesser version, a little more comprehensible and not exactly painful to look at.

Realizing the implication there made Sophia wrap her arms around herself for protection, or perhaps only to reassure herself that she was still solid flesh.

What she did see was a blurred series of images. The closest thing in the mortal world that Sophia could think of was the way air shimmered on a hot day. Cathal stood in front of her, handsome and human. The air waved and fractured. His outline bent at the edges, not to accommodate any concrete change of bodily form but reflecting light outward in rays, like a mirror.

A gust of wind blew suddenly past her. The air had been still, with only the faintest of breezes, but this was strong enough to send her cloak billowing out behind her and her skirt with it, to snatch pins from her hair and bring tears to her eyes. And it was *hot*. Sophia felt for those few moments as if she'd just stepped into the kitchens.

The hair on her arms and the back of her neck stood up. For only a second, there was a low humming in her ears.

Then Cathal wasn't standing in front of her any longer— not the way she knew him. The air stopped shimmering, and she could look at him again, but her mind, even hers, even as prepared as she had been, stuttered and produced only impressions.

Scales: dark green, almost the color of the evergreens around them. Shiny. Claws: the size of her hand. Tail: spiked and pointed at the end. Wings: wide, bat-like. Head: horns, squarish muzzle, huge eyes without pupils, the same lighter green as Cathal's eyes in human form. Huge: three or four times the size of the largest warhorse Sophia had seen.

Dragon. The word felt strange at first, not quite connected properly to the creature in front of her. She'd never truly thought to see one, she realized, and certainly not up close and living. The pages of bestiaries had done very little justice. *Dragon*, she thought again, and this time it seemed to make more sense. *Cathal*.

Unmoving, he watched her, and she thought he was waiting to see what she did next, if she would keep her word. Until that moment, it hadn't occurred to her that she might not.

Stepping toward him did raise a touch of unease, the same kind of gut-and-spine wariness that one felt when looking down over a high precipice—even if the ground was stable and the edge a way off—and just as easy to ignore. She was not her body; she was its mistress, and not vice versa.

"Are all of you this large?" she asked.

In response, Cathal stared at her. Then his back rippled, puzzling Sophia briefly. When she realized that the movement was his attempt at a shrug, she realized a more important fact as well. "You're not capable of speech in this form, are you?"

The great head swung back and forth.

She had to laugh. "One of us, perchance, could have thought to broach that subject beforehand, could we not? Oh well…I'm more attentive to detail in my experiments, I promise you."

Laughter rumbled through Cathal's chest. Sophia supposed it was laughter, at any rate, and devoutly hoped so. Taking another step forward, she clasped her hands behind her back and studied him, beginning to walk a circle in order to get a better look.

Her mind had immediately jumped to warhorses, the largest animals she'd seen at all close to her, for comparison. In truth, Cathal's dragon form was shaped more like an outsize dog or cat, closer to the ground and built to spring. Predatory, of course: she'd seen the results of that after his hunt, and the claws, large as they were, looked very sharp. So did the teeth. The tail, currently still behind him, was long and articulated; she could see it snapping around like a whip, but with far greater force than a man's arm could provide.

Circling, she examined his wings, now folded at his sides. Without scales, they still had thicker skin than a bat's and a sheen of their own where the sun caught them. The geometry was difficult, especially in her mind, but she thought that, extended, they'd fill half the clearing. "You are," Sophia said thoughtfully, emboldened by Cathal's silence, "a terribly *vast* creature. And yet…lack of ambition isn't the only check on your kind, is it? I would wager there are beings as powerful, or greater."

He nodded, a motion like the swaying of the great pines in the wind.

"But then, there would have to be, of course," she said, wrinkling her nose at her own lack of thought and going on. "But worldly beings, or as worldly as you are."

Now she was coming back around, by the other side of his face. Around his eyes and his mouth, the scales lightened in color, becoming a gold-green like spring leaves, and they were smaller. They still looked both shiny and hard, though.

On impulse, she held out a hand, near the base of his head but not yet touching him. "May I?"

Cathal swung his head around to look at her: startled, maybe? Thoughtful? She couldn't tell. Then he nodded again.

Feeling slightly embarrassed, Sophia closed the distance between them and laid her palm on his neck. The scales were smooth beneath her fingers, and very warm—well, that stood to reason. "Does it... Do you feel that?"

Again he made an attempt at shrugging and finished by shaking his head: *not really*.

She smiled. "It's no wonder that you don't wound easily." One shape, of course, lent its qualities to the other, and Cathal's dragon form looked as if nothing but a mounted charge would have left any impression.

Stepping back, she folded her arms again. "It begins to feel awkward," she said, "when you can't speak. If we were to do this often, we would likely need to make a series of signs." Then she felt ridiculous—of course they wouldn't do this often. Why would they? Sophia fought the urge to look away. "If you don't wish to change back, of course... That is to say, I could find my way back to the castle by myself, most likely, or wait out here, as you prefer. You could, ah, cough once for the former option or twice for the latter, or—"

The world blurred again. The transformation seemed faster the other way around, though that might have only been because Sophia wasn't trying to watch this time. She saw a shimmer; then she saw Cathal, running a hand through his tawny hair and half smiling, as if surprised by the last few minutes.

"Truly," she said, laughing, "if either of us is to look so astounded, I would claim the right far sooner than you."

"You do." Cathal crossed the distance between them and put a hand under her chin, tilting it up so that he could look into her eyes. "You did."

The pose and the touch were both most improper. Sophia made no objection. Her whole body hummed with feeling, and even drawing breath to answer made her aware of Cathal's scent—metal, leather, and wine, woodsmoke and man—and of the way her breasts rose and fell with the action. Cathal didn't watch them, though. His eyes stayed fixed on hers.

"And?" she asked, breathless, struggling to find words. "Is there any wonder in that?"

"You weren't afraid."

"Oh." She was slow to grasp the sense of it, and when she did, it made her laugh—and she laughed more as he looked startled again. Not all of the humor was pleasant. "My lord MacAlasdair, you're a Christian, a man, and a lord of men. This place is yours, and more than remote. What danger would your malice hold for me in that form that it wouldn't in this?" She touched the sleeve of his tunic.

The touch or the thought, or both, held him frozen for a moment, eyes narrowed. The hand on her chin tightened, not unpleasantly, and then quickly dropped back to Cathal's side. "Truly?"

Sophia shrugged. "Fire might be less pleasant from a dragon than from a mob, I suppose. Claws or teeth might hurt more than the edge of a blade. I cannot say I've heard much comparison, and I doubt I'd have much time to make it." Reluctantly, she stepped back, away from his touch. "And I think we should be returning."

"Yes. Duties." He shook his head, like a dog shaking off water, and bent down to the edge of the spot where he'd lain as a dragon. Turning back to her, he held out his cupped hands, with three green scales in the midst. "Here."

"Truly?" It was her turn to ask, but Sophia was reaching for them as soon as she saw them. She thought of experiments, of the plans she'd made before reaching Loch Arach and the possibilities that they might open for Fergus.

She stopped, looking at Cathal and waiting for his answer.

"There are always a few after we transform. Usually we bury them." He shrugged quickly. "I've owed you these for a while."

NINETEEN

AFTER THAT, CATHAL KEPT THINKING ABOUT DANGER. He'd thought he understood it, both the rare instances when it applied to him and the more general principles of keeping the mortals in his charge safe. He knew his responsibilities; he'd done his best as a soldier and then as a lord to fulfill them.

He hadn't considered what it must be to be always at risk, even without weapons drawn or battle declared, even without a specific enemy. Consciously putting himself in harm's way was familiar—that was the duty of everyone from a general to a pikeman—but living in harm's way as a part of life, one that he'd never signed up for save for being born, that he could barely grasp.

When Sophia came to him and told him of her second nightmare, she was composed, almost as detached and interested as she had been when speaking of her alchemical experiments. She stood in the hall with her hands clasped in front of her, a small, neat figure in black like the queen on a chessboard, and told Cathal about the same fall-through blackness that she'd experienced before, the same forest and shadowy creatures.

"I ran more quickly this time," she said with a little smile, "and the branch held my weight much better than it had done before. And I believe these things to have been reflections of my will. But that was not the real test."

Around them, the life of the castle went on. A few of the servants walked around them; a few others glanced their

way before continuing, unconcerned, with their duties;
one or two of Cathal's men-at-arms lurked further out in
the hall, playing dice with one of the stableboys. Cathal
noticed these things with the edges of his mind, the part of
him that had over long years learned to take a high-up view
of any situation, lest it suddenly turn violent. The rest of
him saw only Sophia's smile.

"You see, one of them grabbed for me as I climbed.
Like it did before, you know…reaching for my ankle. I
could have moved more quickly, I suppose," she admitted
with another quick smile that chilled Cathal, "but I wanted
to confirm my theory. So I let it reach, and then I pushed it
away, or back, with my mind."

"And?" he asked.

It wasn't a bad idea. In his time he'd ordered men to
scout enemy territory or to expose themselves in order to
draw off ambushes. He couldn't justify objections. Sophia
was being intelligent, as usual. Cathal forced his hands to
uncurl and listen.

Her third smile was downright brilliant. "It worked.
The shadow-thing staggered a little bit even, and its arm
dropped back down. And then, when I reached the top
of the tree and could go no further, I woke myself up
without Alice."

"Good. That's very good."

Sophia nodded. "I couldn't make the shadow-things
vanish, nor give myself more of a road, but that's to be
expected. I think perhaps if I had more information, or
perhaps just more practice… And I begin to have some
theories about the space through which I fall too. It might
the World of Causes, or perhaps the World of Making,
but"—she bit her lip—"I am not permitted to know as
much about those. It certainly resembles a place one of

the Mussulmen told me about, between life and death. A place where the soul and the body are separate. I don't think it's only a dream."

"Then your soul's being drawn elsewhere," he said flatly.

"I believe so. We already know that Valerius can do this. Perhaps the forest is a trap of his shaping, or at least initially. But anything constructed in that other world must, I think, be vulnerable to…" She hesitated, brow wrinkling as she tried to put it into words, or perhaps to translate it for a simple-minded layman. "If he's learned to influence the…the world of souls, it says a great deal for his power, but…it's a *world*, yes? And it's not entirely his. It's as though he built a keep there, and anything built may be overcome, or at least infiltrated."

Her face, turned up to his, was almost shining, her eyes large and filled with the wonder of new discoveries.

"Plenty of men die," Cathal said, "trying to take keeps."

"All men die in the end. All women too." She gave him a gentler look then. "But I will be careful. I've no wish to perish just now. There are my experiments, and Fergus, and…" Sophia stopped and for the first time in their conversation looked disconcerted, her cheeks turning red and her long lashes dropping over her eyes. "And I have a great deal more to learn, I expect. But it is a good sign, don't you think?"

"It is," said Cathal, and he smiled back at her for the first time, unable to deny either her logic or her enthusiasm.

It was well, he thought, that they stood in the middle of the hall, and that there were plenty of people around who would see and comment. It kept him from cupping Sophia's face in his hands and kissing her, or from pulling her into his embrace and proving her wholeness and her safety to himself in the most direct way imaginable.

When he let himself be drawn away, he ached for her, his cock hard and barely concealed by robes and hose, his heart wondering at her courage and at the sort of vision that saw and rejoiced at knowledge even in the midst of peril. Neither would find satisfaction—she was not for him, and she had pulled away since that afternoon in the forest, their conversation having perhaps made her newly aware of that—but Cathal looked over his shoulder and stole a last glance at her, treasuring it throughout the rest of his day's errands.

Sleep took a long time to come that night. He knew Valerius likely had to wait between his attacks. He was glad that Sophia could fend them off, and that every nightmare held potential advantage to them now. He closed his eyes and saw Sophia's face, calm and still with sleep: not a helpless target, but a target nonetheless.

War was much easier.

It was amusing, in its way, that the next development came during one of the few hours when Cathal wasn't thinking of Sophia at all. He was sitting with his steward, going through the long and tedious process of accounts and plans—so much grain, so many beasts, laying in fish for Lent, anticipating the soon-to-come day in spring when the villagers would meet him to submit their taxes.

At first, Cathal thought the touch of cold air near his face was simply a draft. Then he heard the faint sound of music, too soft for mortal hearing to catch: the signal they'd trained into the air spirits for times when they shouldn't simply appear. A message awaited him, almost certainly from one of his family.

He kept his mind on the task at hand and even believed himself to make a good job of it, but it was fortunate that the conference had been winding to a close already—fortunate too that he didn't know the source of the message. Once freed, he made his way up to the roof, read Moiread's name on the parchment, and shouted with relief.

Her hand was as plain as ever, and her wording as sparse. She started by admitting that she'd probably be home soon. She cursed Artair and Douglas affectionately, the rest of the surrendering lords less so, the concept of diplomacy in general boldly, and the English in terms that should have burned holes in the page, using language Cathal had mostly heard in taverns and surgeons' tents.

But we did as well as we could. You gave me good men and, by the grace of God and my own wit, I'll be bringing most of them home alive. Unless the bloody English drop the sky on us after I finish this letter, that is.

I mentioned your "Valerius" to the prisoners.

Yes, I gave quarter. I can see you looking doubtful, and I'll clout you for it when next we meet. I'm only merciless where family's concerned.

A couple had heard of the man. Runs a muster of the worst scum you can find outside the hangman's noose. A few of those are as uncanny as you say. He can summon hellfire with a gesture, might ride with the devil himself. I doubt the last one. The English think too much of themselves. No decent man wants to serve under Valerius, and even Longshanks keeps him well away from court. You don't hold a brand too close to your body.

You know, maybe, how loath most men are to admit there's magic on their side, and the English more than most.

Reading, Cathal nodded. Save Valerius and a few others, the English use of magic in war was mostly indirect: swords that could wound the MacAlasdairs as mortally as steel could any other man, armor that stood fast against dragonfire, traps that exploded or poisoned or brought down mountainsides. A man who didn't want to see magic could pass all of that off as craft or chance.

Most were even worse about Valerius. I bribed, and I threatened, and the ones that would talk in the end talked mostly in hints and in tales.

None could say what name he was born to, nor exactly where, but there were stories.

His lands are on the border, though nobody could tell me where. They're not wide, but he put his stamp on them, by all accounts. God help the man who falls short in his taxes or catches a hare in His Lordship's forest. Hanging's not the worst of it. His vassals' one comfort is that he's not often at home. The bastard's got ambitions, and they put him in the field more often than not.

Here's the part for a winter's night:

Once there was a lord, and he had a son— maybe two, as comes into the tale later, and depending on who you ask. Son grew up, went off, and became a knight, or almost became a knight. The first death may have been there: a fellow squire who ran afoul of his temper, or was better than he was, or crossed him in another way.

Three different men tell three different stories. You know the way of it.

Our young lordling, knight or no, comes back

home. Mayhap he's learned a bit of the world. Could be he's learned too much. He takes up his place and his duties, regardless.

Then—well, the story branches again. One version is his father hears what he's been doing and goes to cast him out. One version is there's a girl, of course, though whether she had the bad taste to choose a younger son—the brother who may not exist, aye?—or a villein or the veil is also down to the teller. And one version is he's just not content, he wants more, and he sees no way in this world to get it.

All the branches come back to the same place. The old lord dies. Messily. Slowly. If there's a second son, or a peasant rival, he hangs for it. If not, I'm sure some poor servant took his place. The elder son, the man of our tale, becomes lord in his turn, only now he calls himself Valerius, and now he has powers that his vassals don't speak of, and he goes seeking a wider place in the world. And whatever the English king knows or believes about him, he sees a tool and picks it up.

One more thing: none of the men know quite when this happened, but those who heard about it heard when they were young. Twenty years past, I'd guess, and could be more. If the man you fought was no more than middle-aged—

Cathal winced, remembering that Valerius had looked no less hale than half the men he'd fought.

—then there too is a thing to consider.

Mortal magicians could do a great deal. Staving off age was a rare power; usually it involved some contact with the great forces of the universe.

> *That's your enemy, brother. If I get back in time, you know you have my aid. If not, may God aid you, and may this woman he's sent you be the ally you need.*

Slowly, Cathal folded the letter and put it down. He would double that last wish in brass, only slightly differently. He didn't doubt that Sophia was the best ally he could hope for, but he wished he could be as certain of her safety.

And as he finished that thought, he heard her scream.

TWENTY

THE FIRST SIGN OF SOMETHING AMISS WAS A FOUL SMELL, so Sophia was less alarmed than vexed to begin with. Unpleasant odors were common enough when alchemical processes went *right*—she'd learned early on to keep a veil over her face during certain stages of compounding elixirs, and to breathe only through her mouth—and far more common when an error had crept in. Not expecting either smoke or sulfur in any of her ongoing experiments, Sophia sniffed the air, cursed, and then swung around to check the crucible over the flame.

No, the mixture inside the vessel was the dark red of Mars, as she'd intended, and the surface was smooth, with no bubbles or other signs that it was heating too quickly, and certainly no more smoke than Sophia would have expected from a properly tended fire. The air around it smelled strongly of herbs, notably garlic, and of hot iron, but no sulfur. Sophia breathed a sigh of relief. This was her first experiment with the protective formula she'd found. It was in a sensitive stage, and she hadn't even added the dragon's scale to catalyze it.

The next potion for Fergus was also in progress but in distillation, and thus, she'd thought, less likely to be giving off a smell. She turned to the glass apparatus and the lead vial anyhow, to be certain, and eyed the black mist within. It looked ominous enough, but she could see the streaks of silver within it that she knew should be there, and Saturn's power was for tenacity. Until she could wrest more control from Valerius, tenacity would have to do.

Meanwhile, the smell was stronger. Had the kitchens exploded? She turned, taking another breath to try to track the reek to its source, and then heard a screeching, clicking sound, like a million insects with very sharp legs were walking across the stone floor.

A hole was appearing in the air.

It hung in the center of the room, a spot the size of her hand that her mind translated as *black* because black was the color of things not there. Looking at it made her dinner rest uneasily in her stomach, and her eyes hurt. Looking at it also gave Sophia the impression that it was getting larger, and that it was struggling to do so, writhing against fences that she couldn't see.

Crystallization: the world went still around her, each piece of it separating from the one adjoining. Into that stillness, her own voice spoke inside her head.

So then. There is a hole in the world here. Likely this is going to get worse. Cathal might know how to repair it, but he's said himself that he knows little of magic. You have no time for research. So—tenacity or protection?

Three silver vials stood on the table, each containing one powdered scale. With hands that felt barely like hers, though they were steady and quick, Sophia opened one and poured the contents into the red mixture heating over the crucible.

Red smoke billowed up, but not enough to block Sophia's view of the hole. Still twisting, it had grown to the size of her head, and now there were other colors than black. She could see flashes of olive green, of sickly yellow. One of the yellow patches turned. Clarified. Became an eye.

Sophia shrieked at the top of her lungs. It seemed the most sensible course of action, considering the presence of armed men nearby. It was also irresistible instinct. When a clawed hand reached out of the hole, she screamed again—and managed to do it even louder.

She started for the door, then stopped herself. Well enough if Cathal or his men could arrive and dispatch the thing. *Not* well if it got out of the door and started running amok through the castle.

At hand she had a knife she used for chopping herbs: sharp, but not nearly long enough, and she was good at chopping herbs, not fighting demons. She doubted she could close the hole in the world now, with the demon already partway through.

In theory, she knew how the potion of protection was supposed to work on a person. She'd hoped that she could have tested it gradually.

The world, her mother had often said, *is almost never the way we'd prefer*.

Before she could think too much, Sophia grabbed the crucible and upended the contents over her head.

Her whole body was already cringing, expecting unbearable pain, but she felt only a moment of heat, as though for a breath she'd stepped into July sunshine, and then nothing. Her skin and clothes were as dry as they'd ever been, and they felt like—well, like her skin. Her clothing. *God grant that means it's worked*.

The demon was most of the way out of the hole now. Even as demons went, or were supposed to go, it was ugly: starved-cat skull with a too-big mouth, six spindly legs with clawed talons on the end of each, body like a mastiff's. It reared up, putting its head almost level with Sophia's, and the rest of it fell out of the hole like a repulsive, oversized caterpillar.

Sophia didn't scream again. Anyone who'd hear and help would have heard the first two times. She needed to save her breath. She thought she heard running footsteps from lower down in the castle; she prayed that she wasn't only hearing what she wished for, or that it wasn't Alice or some hapless and unarmed servant.

The hole closed behind the demon. At least that was no longer a problem, Sophia thought, and gripped the knife.

She didn't know how soldiers managed this: the moment of preparation, of knowing that the enemy would be at your throat in the blink of an eye. She thought it might be easier when the enemy had the right number of limbs and no fangs.

She had time to say half a prayer.

Then the demon sprang.

Scholar rather than warrior, Sophia managed only a clumsy dive sideways. The demon didn't close its jaws on her neck as it had intended, but its body hit hers almost squarely, bearing her to the floor. She heard the *crack* of bone on stone before she felt either the pain in her head or the impact along her spine. The body protected the mind somewhat, even when it couldn't save itself.

In this case, her mind—and her decision—had recip-rocated. The demon scrabbled at her side and shoulders, whipped its head around to bite again at her throat, but neither claws nor teeth could seem to find much purchase, and Sophia felt no pain from either. The potion had given her a suit of armor in its way: invisible, intangible, weight-less, but as sturdy as a knight's chain shirt.

Almost remotely, as men close to death were said to see their own mortal wounds from on high and afar, she observed the weight of the creature, the venom-yellow of its eyes, and the almost boneless flexibility of its limbs. Its smell wasn't sulfur or smoke, but foul-sweet, burned honey or rotting fruit. The scent she'd caught earlier must have come from the hole itself.

Remotely too, she remembered that she had a knife. Bracing herself against the stone as best she could, Sophia stabbed upward, but felt nothing give way before her. Demons had thicker skin than plants, and the angle was bad. She swore, the English obscenities she'd learned as a child, profaning saints she thought to be as mortal as herself and invoking diseases she doubted would bother the creature she fought for a moment.

Pressure and heat reached the side that the demon was currently trying to claw. The sensation was no worse than a hot mug in the hand, but it was a warning. Armor would not last forever, for certain not against an otherworldly foe.

It was not a particularly *heavy* foe—the weight of a good-sized dog, perhaps, but not the mastiff it resembled in size. Later, Sophia would wonder over that and develop theories about hollow bones and magical flesh. Just then, she shoved upward and sideways, catching the demon by surprise and flipping them both over. Its skull made the same crack against stone that hers had, and she took bloody satisfaction from that. It warmed a primitive spirit that she hadn't known dwelt within her, but which was proving quite useful.

In that spirit, she used her new position well, rearing back and driving the knife down into the demon's neck. This time she had leverage enough, and it sank up to the bone hilt. Sophia was familiar with anatomy. If she'd been fighting a man, bright blood would have fountained out of his throat and he would have died in seconds, his jugular clumsily severed. The demon did bleed, a putrid-green substance that glowed and hissed as it hit the stone, and it shrieked as loudly as she had but with a buzzing sound mixed in, but it didn't die.

Rather, it whipped an arm up and batted her hand away from the knife. The claws might not hurt, but the strength of the blow did. Sophia's arm flew backward, and she cried out, feeling tendons strain and snap in her shoulder.

Instantly she wished she'd kept silent, no matter the pain. A new light shone in the demon's eyes—wicked joy in her pain, yes, but also a look she recognized even across species, that of observation and calculation.

Claws couldn't hurt her. Teeth couldn't hurt her. But her body hadn't gained much in strength, and it still had some of its limitations.

Before Sophia even saw the creature's arms move, its hands had closed around her throat. She yanked herself backward and grabbed again for the knife still in its neck, but the demon's grip was strong and sure. Already darkness began to fill in the edges of her vision. She knew what that meant.

And, as she panicked and weakened, the demon easily flipped them again and gained the same advantage of angle and force now that she'd used earlier. Its hands tightened, squeezing and turning. The pain in Sophia's neck was nothing to that now building in her chest, the burning as her lungs screamed for air they couldn't receive. With the last of her strength, she clawed at its face, seeking one of those horrible eyes, but it merely reared up, taking its head out of her reach.

Sh'ma Yisrael Adonai—she hoped her lips were forming the words, or that her mind counted. Everything was going dark. It was a mercy, in a way. She wouldn't have to look at the demon at the last. *Eloheinu*. The words were becoming harder. Words had always been easy. She reached for the next, couldn't find it in the darkness—

A sound. Smooth. Wet. Close.

Then the darkness was reversing itself. Her neck was free. Her chest was free, burning but now taking in air and letting it out again, frantic with possibilities. She lay on stone and gasped, fish-woman brought suddenly to land, but living and not dying.

Her vision cleared. There was a shape above her still, but it didn't crouch on her chest. One hand was behind her head, not around her neck, and the other was roughly sheathing a sword. The shape had legs and hands; it was human.

Words came back and reattached themselves to things. Sword. Floor. Hand. Man. *Cathal*.

Unaccountable joy swept over and through her, despite her throat and her chest, her head and back. She was alive; the potion had worked; Cathal was here.

He was speaking. "You're not dead. You're *not* dead."

"As," she said, and her bruised throat made the words come through gravel, "my lord commands."

It was a lovely line, sardonic and detached and composed, and the look on his face—surprise, joy, affront— was one she'd treasure for a long time. In the next second, though, she spoiled it by flinging herself off the floor and into his arms.

TWENTY-ONE

THIS TIME CATHAL WASN'T GENTLE: COULDN'T BE, NOT with recent danger still setting his blood afire in ways he hadn't felt in months, nor with Sophia's rounded body suddenly flush against his, impelled there with a speed and force that had surprised even him. Her breasts rose and fell against his chest, and their steady movement was a delight both to his quickening body and to the mind that remembered how still she'd been when he'd rushed into the room. His arms closed around her almost at once, and he was kissing her only a moment afterward.

He shouldn't do this, Cathal knew. Oh, he knew it was unwise, and he knew it was probably unchivalrous, even for the very flawed version of those rules that he'd ever bothered to follow, and he knew she might pull away and slap his face in the next instant, but he held her close and took her mouth, his tongue urging it open with very little effort. The last thing on his mind was regret; the next-to-last was stopping.

And she wasn't stopping him, this beautiful girl in his arms. No, she was wrapping her arms around his neck, pulling him down and herself upward so that she could kiss him back, her lips sweet and soft beneath his. At first there was a slight clumsiness about her motions, whether from inexperience or because she was still disoriented from her struggle, but that vanished quickly, and she seemed eager to pick up where they'd left off in the grove.

Cathal had will enough to remember that she *had* been

in a fight, that she might have injuries other than the bruises on her neck. When he slid his hand down her back, he kept his touch light, ready to stop if she flinched or made any sound of pain. She did gasp, when he cupped her arse and pressed her against the swollen length of him, but there was no discomfort there. No, she circled her hips against him and then made a—sound.

It was low in her throat. It was curious and eager at the same time. And it made Cathal's whole body clench with lust. If he heard nothing else in his life, if he went deaf the second afterward, he needed to hear her make that noise again.

He left her mouth for her neck, that long golden column he'd admired across the table on too many nights. He brushed over it with his lips, felt Sophia shiver, heard her catch her breath, then returned to kiss with more strength, to suck and then nibble, careful always of the bruises. Her buttocks were firm beneath his hand, muscles tensed as she pressed herself to him. She was continuing her earlier motions too, little jerks of her hips that brought her sex against his thigh, her stomach against his cock, and then away, driving him mad, and he didn't know whether she knew it.

Another swift motion and his hand cupped the curve of one breast, feeling its shape and weight through the wool of her gown. Cathal circled his thumb lightly upward, rubbing over Sophia's nipple. He longed to feel it better, would have sold his soul for magic to banish her layers of clothing in an instant, but there was still no mistaking the stiffness there, nor the way Sophia thrust her breasts forward at his touch, nor yet the whimper that came from her throat this time. He hadn't known it was possible for her to make a more arousing sound than the last one, and yet there it was.

He bucked against her, feeling her soft and yielding against his aching cock. The drag of fabric and the imperfect angle were a sweet kind of torture, the motion a desperate, almost unthinking attempt at his true goal. The wool beneath his caressing hands became a more frustrating barrier with every second, every sensation, every desperate little wriggle the lady gave. If it had been summer, Cathal thought, if she'd been less respectable— more practically, if there'd been a bed anywhere to hand… There was a table, but even for his lust he couldn't destroy its contents.

He, or what remained of his mind, was seriously considering the floor when Sophia pulled back.

For a second Cathal thought that he'd offended her, or that she'd remembered her virtue, but no. She only stepped back a little, enough to put her hands on his shoulders and, by coincidence, to give him a look at her face, all reddened lips and cheeks, dark eyes dazed with sensation. Her wimple was crooked, half off, and dark curls straggled out and wound down around her face and her neck.

"Yes?" Cathal murmured.

"I should… I want to touch you," she said, and her hands were sliding down over his chest, twin flames through his shirt. Her tongue crept out of her mouth and circled her lips. "You're very hard," she said, and then laughed and blushed, not too innocent for the innuendo. "Not… I didn't mean like that."

"Like that," he said and shifted forward to brush himself against her again, teasing them both. "Too. But not as constant as the other, no."

"It cannot be comfortable," she said and then glanced down at herself, her breasts heaving. "But then, desire never is." Guessing well, despite his clothing, she traced her fingers over his nipples, and smiled at his indrawn breath. "Similar, then."

"Aye. Come here."

She stepped forward, though only a little this time, unwilling to lift her hands from his chest. Cathal couldn't say he objected. Her fingers were brushing lower now, down and then back up again, and his body felt every inch of their journey. Less graceful than he would have liked to be, he plucked the pins from her hair and brushed the wimple onto the floor.

Then he stopped. Lust, strong as it was, stepped aside for a different and far less pleasant sensation.

The white cloth was spotted with crimson.

Sophia had gone still when he had. Now, frowning, she followed his gaze to the bloodstained cloth. "Oh," she said faintly, and stepping back, she put a hand up to the back of her head. "I didn't realize… It hurt when I hit the floor, but I didn't know."

"And now?"

"A little." She flushed. "I hadn't noticed, which I think bodes well. I think a serious injury would hurt more."

"Likely," said Cathal, whose experience with mortals and head wounds was cursedly scarce. Men went into battle with him, were injured when he couldn't prevent it, and whether they lived or died afterward was the realm of God and physicians. He wished he'd paid more attention.

He could hear footsteps on the stairs. His first thought was anger, that the men should be so late, but then he realized that far less time had passed than he'd thought, common enough when both battle and lust clouded his mind.

She probed gingerly through her hair, then winced. "There's a great lump back here, yes, and I think it's bleeding, but…it doesn't feel as though I broke my skull.

Although I'm not at all certain how that would feel." Drawing back her hand, she inspected the reddened fingertips. "But I'm awake, and I'm sensible." Here she stopped and bit her lip, then went on without saying whatever had come to her mind. "So I believe that to be a good sign too."

"Better than otherwise."

Footsteps reached the landing door, and Cathal swung around to meet the new arrivals. Munro and Edan, two of the most experienced of the remaining men, were there, blades in hand, and a square young man named Roger. All slowed as they came within sight of the doorway and presumably saw both people within whole and in no visible distress.

"Sir?" Munro asked, flushed from the long run up the narrow stairway, "Lady? There was screaming, and—"

He fell silent, mouth opening. Clearly he'd caught sight of the demon's corpse, lying in a corner of the room where Cathal had flung both it and its severed head in the seconds after its death. Nobody could have mistaken it for human, even for a second.

The men crossed themselves. Edan swore.

"Aye," said Cathal. "The wizard who cursed Fergus has other tricks up his sleeves, it seems."

In truth, it was almost better to have them staring at the demon. He hadn't been able to get either himself or Sophia into any truly compromising state of undress, and alarm had greatly diminished his own excitement to a state easily hidden by clothing. Nonetheless, they were a man and a woman alone in a room, and clearly both disheveled.

"What is it?" Roger asked. "How did it get here? Are there more?"

They were all speaking in Gaelic, and Cathal only noticed it when Sophia stepped back, taking herself out of a conversation too quick and too worried to follow in a foreign tongue. He switched to French, trusting the men to follow his lead.

"'Tis a demon, as I understand such things. Likely if he could send more, he would have, but I'll post guards throughout the castle tonight, and I'll take other measures as well." There were wards. His knowledge of them was academic, another memory of childhood training for which he'd cared little at the time, damned young idiot that he'd been. He *thought* he could make them stronger. "We'll have Father Lachlann bless weapons. How did it get here?" he asked, turning to Sophia.

"There was a"—she waved her hands in the air, making a circle of varying size—"space that grew larger. It came from that. I smelled rot before then, and sweetness." Sophia's eyes held Cathal's for a breath longer. There was something she wasn't saying, that she didn't want to speak of in front of the guards.

"A bad sign. But as you see"—he gestured to the demon's corpse—"they die like anything else. Munro, gather the men. I'll talk to them soon, let them know the plan. Then two of you can come back here and get rid of the body."

Whatever skills Cathal lacked in running a castle, he'd been commanding men long enough to know how to put dismissal into a tone of voice. The three guards left, Roger crossing himself again before he turned.

Cathal waited for their footsteps to fade before turning to Sophia. She stood farther away from him now, arms wrapped around her stomach. In the light of greater concerns and the eyes of others, their earlier madness had cooled for her too, perhaps. He still hungered to look at her, but it was a fainter urge now, and he could displace it, as he knew he must.

"I think," she said, "that I'm the reason it could get here."

"Ah," Cathal said and wished he could argue the point. But the demon had appeared in her laboratory, and... "The connection again?"

Sophia nodded, hair brushing against her cheek. "I doubt it could appear where I'm not. And I'm not certain what to do about that. If I leave, I'll be abandoning your friend, but if I stay, I will perhaps put you all in great danger."

There was no confusion on Cathal's part, whatever there might be for Sophia. "Then we will put a guard on your chambers and on this room. If need be, I'll stand the watch myself." He glanced down at his waist, at the silver-chased and sapphire-set hilt of his sword. "I had this from my mother's kin. It's not the only weapon of its kind, nor the only one in the castle. And," he added, glimpsing the pouch at his belt and remembering the letter within for the first time in an hour or two, "I have news."

Only after Sophia looked up from the letter with a face of embarrassed regret did Cathal remember that she likely couldn't read Gaelic. Only after he'd skimmed over the first few paragraphs did he realize that he hadn't thought twice before giving her his family correspondence. That was a notion he was sure he'd turn over in his mind later, on an early morning or a sleepless night. For the moment, he repeated Moiread's information without embellishment.

Listening, Sophia stood very still, her hands twined in her skirt. At the news of Valerius's crimes, she swallowed, a quick movement of her slim, bruised throat, and again at Moiread's conclusions.

"And so we can guess where he obtained the demon's services," she said. "I've told you before that I know little about such creatures, great or small, but fratricide seems a sure way to attract darkness, if you seek it." Her voice was quick as usual when discussing theory, but quieter, smaller. "This may help. I can't be certain. I wish I could promise more."

"These things die like anything else," Cathal repeated. "And you held it off long enough this time."

"Barely. And… Oh!" Unlikely joy dawned on her face. "It worked. My experiment, that is. It has certain limitations, but it's entirely promising. The demon couldn't break my skin, and that alone was a great protection. I'm sure it saved my life… Well, that and you arriving when you did, and having the right sort of weapon. I did stab the demon, but it didn't seem to take."

"Steel often doesn't, I hear," said Cathal. "I'll find out more as I can. As for the potion, I'm glad of it. While this lasts, you should make more. Drink them every time one wears off." He reached out and took her chin in his hand, turning her face up to his. "You'll have anything of mine that you need."

Then he left. He had tasks at hand and limits on his self-control—limits that were, it seemed, growing shorter by the day.

TWENTY-TWO

PRACTICALLY SPEAKING, THE DEMON'S ATTACK WAS almost a blessing when Sophia thought about it. For the cost of a few bruises, a knot on the back of her head, and a short stretch of literally mortal terror, she'd tested her potion and found it successful. She'd encountered a new form of life, even if it was horrible and evil. To top it off, as she was cleaning up her laboratory and periodically glancing at the demon's corpse, she'd realized that there lay a potential new source of both materials and a connection to Valerius.

Sophia hadn't worked with demons before, naturally. She didn't know of anyone who had, and what little she did know warned against it—but against calling them up, not analyzing their bodies after they'd met their well-deserved fate. Very gingerly, she pried off two of the demon's claws, wrapped them in linen, and tucked the package into a corner of her box of supplies. The blood would probably burn through any container, she thought, and while either its heart or eye would likely have the greatest power, the risk of mischief from that direction was too great.

The claws would be enough to go on. She'd test half of one for elements and planetary correspondences; that would give her at least a hint to whether the rest could be at all useful. Then too, she wanted to consider the protective elixir further—with time and other processes, it was possible that the effect could last longer, or that it could guard against, say, being strangled—and there was the other potion for Fergus, which had fortunately not been upset during the fight.

Sophia had many roads to go down, many discoveries she could make, much work that she could do—and she rejoiced in it. She always would have, when the projects were new, but for the first time in her life, she felt that she would lose herself in it as a need, and not just as an inevitable result of progress and curiosity.

She didn't—couldn't—regret the moments she'd spent in Cathal's arms. She knew she'd flung herself at him as she'd told Alice she wouldn't, though out of neither recklessness nor despair, and that nothing had changed *since* that conversation with Alice. The reward had been worth the act.

For most of her life, Sophia had thought she understood desire tolerably well for an unmarried woman. Men were part of the world. A few of them were well made. She'd noticed, imagined more than noticing from time to time, and responded accordingly—but she was unmarried, and had never before had the time or the opportunity to be truly tempted into misbehavior. Despite her reading, she'd never really been able to imagine much beyond kissing, if that. It had never occurred to her that she would feel faint and dizzy, that her sex and her breasts would ache, and that she would not only find all of those phenomena pleasant but actually crave the chance to feel them again.

Lust was its own kind of alchemy, it seemed, and as full of contradictions. In Cathal's arms, she'd ached and not noticed pain, had all the strength go out of her limbs while she'd felt full of new energy as bright as the noon sun. It was fascinating.

It was not an area of knowledge Sophia could rationally pursue further. She was glad of the time they'd had. Until she died, she would remember the heat of Cathal's mouth, the intoxicating glide of his thumb across her nipple, the way his manhood had thrust against her. When she was alone at night, or in the depth of age, she knew she would take out the memories and comfort herself with them. Had they not stopped, she would have let him take her on the floor, and she doubted she would have had many regrets after.

They had stopped. She'd started thinking again—and while giving herself to sensation in the moment would have been one thing, there were too many obstacles for Sophia to overlook when her mind was clear.

For instance, the castle and the village might not care overly much about an alchemist in a tower, but people talked about a mistress. She didn't know what jealousy and spite might arise if she went to Cathal and word got around, but she did know that word would get around.

Also, she planned to leave when her job was done. Travel would be perilous as it was. If she had a child with her, in her belly or out of it, she'd be risking her life and its—not to mention the reception they'd likely receive back home. Her parents tolerated and even encouraged her eccentricities. She wouldn't ask them to accept her shame.

Another concern: she hadn't needed to broach the subject with Cathal when they were embracing, only to follow his lead. She didn't know if she could go to the man and offer herself. There was a certain kind of courage there that she doubted she had.

So, later, when she was far away from Scotland and Cathal, she would remember their time together fondly. For now, she wouldn't let herself think of it more than she could help. For now, she would turn her mind to purely intellectual paths and be thankful for the work at hand, that she might concentrate on that and keep herself separate.

For the most part, the endeavor went very well for a few days. Sophia rose early, worked long and late, ate when Alice reminded her, and made polite conversation with Cathal when they met. Her throat and her head healed. She slept as well as she could and had no dreams. She began to research, in what little time remained, the right planetary alignments for visions and demons to anticipate when Valerius might make his next attempt. She went around guarded by men with crosses on their swords. One stood outside her laboratory, while another kept watch over her bedchamber. One had given her a silver dagger.

None of them was Cathal.

Sophia understood that, or told herself she did. He was a busy man, and busier now. Often she heard noise from the rooms below her, or saw light beneath the door when she came up and down the stairs. His duties went far beyond her, or Fergus, or the disruption that both of them had brought to the castle, and perhaps he'd had the same sort of second thoughts she had. A foreign mistress, and one who dabbled in magic, probably wouldn't help his reputation with his men or his tenants. This distance was for the best. She told herself that too.

Then, on a day warm enough for the snow on the trees to melt and splat down to the still-frozen ground, she noticed that she was running short of herbs.

Donnag kept a small house near the edge of the village. It was humble in comparison to the buildings Sophia had known in France, and even more so compared to the castle, but Sophia got the impression that it was spacious for an old woman living by herself in the country. She and Alice both managed to fit around the fire with the midwife, even though Alice's elbow came dangerously close to Sophia's stomach when she gestured.

The midwife also made excellent cakes, far better to Sophia's mind than the ones the castle cook managed, and her ale was none too bad either.

"I don't brew it myself," she said, when Alice complimented her. "Black John down by the river does that. It's come up a bit under him. His father's wasn't near so good. Drank too much of it in the process, I'd say."

When the conversation was leisurely like this, Gaelic was easy enough now for Sophia to understand. She thought Donnag might be going slowly on purpose, being easy on the foreign girl, and she didn't have too much pride to appreciate that. "That happens back home too," she said. "Temptation's a hard thing."

The old woman grunted affirmation. "Black John's got a stronger will. From his mother's side. I brought both his parents into the world, aye, and *she* knew her own mind from the very first."

Alice laughed. "My oldest was that way...even in the birthing."

"From the mother," Donnag repeated, nodding. "Now, Munro there, his sire and dam are both calm, peaceable sorts—you'll not have met them much, saving the blizzard—so the Lord only knows what made the boy go in for a soldier."

Leaning against the wall, eyes alert and priest-blessed sword on his belt, Munro only waved a hand.

"There are these unexpected strains in the blood. Sideways, much of the time. My parents are neither of them scholars. My brothers either. That was down to my uncle, and then to me in my way." Sophia smiled. "But it must be easier to see the pattern from where you stand."

"Anyone old enough. Anywhere small enough. I heard stories of cities, of London, but I never fancied going.

You can't see the patterns there." Donnag crackled laughter. "And here I'll never anger the lord by bringing him a daughter."

"They do seem not to mind girls," Alice said.

"Aye," said Donnag, "and besides, I've not yet been present for one of their births, and it's likely I'll be in the ground before the next."

"Long-lived folk," said Sophia, carefully neutral. The people of castle and village must not be entirely ignorant of the MacAlasdairs' true nature, she thought, but that didn't mean they knew it fully. "And none of the grown children have married yet."

"One of the girls. There was a grand feast, and then she went away. The boys... Well, they're men, aye?" Donnag glanced up at Munro again, shook her head, and chuckled. "At least the village girls have naught to fret over."

The fire was very hot, and Sophia leaned back, letting the cool air hit her face. "That's very...courteous..." she said with even more care than she'd used before. She didn't meet Alice's eyes. She didn't even let herself think past the words.

Unnoticing or uncaring, Donnag shrugged. "Courteous or not, they can't breed. Can't even do it with their proper brides, my gran once said, without going off into the mountains for a fortnight."

"Gossip." Munro finally spoke.

"Could be. But you were a boy here, and a young man. Ever seen a child that took after one of their lordships more than it did its father?" Donnag stretched gnarled hands out toward the fire, the knuckles cracking. "It's generally plain enough to those with eyes. And it's not as though they look common, is it?"

Sophia reached for her cake, took a bite, and didn't taste

it at all this time. She thought of Cathal's brilliant green eyes and the clean lines of his body. No, he didn't look like most people. "They could just be very, um…pure?" she suggested. "Or…keep such things outside the village?"

"Not from what I've heard. Not about old Artair or his eldest, at any rate. Sir Cathal…he's not been around here long enough. But I've never yet heard of a soldier who'd keep his hands off the women, given a chance."

No longer able to ignore Alice's gaze, Sophia turned to her friend and gave a quiet shrug, all the answer she could provide at the moment, and perhaps the only one she'd ever be able to manage. After all, what they'd heard *was* only gossip and the conjectures of a single old woman, midwife though she was.

Even if it was true, that wouldn't change very much. Sophia and Cathal would still be in a castle, still surrounded by witnesses; she would still be leaving; and it would still go against what she'd been taught was proper. One wall had a few cracks in it. All of the others remained standing, remained sturdy.

That was another thing that she could tell herself— another thing that she suspected she'd need to hear.

TWENTY-THREE

FROM THE MIRRORED SURFACE OF THE SCRYING POOL, Artair MacAlasdair gave his youngest son a grave look. Neither distance nor magic blunted the impact very much.

If Cathal was larger than most men, his father was huge: near seven feet tall and broad-shouldered. His hair was almost pure white now, his craggy face seamed with lines, but his eyes were as they ever had been, the cold, clear blue of winter lakes, where an unsuspecting mortal could freeze to death in minutes. When they focused on Cathal, he still had the urge to scuff his feet and look down.

"Demons, now?" Artair asked. "You've made yourself quite the enemy, boy."

Cathal contemplated excuses: *It was only the* one *demon* and *I didn't see much way around it* and *I suppose you'd have charmed Valerius into surrender, then, or mayhap just eaten him?* None became a man of his age and dignity. He settled for a stone-faced "Aye."

"Aye," Artair repeated, not asking for elaboration. "Well. I can remind you of the wards. I presume that's why you needed my presence."

"I'm not overburdened with blood or amethyst, no." Time was also often an issue for scrying. Even aside from waiting until his father could respond to the summons, the ritual to activate the pool was a lengthy one and required a specific alignment of day and hour. Agnes and Douglas had understood the principle. Cathal had simply bludgeoned it into his mind.

He wished he could have told Sophia about it. She would, he suspected, not only understand but see angles of possible improvement.

The entire family would have killed them both. Anyone in the village, and a few beyond, knew that the MacAlasdairs weren't merely human. Other secrets stayed strictly in the bloodline, or on rare occasion with spouses, where the wedding vows provided geas enough for secrecy.

"I thought it urgent," Cathal said into the silence. "If the wards will even work."

"They should. You'll need to take a hair from the lady or a drop of blood. She'll have to stay until this business is over, mind you." Artair frowned, his just-in-case-you-were-thinking-otherwise look. "You've gotten her into very dark matters. She's a door now. At Loch Arach, you've enough power to hold it shut. Let her walk unguarded elsewhere, and in time, people will die for it."

"I hadn't planned on it," said Cathal. "Even now she has guards wherever she goes."

"And she'll not need them once you're done, so long as she stays in the castle. Understand that well. You're at the source of your greatest strength there. The land—"

"—knows my blood. Our blood. Yes."

Artair's eyes glinted. "You still remember, then? I'm glad to hear it. Allow an old man his doubts. A few decades tend to blunt memory."

The young wolf snapped; the old one bared his teeth; no more was needed. Cathal dropped his head. Impatience had only been the easier path, anyhow.

You've gotten her into very dark matters.

If Cathal said that Sophia had chosen her path, that he'd offered a way out, his father would be neither surprised nor moved. He'd spoken as fact, not in accusation. Cathal knew his voice, in his own ears, would have the ring of an excuse, and so he was silent again.

"Howbeit," Artair said, his tone more thoughtful now, "this mischief will have left tracks."

"It came through the air," Cathal said. "Not flying. I don't think any of us could trace its path."

Artair shook his head. "Not that sort. All magic costs. To wrench a demon out of hell has one price. To point it at a target and send it across miles has another. And I doubt your foe is lurking just outside the castle walls."

"Costs," Cathal repeated. He looked down at his wrist, where the cut was already mostly healed. He knew not at what price the oracle chamber or the air spirits had come; that work had been done without him. Sophia's work took herbs and jewels, flame and spirit. The scrying pool took jewels too—and blood. "Messy ones?"

"From all I've ever encountered, very. It's easier to hide death in war, but these would be noticed, unless your man took great care to hide them. He does not," Artair added with a curled upper lip, "seem the careful sort, past what is absolutely needful. There would likely be talk."

"And he'll not be able to send too many demons."

Artair shrugged, massive shoulders moving like stones beneath his plaid. "Not too many. We've both seen war. There's always a few who won't be missed…along with the army, if not in it. The spell itself should limit it more."

"The alignment of the planets?"

His father looked surprised, a memory Cathal would treasure. "You've picked up a few things. Aye, that. And the other costs, which I don't know. And it'll likely take a bit out of the man too, though not enough for my taste."

"I thought…" Cathal said. "If Moiread's sources were right, he made a pact?"

"Likely. But extra services have extra cost." Artair folded his hands underneath his chin. Another man his age might have stroked his beard, but the MacAlasdairs had never been able to grow them. It had gotten Cathal into a few fights in his boyhood. "I'll pass the word along. If... Valerius"—he said the name with the same distaste Sophia had shown at first—"is leaving a blood trail, there's likely a few who will have picked it up."

"They might not be so willing to speak with us."

"Mayhap not. But they'll have talked of it to another, who'll speak to yet another, and in time we'll hear of it if we're listening." Artair's smile was much older even than his face and spoke of centuries of war, and the edges of war, and the fighting men who cared little for their nations or kings. "Have patience, boy."

The old reminder was half reassuring, half provoking. "The matter's an urgent one."

"And we're treating it urgently. Act...and then have patience."

After dinner, on the staircase, Cathal asked Sophia for her hair. He had tried to find enough privacy for the request and had sent Roger away beforehand—his turn on guard was coming to an end, and he'd tell Munro where to find them—but he couldn't think of a plausible excuse to keep Alice absent. Nor could he justify wanting her gone, save that making his request in front of those sharp eyes made him feel like a lad begging for his lady's favor. Matters were awkward enough as was.

Nonetheless, he charged into the face of danger. "It's for the defenses," he said and paraphrased Artair's explanation. "They need to know you. So to speak."

"Yes," said Sophia. She was unpinning her wimple as she spoke, and her face lit with the new idea. "It does stand to reason that they would, especially given that I'm not one of your people. I understand very little of the theory, of course, but from what I know, it makes a great deal of sense."

"I'm glad you think it does," Alice remarked and shook her head as Sophia reached for her knife. "Stand still. If you do it yourself, you'll look like a hedgehog. I know, remember?"

"I was ten," Sophia protested with a laugh that warmed the stone staircase. Yet she stood motionless as Alice lifted a single lock of her hair away and sliced through it.

Alice, in her turn, handed the strands of hair over to Cathal like a surgeon dropping an arrowhead on a tray. "I hope this will suffice. Or do you need to shave her head?"

"No. That should be fine."

"It must be a fascinating process," Sophia said. "This spell of yours, I mean, not shaving my head. I'd dearly love to see it, were you so inclined."

"I'm inclined," Cathal said. As he spoke, he found that it was true. He would have given much to have Sophia at his side during the ritual, both to watch her fascination and to benefit from her advice, if anything went amiss. He sighed. "But no. Chamber's got its own defenses. None but my bloodline can enter or even see inside."

Sophia frowned. "But then, if a spell goes awry—"

"Then it's a truly dark day for us, aye. An uncle of mine lost an eye that way. One of my cousins died. Other mishaps too, more minor ones. The ideal is to have another of us standing by to lend aid."

"If enough of you are in the castle," said Alice, with a look between him and Sophia that he couldn't quite puzzle out. "There aren't that many."

"No. Often we're at least two. Now…war. And love, or at least marriage." Cathal shook his head. "I'd not call that the wisest protection, but neither did I set it up, and I fear to try to change it. I'll only be doing as much as I am by rote and detailed instruction… Could I bring you in, I'd gladly do so. As it is, you must accept my regrets."

"I understand," said Sophia.

All three of them stood silent on the stairs. Much time couldn't have passed, for once again footsteps broke the quiet. Munro appeared only a bit later, but still the moment felt longer. To Cathal's surprise, Roger was following only a little way behind, hopefully not bearing any catastrophic news.

"I bid you good night, ladies," said Cathal.

"Good night," said Sophia. She started to ascend the stairs, then turned back. "Be careful. And if anything does go amiss…call. I cannot say I'll be able to help, but I'll try."

Cathal stared as she left and stopped looking before too long only due to a combination of will and the realization that Roger had lingered and was watching him. Abruptly, he turned and began to head back down to the hall. "Aught wrong?"

"I don't think so, sir. Indeed, I hope not." Roger glanced sideways at him, then away.

"Sounds promising."

Roger flushed. "I've not forgotten that you're the laird's son, nor that you've the castle and all of us in your charge. And I'd not question your judgment lightly, you understand. There's nobody who'd do that."

Christ have mercy. "But you are questioning it. Have out with it, then. I don't bite," Cathal said, trying to remember what little he knew about Roger.

Like Munro, Roger had grown up in the village, and his people had lived there almost as long as the MacAlasdairs themselves. Roger hadn't ever left, even to fight with Wallace's army. He'd been willing enough to go, but his parents were aging and he was their only son. At practice, he wasn't notably worse than his fellows and displayed even a little more alertness, one of the reasons why Cathal had picked him for Sophia's guard.

Now he cleared his throat, folded his arms, and said, "How much do you know about…her?" A jerk of his head upward made quite clear who he meant, since it was doubtful he'd concern himself with Alice.

"Enough," said Cathal. Generally, he tried to be reasonable with his men. He felt little inclination toward reason on this, but forced more explanation out regardless. "She's helping us. You know of Fergus."

"Is she truly helping, sir? And for what cause?" The tensing of Cathal's muscles—or mayhap the way his lips drew back from his teeth before he could stop the incipient snarl—must have told Roger what sort of ground his question had landed on. "Meaning no offense, sir. None at all. It's only that she's foreign, and she's odd, and aye, she's pretty-mannered, but foreign women…"

If he closed his eyes, Cathal could still see the bruises on Sophia's throat or the ring of frostbitten skin on her leg. If he didn't stop himself, he would recall, clear as day, her body on the floor and the demon crouched atop her.

He could hear her voice much more clearly than Roger's, thick with anger and conviction: *What would I be if I turned and ran now?*

"She is helping." Cathal said it with infinite patience, or thought he did, but the words came from deep in his chest. "She's an honorable woman. A woman with courage. And

I trust her a damn sight more than most. You can remember that. You can tell your fellows too."

And when Roger hurried off, Cathal turned and hit the stone wall—not with his full strength, but hard enough to split the skin over his knuckles. It could be that he'd managed that conversation poorly. Anger wouldn't necessarily have helped; it might have just convinced Roger—and whoever he'd spoken to—that Sophia had too much influence. There might have been better, more delicate ways to handle the matter. He couldn't think of any.

Waiting at Loch Arach, taking care of it until his father or Douglas could take the reins again, was less burdensome than it had been originally, thanks to her. It still wasn't where he belonged, nor where he wanted to remain.

He wasn't, Cathal realized, precisely certain where that *was*.

TWENTY-FOUR

AGAIN, SHE WAS UP A TREE. AGAIN, THE SHADOW-THINGS gathered below her. The dead forest stretched far beyond, and the castle lay at its distant edge, dark and almost as lifeless.

This time was different. The branch hadn't broken; indeed, the tree's limbs had all been sturdy, and Sophia thought that there'd actually been less space between them than there had the times before. The shadow-thing that had grabbed for her ankle hadn't even broken the skin.

She'd considered fighting them. The world, whatever it was, had started responding to her will. She might have been able to make herself a sword or a bow. Possibly here she'd even be able to use either—but Sophia thought not. For one thing, her body seemed still to be hers, with all of its strengths and weaknesses, and she saw the sense in that. The body was one of the first and closest ways that a person knew themselves, and thus logically the hardest to change. For another, she didn't know enough about weapons to know how to make herself good with them. For a third, the direct exercise of will itself was still new to her, and she used it clumsily. Her efforts before had been shouting or shoving, not delicate manipulation.

Last and most important, the world might not have belonged to Valerius entirely, but Sophia would have wagered that the shadow-things *did*. Either they were his creatures, dual-natured and thus more at home than she was in the world of the forest, or they were direct projections of his will. Unless she had no choice, she would not set herself against him. She'd never do it and hope to win, nor even to survive.

And so she'd fled. She lay wrapped around a branch near the top of her tree, looked down at the moving mass of shadow, and then peered out across the forest.

She didn't want to go to the castle. Then again, she didn't want to be in the dream at all, and there certainly was no more inviting destination in sight. Now too, she wondered whether the forbidding appearance of the place might not be intentional. If so, if Valerius didn't want her there, it certainly merited further investigation.

Very well, then. Options.

Giant birds—or dragons, in fact—would be difficult. Sophia had yet to try to create anything living, but it didn't feel like a wonderful idea or even necessarily a possible one. If the shadows were dual-natured and pulled into the dream by Valerius's magic, then trying to create anything sufficiently dragon-like might even force Cathal into the forest world, another only-in-dire-circumstances plan.

Bracing herself against the branch, Sophia summoned her will, stared at the castle, and tried just to *think* herself there. Very briefly she felt the fabric of the world respond—a deeply strange sensation—but it was as though she leaned against a very thick door. The frame shifted a bit, then shifted back. There was no real give. She hadn't really expected any—she'd had to climb the tree herself, after all—but she would have felt foolish not trying.

Given that she didn't much fancy going back down the tree and facing the shadow-things, there was only one other way forward.

Sophia stared at the open space between her and the castle and thought of bridges. She pictured slabs of stone, wide enough for horses and carts to cross; sturdy arches; high railings. Other images came to mind too—rotted, gapped planks, dangling from a few strands of rope—and she tried to ignore them, but they wouldn't go.

As she focused on the images, she felt herself push with her mind again, and once more was struck by how odd it was, and how little control she still felt she had. How did one learn to work limbs that had never existed before? How did the mind learn that such a sensation means *grasp*, and another means *hit*, and a third, elsewhere, means *stand*? What did that process feel like? Perhaps children forgot so quickly because the memories were so much work.

Logically, her mind couldn't ache, and thinking couldn't make her sweat, but Sophia's forehead was wet by the time the first side of the bridge appeared, and a low, muscular-feeling pain was starting in her temples. Logic didn't govern everything, particularly not here.

Slowly the bridge took shape. It was a patchwork beast. Sections were stone, others wood, a few like nothing more than solidified light, and the division was not always neat. Looking out across it, Sophia saw a patch near the start where a thin rope handhold supported an immense stone block. Her eyes practically crossed as she looked at it.

She thought it would hold. She hoped it would hold. She hoped that falling in a dream didn't make one die upon hitting ground, or if it did, that Alice would wake her before that moment arrived. Her hands were sweating too now, and the stomach she didn't properly have threatened to disgorge a dinner that she'd never eaten in this world.

The edge of the bridge was a few inches away from her, perhaps a foot below. Sophia wished she'd spent more time in trees when she was a girl and less in her books.

Holding on with both hands, she let her body dangle from the branch, swung forward, and dropped.

It was stone, and it hurt. Her skirt rode up, letting her scrape skin off her legs from knee down to shin. The impact shuddered its way through her body. But the bridge held firm.

Keep going. You don't know how long it'll last.

Her legs weren't broken. Sophia pushed herself up to her feet and began to make her way across. She went as quickly as she dared, but it still felt slow, particularly on the mismatched parts, putting one foot gingerly in front of the other like a child walking a rooftree.

She knew not to look down, and of course she wanted to, even more than she would have on a normal bridge. It helped not at all that the view straight ahead of her was itself disconcerting. The sky was like a festering wound, and near the edge, where the outlines of the trees and castle showed up against it, Sophia thought she saw movement or perhaps gaps. Not everything joined as it should have. It was no pleasant sight, but there was nowhere else to look, and she didn't dare close her eyes.

When she set foot on the first translucent part of the bridge, she truly wanted to. The railing and the bridge itself didn't quite feel real either. They bore her weight and guided her, but there was a softness about them, a sense that they weren't entirely solid, and every fiber in Sophia's being screamed that this was a bad idea. Abandoning her better judgment, she crossed that section with more haste than the others; she hadn't thought that flimsy planks could be such a relief as she then found them.

As if in response, the bridge swayed beneath her weight.

No, Sophia thought at it, even as she grabbed the guide rope and whimpered. She kept walking, though. Stopping

would give her too much time to think. It might also show
the bridge—or the world, or Valerius—that she was afraid,
and she thought perhaps that was a bad idea, as with dogs
and horses. Although she was aware of every movement
of every muscle, even though she cringed inwardly every
time she put her foot down, expecting it to land on empty
air, she kept going.

She began to think of the stone sections as islands,
places of safety, although she knew logically that there
was no reason for it. They weren't real stone, nor did
they have anything in the way of support keeping them
up. Sophia tried not to think about that very much. If the
stone bits felt safer, she would take safety from whatever
corner it came. They certainly felt solid, and they didn't
move. That was enough to be thankful for.

Gradually the distance shrank, until it was a man's
height, then half that, then only a few more steps, and
Sophia finally stepped onto solid ground. She wanted to
collapse then, just as she'd wanted to run the last few
feet, but she didn't let herself do either. She could see
nothing menacing around her, but that didn't mean nothing was there.

Also, as good as solid ground was in comparison to
the swaying bridge, the ground beneath her feet was even
worse than it had been back in the forest: softer, wetter,
more redolent of decay. Sophia didn't want to get any
closer to it than necessary, and her first few heaving breaths
of relief quickly became much shallower and further apart.

Ugh.

Up close, the castle was huge and dark. Not only did
nobody come out to meet Sophia—although she wasn't
certain she would have wanted that—but she couldn't spy
so much as a light in any of the windows. The great doors

were closed, and the portcullis was down. If there'd been a drawbridge, she thought it would have been up.

Why *wasn't* there a drawbridge? If Sophia had been making a castle in a dream world, she'd have put a moat around it. She'd have gone ahead and put in some sharks too, or mayhap vitriol instead of water. One couldn't be too careful.

Instead, she could walk right up to the castle walls. That might have come down to arrogance, but it suggested more what Sophia had been starting to think: this was a place where Valerius had less control. The castle most likely mirrored some counterpart in the waking world—at least to a degree. The actual place probably *was* inhabited and guarded, and she doubted that the walls felt spongy to the touch.

UGH.

Wiping her hands on her skirt did little good. The doors felt just as awful, and they didn't budge when Sophia tried to push them open. Reluctantly, she knocked on one, but received no response.

Standing back, she contemplated the building, thinking of it now not just as a physical object. Half through what few laws she'd observed of the world, and half through a feeling she couldn't put into words, Sophia thought that the castle was an anchor—the inalterable center from which all alterations spread, mirror of and clue to the man behind the dream.

From Cathal's first description, she'd known Valerius for a vain and petty man. Moiread's information had only confirmed that much, but now Sophia thought of lines of descent and pacts forged in blood, strands of information knotted together into a fishing net. Valerius was not isolated, not even as much as another man might be. He had connections; there would be an opening, or—

—there.

Near the base of one wall, a brick had crumbled. Whether it had always been so and Sophia had only just noticed it or whether she'd worked her will on the castle just then, she didn't know. Later it would make an interesting theoretical question. Just then, she knew what she needed to do. The brick was not an opening, but it might be what she needed.

Bending, for she still didn't want to kneel, she plucked the pieces of brick one by one off the bare earth and held them in her cupped hands. Against her skin, they seemed almost to move, or to pulse with a faint and foul heartbeat.

Sophia gritted her teeth, closed her hands tightly around the stones, and woke herself up.

This time there was no disorientation. It was morning. Alice was sitting beside her, watching and frowning. Her face cleared as soon as Sophia opened her eyes, but not entirely. "Your hands are glowing," she said, "and I don't like the look of it."

Indeed, a nimbus of dull light surrounded both Sophia's hands. Any but a close observer might not have noticed, but it was there, and the same red-gray as the sky in Valerius's world. It was repulsive; it was satisfying.

"Bring me"—Sophia bit her lip, held her hands away from her that she might not touch anything with that sickly energy, and thought—"the branch I took the holly leaves from. Please. I think it might be helpful."

TWENTY-FIVE

THIS TIME THE POTION WAS DARK BROWN, WITH THREADS of black and gray swirling through it. The vessel was lead. To magical sight, the whole thing had a dark glow to it, an impression of being more *solid* than anything around it, and a nasty strand of red-gray that Cathal was relieved to see dull and muted by comparison. Standing at Fergus's bedside, Sophia frowned down at him, then up at Cathal and Sithaeg, and her hands were tight on the cup's sides.

"It's the appropriate day and hour," she said, not clearly speaking to anyone in the room but herself. "Yes, and the logic stands."

Still she hesitated. Watching from the other side of the bed, Cathal saw her eyes dart up to his, then again to Sithaeg's. Her mouth opened. "This…" she began, and then stopped.

From the past few months, Cathal recognized the impulse she felt in that moment. Sophia had already presented the facts to them, as best she could with their limited understanding. Saturn would confer strength and bind Fergus's body more to the world of matter. The bit of Valerius's will—or soul, or whatever had gone from dream to Sophia to holly branch—should give Fergus power over the wizard. With matters as they stood, the reverse shouldn't be a worry. She couldn't be certain.

Sophia had told those things to him and Sithaeg. Neither had objected, and Cathal didn't think she had any new information. What she wanted now was to lay the case in front of them again and have them decide to go forward, or not, so that the blame wouldn't fall entirely on her shoulders if the results were dire. She wanted what most men did from their leader or their lord: freedom from decision. Christ knew he'd longed for it often enough.

He was about to step forward and speak—*Go ahead, lass*—when Sophia shook her head. Her shoulders went back and up; her spine straightened. "This one should not explode," she said, "even should it fail. But you might both wish to stand back, in case I'm in error."

Instead, Cathal went to her side. Sithaeg's presence would be chaperone enough, even were the work ahead of them insufficient; his greater physical strength was justification. The hand he put on Sophia's shoulder had no such excuse, but he regretted it not at all. Beneath gown and kirtle, her muscles were taut as lute strings, and he could do nor say nothing just then to relax her, only hope that his presence and the warmth of his hand rendered the moment easier to bear.

He kept his other hand on the hilt of his sword, the blade half an inch out already. The wards should hold; the time wasn't right for demons, but he'd take no chances.

Sithaeg retreated back to the wall, lips moving in quiet prayer as the beads of a rosary slipped through her fingers. Her face was gray even in the morning light, tense with hope and the refusal to hope.

There was more of Fergus now. The other, more mundane potions hadn't brought him back, but they'd kept the gains that Sophia's first mixture had given him. Sithaeg and a few maids had propped him up in bed, with cushions at his back and his hands folded in his lap, so it was easier for Sophia to set the vessel to his lips.

She went very slowly: almost a drop at a time at first,

with a few seconds' pause between each when she leaned back and watched every detail of Fergus's face, the rhythm of his breathing, and the nails of his motionless hands. Cathal almost did the same, but he switched his attention back and forth from Fergus to Sophia herself, noting how precise each movement she made was, and how little she was breathing.

Rather than a glow, this time Cathal's magical vision showed Fergus's body taking on the same heightened solidity as the goblet. His brown hair and the stubble of his beard looked darker, his pale skin at once paler and more vivid in its pallor. The rust-colored aura around him deepened and lost a few of the gray-white streaks that had been winding through it. At Sithaeg's half-choked exclamation, Cathal switched his vision back to the mortal world and saw that Fergus's hands, which had still been largely misty after the previous experiment, were regaining flesh as the seconds passed.

The sound was deeper this time, and more complex. The phantom-plucked string that made the sound wavered in places, or there was more than one being played. Douglas would have known. Cathal didn't feel warmth this time, but he saw Fergus's body settle deeper into the pillows and Sophia's wrists tremble with the sudden weight of the cup, empty though it was.

Cathal reached down and wrapped his free hand around hers.

You're at the source of your greatest strength, his father said in his memory. *The land knows you.*

Cathal only vaguely knew how to reach for that power, and not at all how he might send it to either Sophia or Fergus. He reached clumsily anyhow, and clumsily willed it through him to both of them, and while he knew not if that bore any fruit, it still contented him somewhat that the strength of his arm was there for Sophia.

Movement, even thought, slowed. The dance of dust in a sunbeam became a stately march. For an instant, all lines sharpened, all shadows became darker. Cathal could hear every beat of his heart and every breath that escaped him. When he looked to Sithaeg, each word of her prayers was stretched, exaggerated: *Ave…Maria…gratia…*

Though slow, Cathal suspected those prayers were more urgent now. Her eyes were huge and terrified. He himself felt the hand on his sword hilt tighten in instinct that far outstripped mere thought.

Inside the half-circle of his arm and body, Sophia stood with her face turned down to watch Fergus and her hands outstretched around the lead cup. What triumph or terror showed in her expression was hidden from Cathal's view, but she stood without moving, her breathing slow and regular, and there was no tremor in her body at all now that he was helping her bear the cup's weight.

It came to him that she was not fully there, or not only there—that her wizard-sent dreams were not the only time when she touched other worlds. More than metal and herbs was at work in alchemy, and had been even before the addition of Valerius's maybe-soul. Stars, he thought, and angels, or gods: beings an order above even those whose blood ran in his veins. He wondered how much of that she knew.

He stepped closer. He couldn't put his body between her and what real danger might threaten; nonetheless, he would make the gesture, and hope that whatever sent its power through her now would witness it.

Fergus's hands opened.

The short, sturdy fingers drew back from each other,

spread apart, then came back together. The hands flexed, gripping invisible objects, and turned, and opened again. One hand plucked at the sheets, investigating by touch.

Sithaeg cried out in joy and ran forward, emotion countering the slowness of spell and age alike. Sophia stayed motionless, whether still entranced or, like Cathal, knowing too much to rejoice at once. He himself saved thanks and action both—but he didn't stop Sithaeg when she knelt by the bed and took her son's hands in hers, nor point out that Fergus's eyes were still closed. Let them have this moment. If it lasted, God be praised, and if it didn't, they'd still have had it.

Fergus's hands stilled, but only briefly. Cathal thought the moment was just long enough for Fergus to feel the size of the fingers gripping his, the calluses of sewing and cooking, the raised veins and swollen joints of age, long enough for recognition. The rosary beads fell over their intertwined right hands. Cathal wasn't sure whether Sithaeg had kept hold of them out of hope or forgetfulness, but they looked right.

With evident care, care that he probably didn't need to take after so long, Fergus squeezed his mother's fingers in response. "Mam?" he asked. His voice was barely stronger than a whisper, the word only slightly more articulated than a sigh.

"Aye," Sithaeg said, clear and loud through her tears. "It's me, love. I'm here. Don't try… Lie still. You'll be a while recovering, but you've come back to us—"

With an obvious effort, Fergus shook his head, a slight back-and-forth movement against the pillows that took forever and a day. "Can't stay."

"You can't?" she asked, lifting her head to look into Sophia's face, than Cathal's, in the vain hope that one of them would offer a contradiction. When none came, her lips went thin, and anger flushed her graying skin. "Why not?"

As if in answer, the chill wind Cathal remembered swept over them again, the smell of the grave almost a conscious taunt. He snarled back into it, feeling his teeth turn to fangs and his nails lengthen, but it did no good. The smell and the wind passed on, unresponsive, and in their wake Fergus's hands lay in his mother's grasp, lifeless once again.

The sense of weight and slowness was gone too. Everything went at its normal speed, which seemed too quick, just as Cathal felt both the cup and his own hand to be far too light. Nothing was substantial enough.

"But his hands are still…better," said Sithaeg, responding to the statement none of them had made. She raised one of Fergus's unresponsive arms. "You see, my lord?"

Indeed, there was solid flesh where there had once been misty half-substance. Fergus's hands were too pale and soft with disuse to belong to the man Cathal had fought beside, too motionless to be a part of anyone still living, but they were *there*, entirely there, as they hadn't been before he'd swallowed the potion.

Quickly—everything was quick just then—Cathal switched his vision. The pale streaks hadn't reappeared in Fergus's aura. He still looked, in this sight, to be more solid than the rest of the room, and certainly more so than he had been earlier.

"We make progress, then," Sophia said and turned to Sithaeg. "I know it to be slow, and…and halting, and it must be all the more so for you, but we *do* make progress."

The older woman wiped her eyes with the back of her sleeve and at first said nothing. The room sent back the rustle of cloth as she rose and the click of wooden beads as she picked up her rosary. "You're sure," she said finally, speaking slowly in Gaelic and looking straight into Sophia's eyes. "This will work. He's not just suffering more. You're certain."

Cathal wished that Sophia hadn't stepped away from him to address Sithaeg. When she flinched, he would have given much to put his arms around her. The weight of the question could crush a man, and there was nothing he could say in response. His certainty wasn't what Sithaeg looked for.

He watched Sophia draw her hand across her mouth and heard her speak carefully, in measured tones and at a slow pace that had little to do with her command of the language. "I'll make no false promises. I can't be certain that it will work. This is a new thing we do, and a powerful man who opposes us, and I"—she raised her hand and let it drop—"I know less, far less, than I would like in this matter. I am certain that we have a chance. I wouldn't leave a man in pain if I thought otherwise."

Neither of them looked at Cathal, nor even seemed to remember that he was there. Sithaeg stood as a woman in a rainstorm, letting the words hit her and sink in. "Aye," she said. "Very well."

They both bowed to the old woman when they left. It seemed the thing to do.

Out in the hall, the door closed behind them, Sophia sighed and leaned against the wall. With her guard coming toward them—Edan, this time—Cathal could still make no gesture of comfort. Words had never been his strong suit, but he tried nonetheless. "Progress. You said it yourself."

"True. And...maybe we won't need his name, though I begin to think it'll be required, and perhaps another planet—" She broke off and shook her head. "I ramble. Forgive me. And I ramble because of what I wish not to say: that we know *our* progress. I don't believe that Valerius is idle."

TWENTY-SIX

THREE DAYS OF CLEAR SKIES AND A WIND FROM THE southeast had melted most of the snow, and when Sophia went down to the hall for dinner, she stood awhile outside without a cloak, hands and face stretched out to receive the sunlight. There was strength to its heat now, a promise that spring would come even to Loch Arach. Grass was sprouting in the corners of the courtyard, and a few of the trees even had started to bud.

Time went ever onward, and though Sophia knew she might work against it where Valerius was concerned, just then she was glad of the reminder. The world did turn— even if she couldn't celebrate those turnings properly, her family would, and knowing that was a comfort—and men would move with it, not stuck in one place but making progress, even if they generally knew not their destination.

A row of sealed bottles in the room above doubtless helped her mood, she knew. The last of the defensive potions had come to what looked like a fruitful finish. She'd added some of the solar herbs she'd used with Fergus in the hopes of promoting a little more internal resistance, and had let the dragon scales blend for more time, but hadn't made many changes to the basic recipe. It *worked*. If she could ask Cathal for more scales, she might try others, but the mere success was enough for the moment.

With spare time and herbs, she'd made up another few elixirs—simple herbals in those cases, suitable for women's ailments and diseases of the gut, or for the ague in the lungs that always struck around springtime. On the road, she might be able to trade them; if she stayed at Loch Arach, she could perhaps use them to buy favor and avert suspicion.

With a pleasant feeling of accomplishment, therefore, she leaned against the doorframe and breathed deeply, noticing how the aroma of wet earth and new growth now mingled around the edges of roasting meat. Munro waited a few feet off, talking with one of the other men and sounding involved enough that she felt no need to worry for his sake. Tilting her face into the gentle wind, Sophia closed her eyes.

"Good," said Alice from behind her. "I won't have to climb all those cursed stairs. Has Sir Cathal had any words with you yet?"

Ever since the conversation with Donnag, and perhaps ever since Cathal had come to Sophia's rescue—though she'd breathed no word of their embrace afterward—Alice had spoken his name with great care to seem careless. She hadn't tried to talk with Sophia about him either, which was odd itself.

Sophia, therefore, slipped into caution as she shook her head. "I've not seen him yet today. He wasn't awake when I went up to the laboratory. What's amiss?"

"Visitors," said Alice. "In a few days. Distinguished ones too, if you trust the gossip, and I often do. Which is all very well and good normally, but I hope they're aware that *things* come and attack us out of nowhere here. It could be a nasty surprise for them to find a demon under their bed."

"The demon only attacked me," Sophia said, though she couldn't object too much. She doubted that the creature would have stopped with her, or scrupled to kill anyone in its way. "Anyone worried has only to stay away from me. And if it happens in the great hall, we'll be surrounded by armed men. Sir Cathal dispatched the last one easily enough, once he arrived."

"He has a few advantages that the others don't," said Alice. "And if the guests are important, he'll likely be with them much of the time, so that solves the problem rather neatly."

"I'm quite the man for neat solutions, when I can manage them," said Cathal from behind them.

For a big man, he moved very quietly. Alice and Sophia both spun around to face him, and Sophia felt herself blushing. No matter that he'd overheard a compliment, if anything, or that their subjects had been only reasonable ones for common discussion, she'd still been talking about him. Besides, every time she met his eyes, her clothing felt too tight, and she was afraid it showed on her face.

She cleared her throat. "I hear you're to expect guests, my lord."

"Not quite. You're to expect a proper host." Standing in the shadows of the doorway, Cathal looked more silhouette than man, but Sophia could hear relief in his voice, and she thought she saw a genuine smile. "My brother, Douglas, is coming back, though God knows for how long. He'll be bringing a few others too…an English hostage and a few allies, or men who might be. And he can handle a demon as well as I can."

"Will he…" Sophia looked upward toward where she knew her laboratory and Fergus's room to be, though she could see neither from her angle. "Is he likely to permit me to continue my experiments, do you think?"

"Aye. He'll do that."

Cathal spoke not with trust so much as determination, but that satisfied Sophia nonetheless and left her smiling in a way that confidence in his brother might not have done. Conscious of Alice's presence, she schooled her voice to casual curiosity and asked, "And will you be going back to the battle?"

"There's not a battle to rejoin," Cathal said, and Sophia's heart unclenched. "Not just now. 'Tis why Douglas is coming home, and Moiread soon enough. It's to my father to handle the treaties. I know not where I'll go, but I'll not leave the castle until Fergus is…well."

One way or another, Sophia finished silently for him.

"I'm glad to hear it," said Alice. "Though sorry it's not the outcome you'd have wished…but you seem to have gotten your family through it alive."

"I'll take that any day," said Cathal. "This is no surprise."

"Will you…" Sophia glanced away, wishing she'd learned more of courtly etiquette. "If we're to move tables for dinner, only let us know."

"No. Not at all. There's room enough, and probably not many women." He'd shifted position just slightly, or the light had changed, and this time Sophia did see him smile: rueful and almost boyish. "Besides, I'd be right glad of a friend."

"Then I'd be glad to help," said Sophia.

"And I'll see if anyone here can get the scorch marks out of *one* of your gowns," said Alice.

"Ach," Cathal said offhandedly, "use one of Agnes's. She left half a dozen when she married, and she's not much taller than you are. One of the serving maids can help you."

Then he bowed and went inside, clearly thinking, manlike, no more of the matter at all.

Manlike too, or speaking from a vantage point of well over six feet tall, Cathal had been wrong about *not much taller*.

Judging from her gowns, the absent Agnes had overtopped
Sophia by at least a head. The skirt pooled on the floor
around Sophia when she tried the dress on, and the sleeves
hung well past her fingers.

She and Alice were both decent with a needle, however,
and taking clothing in wasn't nearly as difficult as letting
it out, particularly when it was merely a matter of making
the gown shorter. In figure, Agnes and Sophia were evidently close enough not to cause trouble in clothing cut
along slightly old-fashioned lines; a belt easily settled any
discrepancies there.

The dress itself was beautiful: white wool and a surcoat over it of burgundy velvet, thick enough for Sophia
to run her fingers through as she otherwise stood still and
let Alice dress her hair. Long ago, she'd resigned herself to
plain clothing as more suitable for experiments and travel
both, but her eyes and heart delighted in the rich colors, and
she was glad to have the excuse for finery.

Alice, who'd been gentler to her best clothing, wore blue
and green, though cleaned as best the castle could manage
in early spring. Sophia had offered to help with another of
the dresses, sure that Cathal had meant them both.

"I'll do well enough with my own," Alice had said in
response. "I'd rather not be obliged."

"But you think I am?"

"I think his friend wouldn't have lived this long without
you, and you've put your life at risk for him. A few scales
and an old dress are no more than you've earned."

She'd spoken very firmly, and Sophia had wanted to
ask more, to say that she wouldn't have gotten to the castle
without Alice, nor survived long enough to succeed, but
one of the maids had joined them then. In the day or so
since, Alice hadn't encouraged conversation along those

lines, and Sophia hadn't had the energy or the nerve to take the subject up again.

When they went into the hall together, though, Sophia reached for her friend's hand and squeezed it, then whispered *thank you* when Alice turned to look at her. Both knew it was for more than the dress or Sophia's hair, now neatly braided and pinned into a coil near each ear, and when Alice smiled and returned the pressure, Sophia didn't much mind that the guests were staring at both of them.

There were four. Cathal's brother was easy enough to recognize, though his hair was red and his eyes ice blue. More than the build they shared, or the strong outlines of both faces, each brother carried himself with a confidence lacking in anyone vulnerable to bad meat or steel blades. With him sat a middle-aged woman, slim but not frail, and two men, clearly father and son themselves. The elder was the shorter of the two, and his hair was more white than black now, but he had the same gray eyes as his son and the same sharp features.

All the new arrivals were dressed very well. Sophia marked silk and fur, jeweled rings, and a silver fillet around the woman's head, and was glad for her made-over gown. If Douglas recognized it, he didn't say as much, but bowed to her and Alice with sober politeness. "My brother speaks well of you."

"That's good of him, my lord," said Sophia. She knew Cathal had probably restricted his praise to her alchemical skills—she wasn't certain that her performance elsewhere even merited remark, though Cathal had seemed to enjoy it at the time—but still she blushed. "And he's done the same of you."

"That's kind to say," said Douglas, with a mocking grin and a sidelong glance at Cathal. He didn't wait for an answer but moved on to indicate his guests. "Lady Eleanor Bellecote, late of England. Rhys, Lord Avondos, and his son, Madoc, of Wales."

"I'm honored," Sophia said and curtsied.

"Rhys knows my mother's people," Cathal said when Sophia and Alice had been seated.

"Yes," said Rhys, looking carefully back and forth between Sophia and Lady Bellecote before he responded, "though not, I fear, his mother."

"Not save in stories," Madoc added. "But there are many for those of us who take the time to listen."

The look that passed between him and his father was the sort that Sophia knew well—well enough not to comment on. Family was family, whatever part of the world it was in. "Legends can take patience," she agreed, steering for a neutral path, "though I suppose that yours are near to home, and that must help."

"Mistress Sophia is a scholar," Cathal said. "I think I mentioned."

"Your brother certainly did," said Lady Bellecote. "And your father as well." Her voice was low, befitting a gentlewoman, but she spoke with conviction. "It was for that reason, among others, that I offered myself as hostage when the bargains were being made."

"How do you mean?" Alice asked.

"Firsthand is the best way to gain knowledge. Even such imprecise knowledge as I have to offer. I heard the legend you had from your sister, you see, and it was familiar to me. Unless there are two such men, my brother's lands border his."

TWENTY-SEVEN

LADY BELLECOTE'S FATHER WAS SCOTTISH, SHE EXPLAINED. In friendlier times, she'd wed an Englishman, who'd died of a fever a few years before, but her family had always lived on the border, and her brother even closer to the English.

"I visited from time to time in my girlhood," she said, and a nostalgic smile had only a moment to live on her face before her lips tightened. "Even then, I heard a few of the stories, and in time I managed to get the rest out of my brother… What he knew of it, at any rate. I was only curious then. What youngster doesn't like a grisly tale?"

Madoc chuckled in agreement. "I think I knew of every ghost supposed to be on our lands by the time I was ten, and I might have made up a few that I felt were wanting. But you sound as though your brother took this other man more seriously than I ever did my ghosts."

"Quite so. Richard's men are well trained, and there are many of them. In those days, there was not the war to give a man license for a little private conquest. He was safe, and yet he was always wary. The guard was ever heavier to the west, and the scouts more vigilant, and he wouldn't visit Valerius as he did any other lord close at hand." She gestured in apology, the light catching on light-blue and deep-pink gemstones as her fingers moved. Topaz and beryl, Sophia thought immediately: protection, healing, and calm; the sun and the moon. "I saw nothing of the land over the border."

"But you heard accounts." Cathal was leaning forward in his chair, hands together on the table in front of him.

The tension about him, the air of waiting and yet preparing, reminded Sophia of the moment before his transformation.

Lady Bellecote nodded. "Merchants would pass through on occasion. The occasional freeman would flee...though I was given to understand that Valerius's rule was livable for most people, most of the time. Particularly those farther away from his lordship's castle itself. His eye and his whims did most of the damage—his and the worst of his men—although..." She stopped, looking uneasy.

"Whatever you say, I swear the rest of us will believe it," said Douglas.

Won over, but not entirely convinced, the lady spoke the rest of her sentence quickly, as if not wanting to think about it herself. "Although they say that the land is poisoned. And it was true, from what the merchants say, that the crops were never truly *good* there. Adequate at best. And that, again, was better the further out one went."

Sophia remembered the wet earth in her dreams: the sucking noises with every step and the smell of rotting meat. Her breath stuck in her throat.

"What was the cause of that, then?" Madoc asked. For him, as with his quieter father, Sophia could see that the interest was casual. He was serious, not mocking, but it was curiosity with him, not the weighty matter that it was for her and Cathal, or even for Douglas and Alice.

She was glad of it. That meant he could ask questions, perhaps even those she wouldn't think of.

"Any number of things, depending on who you asked," said Lady Bellecote. "But always death. There was a tale that he'd married five wives and killed each when they got with child. There was one that he had to eat a human heart every full moon. And then there was a tale that he made a bargain with the devil and killed his father to seal it.

That one made me think of what your sister said, my lord. Peasant superstition, mayhap, but…"

The Welshmen crossed themselves, and Douglas belatedly joined them. "No way to know, I suppose."

"Well, his father *was* killed, I think, and a man hung for it. There were people, when I was a girl, who remembered that much for a fact, only…" She hesitated again, but this time not long enough for anyone else to urge her on. "They were all old. That could have been a child's perspective — everyone is old when you're fourteen — but even so, the man must have sixty or seventy years by now."

Cathal nodded. "Moiread hinted at that much, and that's a grim notion. I didn't fight an old man. Not to look at."

"The wages of sin," Lord Avondos said. "Death, mayhap, but a death long in coming?"

"In truth, the tales I heard of his behavior would make the pact with Satan in character, whether it existed or no. The merchants were spared the worst of it, but they saw enough, and those who fled went for good reason. I'll not repeat details unless you request it of me, gentle sirs," she added, her nostrils flaring with remembered revulsion, "and certainly not at table."

"He must have friends at court, then, to get away with it as long as this," said Alice.

"And so it could be," said Madoc, his gray eyes thoughtful, "as he seems to be doing the English bidding now, but it could also be that he dwells on the border. His estate would be a long way from the places and people the English kings value, yes? Would Longshanks or his father have cared overmuch what the man did with his own vassals, so long as he kept the likes of our hosts out of London?"

"Didn't succeed, then, did he?" Cathal said, breaking the tension further with a wolfish smile. "I've been there.

Douglas in Westminster, though, is indeed a prospect to make a man's blood run cold—"

"You should thank Christ there are ladies present, pup," Douglas said amiably.

Laughter rippled around the table, and there was ease in it, but Sophia couldn't let herself be drawn away from the original subject, unpleasant as it was. "Your pardon, my lady," she said, "but in all of these stories, did anyone ever speak Valerius's name? The one he was christened with, I mean to say."

Closing her eyes, Lady Bellecote was silent for a long moment, during which Sophia did her best not to hope—and finally justified that effort by shaking her head. "If they did, it's slipped my mind long since. I'm sorry."

"No, not at all," Sophia replied.

"But," said Cathal, "you could tell us how to reach his lands, aye?"

"Oh, certainly."

The directions Lady Bellecote gave would have taken a man with a horse several weeks to follow. "And that may be the best way," Douglas said, when Sophia and Alice had joined him and Cathal in private quarters, "even if it's not the fastest. No question that Valerius would dearly love to get one of our family nearer to his place of power."

"He may not even be there," said Cathal. "He and his men were far afield when I met him. Truce or no, it'll take them a fair bit of time to return, unless he has greater powers than I've yet seen."

"Aye, or he'd been closer to home at the time of the truce, or gone home with his missing arm."

Cathal shrugged. "Then we'll settle the matter all the

quicker... Ah, *damn*." He glanced to Sophia, clearly hoping that his sudden thought might not be accurate, but she had to nod confirmation. There was no knowing what Valerius's death might do to Fergus.

"And dawn breaks," said Douglas. "The tricky bit when the other man's taken hostages, lad, is that setting fire to the building generally doesna' work very well."

"Thank you," Cathal said, not quite through gritted teeth. "But every day that goes by is another day when Valerius might find a way to make the curse go forward again...or another means of attack," he added with a glance toward Sophia.

"There *is* that," Douglas admitted and turned himself to regard Sophia, who sat still and tried not to squirm under the collective attention. "The dreams and the demons. The man's too familiar with other worlds."

"Other worlds?" Sophia broke her silence. "I knew the demon wasn't from the earth, of course, and I had my suspicions about the place of the dreams. I'd read things, but I'd no way of knowing it was true. My lord," she added, aware of Cathal's grin.

Douglas didn't smile, but neither did he look reproving, only solemn and thoughtful. "It sounds true. This world contains, or touches on, many others. You can reach some of them by dreams or trances, sure enough, and if you've taken both harm and plunder from the place you visit, I would wager it's real."

"Do you know it?" Alice asked. "Could you go there?"

"To the portion that Valerius has shaped? Mayhap, if Sophia were there already. Not, I think, without a link of that sort. And once there, I doubt I could do more than she has against the wizard. Until we know more, his defenses will hold." Douglas took a slow sip of wine.

"Best we find out quickly," Cathal said, "as was my point. As I can't kill the man, I can be human and stay out of his sight while I ask questions."

"Can you? With a magician who doubtless knows what to look for?" Douglas snorted. "I very much doubt it. He's seen you before, and he'll know you've reason to come after him. The man or his creatures will mark you five minutes after you've crossed the borders."

Cathal leaned forward, hands on the table. The firelight showed the rich colors in his plaid, the same pattern as Douglas's, but the faces above them were far apart in expression. "You can't be sure of that. We can't wait. And with you here and Moiread returning, it's only my neck that I'm risking."

"Unless Valerius claims your mind and uses you against us. Or uses your body as a way into the castle," said Douglas. "You never understood magic, and this is more complex than charging a line of spearmen. Be guided by wiser heads, will you?"

The way the two of them glared at each other, there might have been nobody else in the room. Sophia didn't know whether she expected the air to burst into flames first, or one of the MacAlasdair brothers to throw a punch, but she knew she had to nerve herself to speak before they did—and she knew that Douglas was right. Connections made magic.

"Honestly," said Alice, shaking her head the way she'd always done over her sons, and her siblings before that. "Good sirs, *I'll* do it."

Both men swung their heads around to look at her, and although their forms didn't change at all, in that moment Sophia could easily see the dragons under their skins. If they hadn't both looked poleaxed, it would have been terrifying. As it was, she bit back the urge to giggle.

"You?" Cathal frowned, but not angrily. "Could work."

"Yes, it could," Alice said. "You fly me to the border of Valerius's lands, or as far in as you think you can get before he notices you. I'll go further in and ask questions. Sophia can tell me what I seek, though I suspect I know much of it already. Once I find it, I'll return to you, and we'll fly back here."

She said the word *fly* as if it were poison, but otherwise she spoke briskly and unflinchingly.

"It's dangerous," Douglas said. "You do know that, madam."

"I think I'm more aware than you are, my lord," said Alice, "having seen at least the signs of his creatures. If I sought perfect safety, I would have remained in France. And if you," she added, rounding on Sophia just as she'd been about to protest, "can draw this man's attention such that he's throwing you into other worlds and setting demons upon you, then I can very well go to this man's land and talk to his people. I'm quite human, and quite ordinary, and nobody notices women unless we've titles."

"He'll have human minions, as well as the magical sort," said Cathal. "Not pleasant men."

"There are plenty of unpleasant men in the world. I'll do my best to avoid them. With any luck, most of them will still be out looting battlefields."

Sophia bit back her protest. The errand was necessary. If Alice was willing, Sophia wouldn't degrade her sacrifice by trying to talk her out of it. For the second time that night, she reached over to Alice and took her hand.

From her other side, though there was no physical touch, she felt Cathal's gaze on her face. "I'll do all that I can," he said when she turned to look at him. His eyes met hers squarely; he wouldn't insult her with more reassurance.

TWENTY-EIGHT

"Generally speaking," said Munro, "you'll want to kick a man in the knees or hit him in the nose. They both hurt like a right ba…devil, aye, and then with the nose, he'll be blind for a space. With the knees, he'll no' be able to run."

"Not…" Sophia gestured vaguely to the air around her groin.

She and Alice, for whom the lessons were really meant, made strange figures, standing in the practice yard while the wind blew their gowns around their legs and tugged at their plaited hair. Such a sight was not unheard of at Loch Arach—Moiread had mostly worn breeches and a tunic, but she'd practiced a time or two in women's dress, "just in case," although those occasions had been rare. Sophia had never listened so quietly or looked so uncertain.

Munro grinned. "Oh, aye, the ballocks are a grand target as well, mistress. Only not for the first strike, not unless he's by way of having other things on his mind. A man in a fight will guard the jewels well, and a man fighting a woman will expect her to strike there first. Knees or nose, sir?"

Cathal pushed himself off the wall and stepped forward. When he'd found that both women carried daggers, but neither had been trained, he'd thought to give instruction himself—until Munro had pointed out that few of *his* skills would be of use in any fight Alice might face. He was a big man. Even if he'd been purely human, a punch from him could have broken bones. He'd learned to be on guard against dirty fighting, but he'd never truly thought to learn it, not to the depths a man like Munro had, because he'd never even considered a time when he might need it.

And so he'd become a set of pells.

"If it please you, sir?" Munro asked.

After a quick bow of apology, Cathal caught hold of Alice's shoulders—the typical *Explain yourself, woman, and do it quickly* grab—his grip firm but, he hoped, not too tight. She kicked out and connected a solid blow to his upper shin, but well below the knee.

"Skirts," Munro said, shaking his head as Cathal released Alice. "Nothing for it but practice, I suppose."

"I don't think I can pass as a boy," Alice said, sighing, "so you're right. I'll see if I can't get the motion down, at any rate. Sophia, you try."

With Alice, Cathal had only hesitated to gauge his strength; she might have been one of his younger men. When Sophia stood before him, her face sober with concentration, his hands at once felt larger than usual and less a part of him. He took her by the shoulders and felt desire flare up at once, quick and consuming.

For a second her eyes widened, darkened, and he knew she felt it too.

Then she brought her fist around and up, and hit him squarely in the nose.

It wasn't a strong blow. Sophia dropped her hand back to her side no more than a breath after the contact. "Oh!" she said, dismayed, but with a hint of pride underneath it. "Oh, I didn't think that would *work*. I'm sorry."

"No. No, don't be." Cathal blinked quickly, shaking his head to clear it. "That was the point."

"Don't worry about Sir Cathal, mistress," said Munro, chuckling. "Might sting a bit for him, but you can damage the castle as easily as you can truly hurt him. That's why he's out here with us… Aye, sir?"

"You have the right of it, man."

He'd also wanted to be around Sophia. Not wise, that, but he was going to go off and perhaps die in a few days, so he would give himself that indulgence. He'd also wanted to be useful—and truth to tell, he'd longed for a task.

They waited on the weather because a cloudy night would give Cathal the necessary cover. Naturally, the skies had been fair, and while Douglas settled into the running of Loch Arach, Cathal had found himself with time on his hands.

By God, it was nothing to complain about, being free of the duties under which he'd chafed for months. He wouldn't have taken them back again if Douglas had offered. It was only that he'd been used to activity. Now there was waiting, and then the journey, and then—if they were fortunate—Fergus's recovery.

And then?

Once he'd had a ready answer to that question. Only, looking back on the last few years of his wandering life, Cathal was no longer sure that was the answer he wanted— battles for causes he didn't believe in for a succession of lords who would come and go like clouds crossing the sun. That path had satisfied him once. Had the war not come to Scotland, would it have done so indefinitely?

He knew not.

"Now," Munro said, "we'll get to knife play shortly, but remember that a weapon can be taken from you. Your feet and hands, well…" He glanced at Cathal and made a face, as both of them remembered Valerius. "They *can* be taken, but it's a sight harder. And you'll see how even that little tap made a man like Sir Cathal go cross-eyed. Speaking of eyes…if you'll come over here, sir? It's hard to explain this next one without demonstrating."

"Don't get carried away," Cathal said. "I've only the pair, you know."

The ladies both laughed, as Cathal had intended. If he didn't survive the next few days, his last memories might as well be of Sophia, eyes shining with mirth. If he did survive, he'd want those memories too—wherever he ended up going.

He'd been a warrior for most of his life. Blood was the price of every battle; he didn't seek death, but neither did he fear it. Perhaps that was why the second possibility lay as heavily on his heart as the first did.

This time, things went awry without the help of demons or dreams, and Cathal had no suspicion of a problem besides the ones he'd already known himself to have.

He sat with Douglas in the solar, drinking ale and planning as best they could: lists of provisions for him and for Alice, likely times and sources of cover, how long he should wait concealed before taking action, and what kind of action that should be. Douglas had voiced his opinion in favor of abandoning the quest and returning to Loch Arach—and had done so in such a way as to make it seem the only sensible option.

"And leave the girl to Valerius?" Cathal snorted and shook his head. "Don't be an ass—"

"Then don't be sentimental. You know how such matters work. You've left men behind before, I don't doubt."

"*Men*. Soldiers who took pay. Not women who volunteered to help us and couldn't win a fight against a kitchen boy with a meat knife. And I left them to other men, not creatures like Valerius. *And* those were fights I knew I'd never a chance of winning."

"You've no great chance of winning this one," Douglas pointed out. "You can't even kill the man, remember?"

"I could take him prisoner. After that…" Cathal shrugged. He didn't like torture, didn't think it did much in most cases, but if he could bring Valerius into a room and cut bits off until Fergus came back all the way and Sophia was out of danger, he'd live with the memories.

Douglas shook his head. "And if I were him, I'd have safeguards for just that moment. Spells to call demons down on all of us, mayhap, or throw Fergus's soul out into the pit. 'Tis much easier to cast the deadlier ones when you're standing in front of your target. That's assuming you can even reach the man, much less capture him, mind you. You've *not* thought this through."

The dragon-blooded had few children and spread them apart a fair way in time. At Cathal's birth, Douglas had been a man full grown and more. He showed his maturity, as neither Moiread nor Agnes would have, by not adding *of course* out loud, but Cathal heard it nonetheless.

"I'll have you know…" he began, standing up from the table, and then he heard the footsteps running up the stairs.

Whatever their differences, their blood and their training was the same. Douglas's hand fell to the hilt of his sword in the same moment that Cathal's did. Douglas was the one who called "Come in" warily at the knock on the door, but they both turned to face the visitor, not expecting an attack but ready for one nonetheless.

Edan was there instead, his face creased with worry. His bow was quick and clumsy. "My lord. Sir Cathal. There's been an accident, and Mistress Sophia bids you come when you can."

That it was Sophia doing the bidding kept Cathal a shade calmer than might have been the case, but only that shade. Plenty of dying men could send for a confessor. He practically raced his first few steps down the stairs, and he didn't slow until Edan managed to tell him and Douglas more of the story.

By the time he reached the room where Alice lay, with Sophia bustling around at her side and the sharp smell of herbs in the air, Cathal no longer had the sick feeling that the world was tilting beneath him. Still he couldn't be completely relieved. In addition to pitying Alice, he knew that this latest mishap might bring on the question he and Douglas had been debating much sooner than either of them had hoped.

"Her ankle's broken," Sophia said, dipping strips of linen into a bowl of water. She'd spared a quick glance for Douglas and Cathal, but didn't look at either of them as she worked. "I've sent for Donnag, but it's obvious."

"My lord," said Alice, her face green-white and her voice unsteady, "have you ever considered that your castle has too damned many stairs?"

There it was: the stairs being washed, like the floors, to prepare for Lent and the end of winter, the stone slippery, and Alice hurrying to dinner. A hundred such falls happened every day, and people had broken worse than ankles before. It was *probably* just ordinary mortal bad luck that it had happened now to Alice.

Cathal thought so, at least, but he glanced at Douglas, for whom distance and time still evidently hadn't removed all ability to speak with a look. "There'll be no magic about this," he said. "The wards would have told me, if I didn't know already."

Alice shook her head. "Believe me, I'm more than

capable of doing myself a bad turn *without* sorcery. I'm…
aaaagh—" She broke off as Sophia started to wrap her
ankle, the bandages wet and smelling strongly. After a few
moments she added, panting, "—sorry for it, considering."

"Don't be stupid. It's not your fault," Sophia said. "I
only wish that… Well, never mind." She'd glanced at
Douglas before breaking off, and Cathal could guess that
she'd been about to wish for a real bonesetter or even a
physician, but didn't want to insult her host. "It should heal
well enough, if I'm doing this right and you don't move."

"It'll take months, though," Douglas said, "unless you've
magic beyond what I've heard. None of us can heal humans."

"Most likely," said Sophia, turning back to the bowl of
water. Even dismayed, Cathal couldn't help watching the
sure, steady motions of her hands and the rhythm of her
movements. "I'm afraid we'll have to trespass on your hospitality longer than anyone expected, and if I don't return,
I ask that you give Alice shelter and protection until she's
well enough to travel."

"I… Yes," said Douglas, blinking. Cathal watched, torn
between pride and fear, as he went on. "Do you mean to
say you'll go with my brother, then?"

"Of course. There's little else to do, considering the
situation. I wish I weren't the one who knew how to
make potions, and I hope he doesn't have the resources
to summon another demon while I'm there, but…well, if
I fail, I doubt that will matter very much, will it?" She
turned back to Alice. "I'll begin packing as soon as I've
finished here."

TWENTY-NINE

WHEN SHE'D THOUGHT ABOUT LEAVING LOCH ARACH, Sophia had always pictured herself and Alice joining a group of travelers once more. She'd hoped they'd be triumphant, recognized they might be defeated, and never once considered that dragons would still be involved, nor that the journey would be not the end of her mission but, with good fortune, the beginning of the final stage.

The very word *preparation* was a bad jest. Nonetheless, she tried. It was probably for the best, as she told a skeptical and still-groggy Alice, that she'd done so much damage to her clothing. Scorch marks from braziers could be souvenirs of forgetful moments in the kitchen; holes from vitriol could point to soapmaking. She could look the part of a servant or a peasant girl.

She bought an old tunic and hose from Munro as well. Nobody would mistake her for a boy in good lighting, but at night, with her hair up and a cloak to hide most of her body, perhaps she could fool a man at a distance. Even if not, it would be easier to run in male costume.

Running was the second-to-last thing Sophia wanted to do. Unless she revised the list to include death and capture, fighting was at the very bottom. She felt like a porcupine with all her knives—the innocent-looking one at her belt, one in each boot, and a tiny one between her breasts—but despite Munro's lessons, she had no confidence in her skill with any of them.

"You stabbed the demon," Alice said when Sophia was packing and fretting.

"Yes, and that did me very little good," Sophia said, though the reminder was bracing.

Men bled more, they hurt more, and they died more easily. She tried to keep that in mind. As a source of reassurance, it turned her stomach. It was all very well and good to say that Valerius's sworn men were nigh as bad as he was, but that didn't preclude a wretched gamekeeper or night watchman who simply wished to save his own skin, or his family's. Sophia thought she'd use the knives, or try, if she had to, but such self-knowledge made her no happier.

She turned to other sources of comfort. In the small bag that she'd carry, she packed two of the armoring potions—both wrapped with the greatest care, and then more usual herbals on top of them for camouflage and in case circumstances arose on the journey. She took Douglas up to the tower room, a long and slow process, and showed him the golden goblet and the potion within it: Fergus's solar elixir, waiting for the final ingredients, in the last stable state in which she could leave it.

"Should I not return," she said, and the words stuck in her throat, such that she had to look away and cough while Douglas politely took no notice, "I've written out the instructions here. The processes, the hours and days, the substances…enough to make it over again. For this one, start at the second paragraph. The powdered topaz is in the wooden box with the stars on it, in the trunk. I don't know… Forgive me, but I don't know if you'll be able to complete the work, but if you can, it should buy you time."

"Aye." He looked at her gravely. "I'm obliged to you, mistress. My brother all the more so, I'd imagine."

There was a quality in his voice that was like Alice's

tone when she'd lectured Sophia about Cathal: not the same, but similar, copper and gold. Sophia flushed. "My lord, I assure you that I have no designs on your brother."

Her blush was in part because she didn't quite speak the truth—but she was close enough. What matter that she dreamed of Cathal by night and could barely see him without wanting to touch him? She'd not try to trap him in marriage, nor turn him against his brother, and that was good enough.

"Mistress Sophia," said Douglas, "if you'll pardon my bluntness, I give not a single damn for your designs. Have them or no. My worry is that he'll endanger himself for your sake. He wouldn't heed me on the matter of safety when Mistress Alice was the one going. With you, he'll be ten times worse."

"Ah…" Sophia said, glad and dismayed and disbelieving all at once.

"I doubt you can persuade him. I'll not ask you to. But bear that in mind when you're asking your questions. It's more than your neck on the block."

"Yes, of course, my lord," she said, dazed, and with a curtsy, fled.

It would have helped had she been angry at Douglas for so burdening her, but—no. Upon consideration, Sophia found that he'd said nothing she wouldn't have said in his place, as incongruous as it was to think of Cathal and her brothers in anything like the same context. She kept silent, therefore, and worried, and when she had finished her packing and there was nothing else to do, she prayed that if she couldn't succeed, at least her failure might not doom Cathal and his kin.

And then it was the night of their departure, the sky thick with clouds and Cathal waiting in the clearing where she'd first seen him transform. Sophia had embraced and kissed Alice already, and her eyes were still red from that leave-taking. She was glad of the poor light, particularly since Douglas was also there, a sturdy length of rope coiled between his hands.

"We don't have riders often," Cathal said with an apologetic gesture. "I don't have much to hang on to. But I won't let you fall. You've my word on that."

"You don't need to give it," said Sophia, wanting to say more with those green eyes holding hers, unable to do so perhaps even if Douglas hadn't been standing there. "I... We'll speak again when we arrive, I'm sure."

The transformation was as fast as it had been before, though slightly less painful to watch, as if bits of her mind had started to relent. She was *clearly* set on looking at things human beings weren't meant to see, they seemed to say, so who were they to interfere? Sophia still saw little, or little that she could recall: there was Cathal, and then there was...dragon-Cathal, putting his neck down so that Douglas could tie the rope around it.

He made many knots in it, and complicated shapes, so that the end result was a kind of harness, with loops for hands and feet and a larger circle for the waist. "It'd be best if you still held firmly," Douglas said when he was done, "but this should take your weight if your arms grow tired. Ready?"

Sophia stepped forward in answer, not trusting her voice. That Cathal wouldn't deliberately hurt her remained as true as it had been, but now, close up, she was aware of just how horrible a sudden clumsy move on his part could be for her. He might have been aware of it too, for he might have been a statue as she got herself into the makeshift harness.

No statue was ever so warm, though, save in the hottest of summer noons, and a statue wouldn't have thrummed beneath her with—breath? Heartbeat? Both? Trying to figure it out stopped some of her fear. Heedless of indelicacy, which might not even apply in this instance, she leaned forward against Cathal's neck, wrapping her arms as far around it as she could get. That helped too.

"Very well," she said before she could lose her nerve.

"Be careful, both of you," said Douglas.

The huge body beneath her gathered itself. For the space of a heartbeat, Sophia felt the bunching muscles. Knowing what was to come, she held her breath. Then they were shooting upward, and the ground below trying to tug them back down, a *pull* that she could actually and unexpectedly feel. As the harness jerked tight around her body, she clutched at Cathal's neck, trusting that she wouldn't do any damage that way and desperate for a handhold.

Immense wings snapped out behind her, pushing the evening air back behind them with small thunderclaps. The wind streamed past Sophia's face, yanking her hair out of its confinements and sending it snarling behind her, and she shut her eyes against the pain of it. Just as well, for she couldn't bear to look down.

This is normal. He's done this before.

And yet, had he done it with a passenger? And how would she know if all was proceeding normally? She had no way to speak with Cathal, and even such information as his expression in dragon form might give her was now invisible, as all she could have seen with her eyes open was the back of his head.

The rope was holding. They were still going upward. Sophia clung to those facts as she clung to Cathal himself. She would have screamed, she was sure, despite her best intentions, save that her body refused to move even that much. Instead, she rode upward, silent, frozen, and rigid.

When a cold mist enveloped her, she did force her eyes open, just long enough to see a gray fog surrounding them.

Fog?

No—clouds.

They'd talked about flying above the clouds—the plan had depended on it—but Sophia hadn't fully comprehended that until just that moment, when she looked left and right to find herself in a place no human she'd heard of had ever been.

"Oh," she said, or rather, her lips made the sound. If terror and speed hadn't taken her breath away, wonder would have.

"*Oh*," she repeated, a moment later, as they broke through the clouds and a sky full of stars spread out over her head, closer and more brilliant than she'd ever dreamed of seeing them, with the clouds smooth and gray below. Her grip didn't loosen, nor did her heartbeat slow, and the copper taste of fear still flooded her mouth, but now fear had a rival in wonder.

Cathal's flight shifted then, slowing and becoming level. The wings beat less often, though louder each time, and the pull of the earth slackened. Sophia felt the pressure of the rope decrease, though it was still a comforting weight, and the wind died down. They'd reached the height Cathal had wanted, she thought; they'd put the clouds between them and any observers on the ground. Now they were going forward.

For the first time since they'd left the ground, she took a deep breath. Breathing was hard here, but no worse than it had been crossing some mountain passes. The air around her was very cold, despite her layers of clothing and Cathal's proximity, and she knew this was no place for humans to remain very long.

But oh, it was beautiful.

Above her she could see Arcturus and Leo, Castor and Pollux: old friends from summer nights, but never as clear as this, nor as bright. Around the constellations, other stars glittered against the rich blue of the night sky. Sophia thought that she felt their light as well as saw it. She was almost vain enough to believe it greetings and best wishes for her journey, and even knowing herself to be insignificant, she sat up enough to smile in return, though waving would have meant freeing a hand from the harness.

She discovered that her balance was sounder than she'd feared. Cathal's neck where she sat was no wider than the back of a horse, but neither was it narrower, and in level flight like this he barely moved. Once in a while he would turn or bank with the wind; betimes he'd rise and fall with a draft; but the movements were, to Sophia, very slow and steady. There was only the wind blowing past her face to remind her what a pace they truly were setting.

Around her, all was starlight—and silence, for no birds ventured to such a height. She was alone, save for Cathal and the stars, but she felt no loneliness. As they went on, even fear fell away from her, lost in the clouds below.

It was not that she knew herself safe. Even assuming that she and Cathal landed without incident, *safe* wouldn't be true for days, if that. Up above the clouds, she couldn't feel that it mattered.

Should I die, at least I'll have seen this. I'll have been here. Whatever Valerius does to me, this *is worth any price.*

She leaned forward, not out of fright this time but to rest a hand against Cathal's neck, a gesture she didn't even know if he could feel. Together, they flew on through the night.

THIRTY

Carrying a passenger was a new experience for Cathal, made doubly tense by the urgency of their errand and triply so because it was Sophia astride his back. He climbed above the clouds as smoothly as he could, and as quickly, since hesitation wouldn't be useful. When he leveled out and felt Sophia's weight still securely in place, with her breathing steady next to him, relief ran through him like strong drink.

Navigating by the stars, he flew slowly toward the south and Valerius's lands, avoiding when he could any winds that would make him rise or fall too steeply or angle too sharply. It was not the most exciting bit of flying he'd ever done, but he wasn't eager for it to end. Having Sophia close, even when he wasn't in human shape, with the stars arcing overhead and the whole wide sky spread out before him… He could have stayed for far longer.

In time, reluctantly and more gently than he'd ascended, he dove back under the clouds to look for landmarks. He noted the small flecks of light from manors and stayed as far away as he could. Cottages were only lumps in the darkness, far harder to avoid, but they mattered less. Any peasant could claim to have seen a dragon, but it would take far longer for the story to reach anyone who knew its significance, and by that time, God willing, they'd be gone and Valerius dead.

For a while he could hear owls and bats, the few among his fellow creatures of the air who went abroad at night.

Like most animals, they stayed well away from him, but he knew their cries as part of a familiar chorus.

As they approached Valerius's lands, that chorus faded. They didn't travel in silence as they'd done above the clouds, but the night birds' calls were few, and many sounded weaker. Odd: he'd have expected more bats and owls near the sorcerer's domain. Most said they were creatures of the devil.

Granted, most said that about dragons too.

Near the same time, the air changed. Cathal didn't think anyone human would have noticed the faint staleness to it, or the slight suggestion of rot, but both were there, and got stronger the closer he flew. The colors of the land below him were muted too, even for early spring, and about them there was a hint of grayish-red, like a wound gone bad.

The land is poisoned, Lady Bellecote had said.

No wonder the birds sounded unhealthy; no wonder the crops never did very well. Even the edge of Valerius's domain was *wrong*, though wrong in a way few humans could have pinpointed or even spoken about. Cathal didn't think he needed to view the place through magical sight. For certes, he desired no such thing.

With everything in him, he wished to turn back. The thought of setting foot on the corrupted land was repugnant, and the idea of sending Sophia alone into it was worse. He felt his lips pull back into a snarl, exposing his teeth as if he could threaten Valerius from this distance—or rip his throat out—and he knew both impulses to be futile.

Only one course of action stood a chance of helping.

Near the border was a small stand of trees, far enough from any cottages that Cathal doubted anyone would come here until high summer, if that. He circled slowly down to a landing, wincing at the first contact with the earth.

It didn't hurt, precisely. But it felt more yielding and more clinging than snowmelt or rain would explain, and he thought of how Sophia had described the earth in her dreams.

He could have no doubts about whose land they'd found.

Holding still, he felt Sophia extracting herself from the harness, then watched as she slid to the ground. Their surroundings didn't seem to disgust her. She smiled brilliantly up at him. "That was wonderful. Amazing. I-I would write a book, would anyone believe me, and did it not expose you and yours too greatly. I... Well, I thank you."

On the last, she ducked her head, her dark lashes long against her cheeks, and then began to undo the harness until Cathal shook his head at her.

"Oh? Very well," she said and stepped back.

He changed. The world became bigger and higher; as always, it took a moment or two before he felt as though he moved right. He was standing in the middle of the harness, within a loop quite large enough for his body. Sophia comprehended, and laughed quietly.

"I believe I can get it back on when I return," she said. "I hope, at least."

"It won't matter so much then. We'll likely not have to hide on our way out, so I'll not need to go so high so fast."

"Oh," Sophia said, and smiled again, equally brilliantly. "It's almost a disappointment, truly. But then, if it's in the day, it might be just as interesting to see the world from on high—and I suppose I shouldn't be anticipating anything just yet," she added, the smile dying.

Cathal wished he had the words to bring her smile back, or that it would be just to do so. All he could do was nod. "Seven days?"

"I should think that time enough, or as much time as we can afford. It's not a large place." They'd planned all this at the castle. Now they confirmed it, as much because a plan was reassuring as to keep the details fresh in their minds. "Should I need to stay longer, I'll do my best to come back here and give you that message. And if I'm not back in seven days, you will go back to the castle."

It was not a request, nor even a recommendation. "You've been speaking with Douglas."

"He told me nothing I couldn't have reasoned out for myself. If I... If the worst happens," she said, and smoothed her hands over her skirt, "you'll need to get word back, and it'll do no good to have you come in breathing fire from above, most likely. If you go back then, you and your family can perhaps send men in, or come yourselves, or... or try the sorts of magic you know."

There was no gap in her reasoning, no hole that Cathal could find to justify any argument. He would've given years of his life for one, but there was nobody to take him up on that offer, and so he could only nod. Where Sophia was going, he'd be more hindrance than help. Again he had to wait, and hope, and know himself to be useless.

Just so, it came to him, how the women in the camps must have felt before battles. His mother too, mayhap. Real war had been more distant in Cathal's youth; his mother had been a sorceress who could aid her husband from a distance; and even in age, Artair was harder to kill than the rocks around them, but there were always threats.

If they endured, so could he. It was no new thing, sending one's—

Before Cathal's mind could supply the word and shock him further, Sophia spoke again. "I believe I'm well supplied enough for the journey. If you think you'll need food, waiting, I can leave some."

Cathal shook his head. "I'll hunt. Should I get desperate,

I'll take a sheep and leave the coin for it later. And I've gone a fair few days without food before."

"If you're in danger," she said, "if we were wrong and he can track your presence even here, if you have to leave, you should. Leave me a sign if you can, but if I return and you're not here, I'll wait a night, then try to make my way back to your lands."

"My father's."

Sophia waved a hand, not understanding why the distinction was important. In truth, Cathal wasn't sure why he'd felt the need to make it just then, but it had been irresistible. "I'm only human, and there's nothing exceptional about me. And I have coin and skills. I'll be all right."

"Don't," he said. It was almost a growl, but she didn't flinch.

"Very well. I have as good a chance as anyone of being all right. Better than many people would have. It…" He saw the whites of her wide eyes, the swell of her breasts as she gulped air, and the swift motion with which she pushed back a stray lock of hair, as if she could tuck away fear as quickly and completely. "It shall suffice, yes?"

"It must," said Cathal.

He wanted to tell her again that she didn't need to do this. She could turn away from the path before her and the blighted place to which it led. She'd done enough. But that would be insulting, he knew, and besides, it was no longer the truth. The journey into Valerius's domain was the best hope that any of them had. Sophia was the best person to make it now.

And so there was nothing more he could do.

"We will come for you," he said. "If you're captured. I'll pluck Agnes out of her tower if I need to and get her to weave spells for us, or I'll drag my father home from his treaties. Or I'll manage what's needed myself. I can, given time."

Unexpectedly, she smiled again, and in her smile was an echo of those hours flying beneath the stars, with only the two of them and no need for words. Even Cathal didn't see her move when she stepped forward. She flowed toward him, reached up, and cupped the side of his face in one hand. "I would never doubt it," Sophia said.

"You're wrong," he said thickly, and clasped her shoulders in his hands. She looked up at him, startled, about to argue the point. "Not about rescue. Earlier."

"Wha—"

"*Everything* about you is exceptional," he said, and kissed her before she could reply.

Rather, she didn't reply in words. Her response was as desperate as his embrace. Sophia didn't melt into his arms so much as throw hers around him, grasping him with the urgent strength he remembered from the flight, now colored and transformed by sensuality. As her mouth opened before his, her hands roamed his back, short nails almost scoring his skin even through his clothing.

He kissed her as if by sheer force he could make them both forget what waited, as though with his lips and tongue and his hands on her breasts he could himself cast a spell to banish Valerius to whatever hell would claim him in the end. He drank Sophia's little gasps of desire like the strongest wine and wanted nothing more than to hear those sounds, to feel her fingers twined in his hair, to think of nothing else, to think nothing at all.

When he pulled away, far more gently than he'd kissed her, it wasn't only his cock aching. Reality sat heavily on his chest, and the sight of Sophia's face stirred a longing even more painful than the feel of her body. He'd managed to move his hands to her shoulders once more, but couldn't let them fall back to his sides, not yet.

"I…" Sophia raised a hand to touch her lips, swollen and possibly bruised. A chivalrous man would have apologized, but as she wasn't complaining, Cathal couldn't even pretend regret. "I should go, shouldn't I?"

No, he said silently.

Aloud, forcing every syllable, he replied, "If we're to do this—"

"Then leaving won't get any easier for waiting, will it?" she finished, smiling sadly.

As usual, she spoke accurately. Every moment that passed made Cathal more reluctant to let her go at all. He shook his head.

"Then…stay safe, as much as you can. I'll do the same."

"Aye," he said, and couldn't get any other words through his throat.

She turned. A small path, not much more than a game trail, led off through the forest and toward what Valerius probably called civilization. Cathal watched as she walked down it: small, fragile, and valiant in the shapeless night.

THIRTY-ONE

OVER SEVERAL WEEKS, THROUGH BOTH ANALYSIS AND experiment, Sophia had come to acknowledge that the Valerius-sent nightmares could serve her cause. She'd never been glad of them, nor imagined that she could be. Her journey into the wizard's lands changed that.

A map of the two places would have been similar, accounting for the wayward nature of dreams: a forest on a hill, leading down to a valley with a large, dark castle in it. The dreams hadn't shown the village and fields in between, and even from what little Sophia could see at a distance, the castle looked less dark and impregnable than its nightmare twin. More obviously, the sky was only normally overcast, the ground only vaguely damp, and no shadow-beasts chased her.

It could be worse.

Had Sophia not just known but also lived it, her walk toward the castle would have hit her like a runaway cart.

She supposed the land itself wasn't so very bad. The fields were stark and barren, but so would any field be, early in the year; the cottages were squat and dark, but that too seemed typical. She couldn't see rivers of blood or heads on pikes. Mayhap the village she was approaching was no different from the ones she and Alice had occasionally passed through with their merchants, and she was only letting her task nibble around the edges of her mind. Or the difference might have been that she was alone and aware of the danger ahead and its nature.

Yet there seemed a quality to the air that she couldn't name, not quite the smell of rot nor a feeling of chill clamminess, but akin to both and just out of her perception.

She remembered that she'd thought Loch Arach unwelcoming when first they'd arrived—and it still seemed less than precisely *welcoming*—but its remoteness had been honest. Walking toward the village, Sophia kept looking behind her, thinking to see…she didn't know what, and she wouldn't have wanted to name it if she had, not even in her own mind.

When dawn broke and she saw the first villagers emerging from their cottages, heading forth to milk goats or cows and do various other farming tasks she found more mysterious than Greek or Latin, she approached one of the larger buildings and tapped on the door.

The woman who answered was a year or two older than Sophia, dressed plainly but not poorly, but her face was more lined than Sophia would have expected, and very white until she saw who her visitor was. "Don't have aught to spare for beggars," she said.

"I'm not," Sophia protested, trying to keep any hint of an accent out of her English. "I'm looking for work. My aunt—"

"I'm not your aunt, and I've got no work. You don't want to stay here," said the woman, and shut the door.

Having half expected a response of that nature, Sophia nonetheless found herself blinking, startled and disappointed to have her suspicions confirmed—and more nervous as well, because of the woman's caution and her wary expression.

The next cottage was smaller, and the girl at the door almost a child. She stared at Sophia with wide eyes, but shook her head when asked about work. "Should I try the castle, then?" Sophia asked.

"Well…" The girl looked her over, taking in face, figure, and gown with a gaze older than Sophia had seen from most, even the poorer girls in Flanders. "Could be. You might do all right there for a bit. I…wouldn't think to stay, though."

"No," Sophia said. "I'm not staying."

She pulled her shawl tighter around herself and continued up the road. She'd hoped to gain admission long enough to ask questions, and that well before she got to the castle, but if she couldn't even ask for work without meeting hostility, she didn't think questioning would go very well. The castle it was, then, even if the sight of armed men in front of the main doors did tighten her stomach and make her skin crawl.

They're soldiers. Every lord has them. Cathal does.

The back of her mind refused to accept that, and the rest of her feared that it was right. None of the guards offered her direct insult—Sophia guessed that the worst of the lot were away fighting with their master, and even here there seemed to be a few standards of civilization—but she wished it were still night, that they might not see her as well or at least that she might be less aware of their gazes.

"Kitchens. Maybe. Doubt it," one of them said and shrugged a shoulder, then glanced to his companion.

"That's Cook's problem. Go on."

In the courtyard of Valerius's castle, there *were* smells, and not the unavoidable sort that Sophia was used to from both cities and Loch Arach. One could never do much about waste or spoiled food, but there *were* methods of avoiding at least the worst. The people she'd grown up with had used them, and so had those at Loch Arach. Here, either those in residence couldn't afford to do so or didn't care.

She endeavored not to think overmuch about it, averted

her eyes, and breathed through her mouth. Up above her was the castle proper. She'd need a way into that, in case what she sought was written down. How did one become a maidservant?

A hand grabbed her by the elbow, interrupting her thoughts. Sophia yelped and turned to glare, then closed her mouth and cast her eyes down when she realized it was another of the men-at-arms. "What's your business here, girl, and why aren't you about it?"

"I-I was looking for the steward. For work."

The man—scrawny and tall, with lank hair and the smell of wine about him—grinned. "If it's a few coins you want..." He pulled her toward him, strong enough to ignore her resistance.

This would not be a good time to stab a man. "Sir," she said, preparing an excuse, when another voice cut in.

"She's here for us, Adney. Leave off, unless you want to wait *another* fortnight next time your horse needs shoes."

The speaker was young, female, and very plainly dressed, but when she spoke, the guard let go of Sophia's elbow. "Another girl, Gilleis?" he asked, looking Sophia over again and now with more dubiousness than lechery.

Gilleis tossed her dark head. "Well, since all the *men* are away at war—"

The slight was clearly intentional, and she was just as clearly prepared for the blow, ducking out of the way before Adney's hand could do worse than clip the side of her head.

He spat. "Go, then, both of you. And Gilleis, you run your mouth while you can. Not much time left for it."

The girl grabbed Sophia by the arm—it was getting to be a pattern, though her touch wasn't nearly as offensive—and guided her across the courtyard, walking slowly enough that spectators couldn't say she was fleeing. "Wouldn't leave a dog with that pox-ridden son of a bitch if I could help it," she said.

"He seems a bad sort," Sophia agreed tentatively.

"A drunk pig," Gilleis said, shrugging skinny shoulders. "There's worse. Adney can't do much more than box my ears, and he misses that easy enough, as you saw. You're lucky you came here while his lot's got the run of the place—seeing as you're unlucky enough to come here at all. Or stupid enough, but you don't look that."

"It was… I could find no other work," Sophia said. They picked their way across the courtyard toward the outbuildings, headed toward one where she could see smoke rising from the roof. "You're a smith?"

"Apprentice." Sharp black eyes took in Sophia's stained dress and plain shawl. "Might you know anything about the work? Don't be scared to say no. We won't turn you out tonight, and I'm mortal sick of sweeping."

"I know fires, and the bellows a bit. And a little about metal, though I've not done any proper ironwork. And I *can* sweep."

"That's a sight better than I'd thought you might say. Besides, I meant what I said to Adney, and Harry's last apprentice took a Scottish arrow through the eye, from what we heard. Poor boy." She spoke with genuine pity, but didn't go on either to lament or to curse the Scots, for which Sophia, wincing inwardly, was grateful. "So he took me on, his father and mine being all but kin. And we've work enough for another pair of hands. Here…Harry!"

She called to a man who stood by the forge, and he raised his head to look at them with slow, unhurried curiosity. Sophia saw that he was middle-aged and towheaded, tall and muscled as befit his profession, with a full beard neatly trimmed short.

"Christ's blood, Gilleis, and who's this?" He swore genially and didn't step out of the smithy but rather beckoned them in.

Once she'd crossed the threshold, Sophia felt better. The feelings of wrongness didn't lift, but it was as though a wall went up between her and them—thin enough that she knew what was on the other side, but a barrier nonetheless. She stopped short, blinking.

"Come along," said Gilleis. "He's not as bad as he looks."

"No…not at all," Sophia said, smiling an apology. "I only felt faint for a minute. It's been a long day."

It was a weak excuse, but she'd use what she could. It both heartened her and shamed her to see the concern on both faces. She didn't want to deceive good people—but oh, it made her glad to have anyone well-meaning at hand.

"She's looking for work," Gilleis explained, pushing a stool in Sophia's direction with one foot. "She says she's used to fire and metal, some, and she can sweep. Adney was drooling down her neck, and I thought—"

"I know well enough what you thought," Harry said and sighed. "The time will come, and soon, when you'll have to watch your tongue around the guards."

"I *know*. But it's only Adney."

"For now." He turned his attention to Sophia. "Sweeping will be a start. You can show me your other skills in time… if you think that's wise."

"What do you mean, sir?" she asked, wondering if he'd already thought of alchemy.

Harry regarded her gravely. "What's your name, mistress?"

When she'd set out, she'd planned to go by *Meg*—a common-enough name, and one with no connections to her real identity. Standing in the smith's yard, however, she felt, as strongly as she'd felt her way in dreams, that she should speak the truth. "Sophia," she said.

"Well, Sophia. I can give you a place by the fire and food for as long as you want, and I can keep you safe as long as you keep sensible. Come tomorrow, I can also give you food to be journeying on with. And that would likely be the wiser course. A few days from now, this castle will be…"

"No place for a woman alone?" Sophia filled in when he hesitated.

"No place for almost anyone, if they can help it."

THIRTY-TWO

CATHAL SPENT MOST OF THE FIRST TWO DAYS IN A TREE.

He could have wished for a better season. The evergreens were the only trees that would hide his presence, and it was difficult to go very far up them without breaking the branches. He settled for a point about halfway up that offered a keen lookout for anyone coming. There he sat, or lay with his face pressed to the branch, and waited.

He'd passed more interesting days. In his youth, he'd learned stillness, and at least how patience could serve a man on a hunt or a battlefield, and he was glad of both. Cathal watched the flight of birds: the owls that were now waking up from their winter sleep, the smaller birds that were beginning to arrive back, and the grouse that simply sought warmth in one location or another. He noted squirrels, when they'd woken up, and once saw a deer at the very outskirts of the clearing, though he wasn't surprised when it moved no closer. They were as nervy as horses about smell, even when he was in human form.

When the first night fell and he could be certain that nobody would see him, he killed one of the grouse — caught it quickly, broke its neck, and risked a very small fire to roast it, then buried the remnants with the ashes. As a dragon, he could have eaten it raw and whole, but he judged that course of action riskier than the fire.

He woke on the second day with a crick in his neck and bark in his hair, and it started to rain midway through the afternoon. Sheltered by the branches, and thinking the weather would keep most men inside, woodcutter and hunter alike, he broke a small branch from higher up the tree and began idly to carve it. Cathal had no object in mind, either of use or of decoration, and yet it came as no surprise when the lines of the branch turned into a gowned human figure beneath his knife, and the face took on Sophia's expression of delighted curiosity.

Wondering about her whereabouts, or her safety, was useless. He found that he could stop himself from doing so. It took slightly more effort than had been necessary when he waited for reports back from scouts, but he had practice. He didn't expect other reactions.

Not to put too fine a point on it, but Cathal missed her.

He heard her voice in his head, commenting on or questioning everything that happened, be it the flight of an owl, the sunset, or the way pine felt beneath his knife. More than that, he found himself explaining such things, putting them into words as if she was there and he would interest her by so doing, making a gift of his observations and knowing that she'd appreciate them.

He was not a man used to loneliness. From time to time he'd had companions, male and female alike, but he'd spent long stretches of his life fundamentally alone, and he'd never felt the lack of company. His family, like Loch Arach, was something to return to every so often, but he'd never wanted to stay there, nor with any of them, for very long.

It was passing strange to feel an absence where he'd never even known there was a presence. He gave the carved figure two slim hands, clasped about a goblet with unknown contents, and wondered what Sophia would think of it.

The sun was sinking behind the hills as Cathal finished the carving's hands, and his own hands went still, along with the rest of him, when he heard men approaching along the nearby road. More than one came, he could tell, and their pace was too regular for peasants out hunting. These were soldiers. Quickly, he pulled himself upward to a branch that would give him more cover and still hold his weight, and then listened as three of the men came closer, until he could hear their voices over the light rain.

"Damn well better have kept it up, if they know what's best for them."

"And if they weren't lazy buggers, they'd be here with us. Doesn't matter. What matters is I don't want his lordship coming down that road and getting stuck behind a deadfall…or his carriage overturning on account of a hole. And neither do you, if you like your skin."

"Then we take the road around."

"That's not orders. Orders are we take this one, get back three days quicker, unless there's reason to do anything else. Which means *your* orders are to scout ahead, smart-like, and let me know what's in the way. Or I can tell the captain about that nice set of jewels you've got hidden in your saddlebags… *Such* a shame the house caught fire before we could loot it proper, aye?"

Curses in several languages followed. The scout didn't sound like an educated man, but he was a worldly one. His footsteps went forward down the road. The others stayed behind, and Cathal swore in a few languages himself, if only in the back of his head.

Sophia hadn't even been gone half the allotted time. She was quick, but he doubted she could find what she needed in two days. She was subtle, but Cathal didn't like to think of her spending any more time in Valerius's proximity if he could prevent it.

The hours between sunset and full dark felt very long.

He watched the glow of campfires a distance down the road, heard drinking songs and brawls begin, and then slipped down out of the tree, thanking God that the night was cloudy again. He stayed human for a while nonetheless, pushing himself to run for four hours into the forest—double that time for a mortal man on foot— before he changed and took to the sky, skimming low atop the trees.

Before long he picked out the spot where he and Sophia had arranged to meet: midway toward the castle, about half a day's journey for a lone man on foot, twice that for a group of soldiers—and who knew how long Valerius's carriage and possessions would take? The village was still an hour or two off; the scout on the road ahead of him, making sure all was in readiness.

Cathal folded his wings, dropped, and waited in the darkness, watching through slit eyelids so that even that light wouldn't give his presence away. He saw the scout in the distance: a tall, skinny man with the hardened look of a man who'd killed a few times for pay—a look that, for the first time, it was disconcerting to recognize on himself.

He grew old, perhaps.

The man reached the edge of the village, turned, and headed back, unable to run but still keeping up a good pace. Cathal watched him round a bend in the road, then crept out and began the first part of his plan.

Large as he was, and wet as the road was, it was no great challenge to scoop out a hole. Feeling a bit like a boy playing in the mud, he made it big enough and deep enough to truly ruin a rider's day, then dragged branches close to it and smoothed down the nearby dirt. Valerius's men would likely notice before the hole did any serious damage, but it did no harm to try.

Sneaking away, he crept further back toward the castle, found an old tree, and gave it a shove—more of a determined lean, really, for that was all it needed. It crashed most satisfactorily to the ground. Sitting back and surveying it, Cathal was confident that no horse and none but the skinniest of men would be able to get around it.

The soldiers could shift the log and fill the hole. That would take time, though—more perhaps than the three days of the longer road, if they ran afoul of either obstacle—and if Valerius had any magical means of travel, Cathal doubted he'd have subjected himself to a spring journey by road, even if it was in a carriage. Both obstacles could have come about naturally; the earth was wet, the trees were old, and one man on foot might miss a hole that would cripple a horse or break a carriage.

Knowing Valerius even as little as he did, Cathal did wince for the scout and his likely fate—but that was war. He'd done worse, and more directly, to men a thousand times over in his life. Nobody lived forever, not even the MacAlasdairs. He'd bought Sophia half a week free of Valerius and his men, possibly more than that.

That was, if she stayed so long in the village. She'd likely used the same road. If she came back early to their meeting place, she was likely to walk right into the arms of Valerius's men.

Cathal hissed, breath steaming in the night air. Going back further would mean crossing paths with Valerius himself, and Douglas might be right—the wizard might well be able to sense Cathal's presence and to have planned for just such an occasion.

Yet Cathal couldn't stand by and wait any longer. He'd been resigned to Douglas's instructions when the original plan held, in part because Sophia had seconded them.

Plans changed when the enemy made contact. Any soldier knew that.

He folded himself back into human shape and started running again—toward the castle this time, and at an angle away from the road.

He had no idea where Sophia had ended up; nor was there a man or woman in this blighted land that he'd trust to send a message. He'd have to rely on his own senses—and hope he got to Sophia before Valerius's men did.

THIRTY-THREE

THE HUMAN BODY WAS TRULY AMAZING. SOPHIA HAD thought she'd been used to working with her hands, and yet she'd gotten blisters after three days with Harry and Gilleis. Her arms and back ached too, but she'd expected that. While she'd done her fair share of sweeping and lifting in her youth, it had been a long time since.

She'd slipped into the castle proper a few times and even made her way, under the pretense of being lost, to the upper floors, but she'd found nothing there that she could use. The man's bedchamber was anonymous, his trunks contained only clothing, and he had no books, or had left none, other than household ledgers. What questions she'd managed to ask of the maids and men—though she'd left the soldiers alone as much as she could—had been met only with silence: tight lips, white faces.

Much was wrong here. Sophia couldn't see how to make it right.

Harry had made good on his offers. She'd not lacked for food or safety, and the smithy was warm and clean at night. Sophia had left on as many errands as she could regardless, seeking to learn more about the castle, but by the evening of the third day she'd almost given up. When Harry sent Gilleis to the kitchens instead of her—"They know her better, and the cook's got a soft spot for her"—Sophia barely had the will to protest.

Sitting on the bench, she opened a small jar of salve that she'd brought with her and began to smear it on her blisters.

Her mind was more numb than her hands. Tomorrow she would consider the next path to take, but just then she couldn't face the effort. She listened to Harry moving about, to the sloshing of water and the clanking of iron tools.

All of a sudden there was silence, and when she looked up, it was into his solemn face. "You're here for a purpose."

Caught out, she stammered. "Wha... I—"

"You'd have left otherwise," he continued, quiet and relentless. "You've no family here. This isn't such good work as to keep you...not when there's likely plenty of need for a good woman on any other land. And I know you've been talking to folk."

He was large. The wall was at her back. Sophia dropped her blistered hand to her waist, not sure she could reach any of her knives without Harry noticing.

If he saw the movement, he didn't show it. He raised his hand, and she flinched, but it was to pull at a cord around his neck, drawing out an iron cross. He closed his hand around it. "I swear by God and Saint Clement, I mean you no harm, and you know I'm not *his* man."

His was a jerk of the chin toward the castle, and a curl of the lip that Sophia had rarely seen from Harry.

"You've never seemed to like him," she said slowly.

"No." They hadn't talked much, though Gilleis had ranted occasionally at the foolishness of this soldier or that dairymaid. Otherwise they'd kept quiet, and now Harry drew a hand across his mouth. "If you're here... My father was his smith before me, aye? And he thought as I did, once. Your lord's your lord, and if you get a bad one, well, mostly God sees to it in his time, and it may be the next one is better. Best just to wait, not upset things."

"That could be," Sophia agreed. It was a cautious thing,

this conversation: another bridge, perhaps, but this one made of ice. "And you stayed."

"I'm a skilled man. Hard to get another… And iron's got its own kind of honesty, and its own defense against men like him. I thought…think…I can keep a few people safe, wait him out. Works often enough. But—"

Sophia braced herself and spoke. "But it begins to seem, mayhap, as though there won't be a next one?"

Harry's eyes widened. He nodded once, as if afraid to let his muscles move any more than that. Then he reached for a jug of wine.

Silence was best, Sophia decided. Silence let the moment draw out, let him realize that she'd actually said what she had, he'd actually confirmed it, and the world still went on. She lifted her hand away from her waist and stretched it, feeling the pull of the skin on her blisters, but she didn't look away from the blacksmith.

"My father served his," Harry said finally, "and his lordship was already a man when I was a boy. Here I'm old enough to have children grown, and he looks no older than me, nor acts it. In a good man, that might be all right."

She nodded. "He isn't. And he's not keeping himself to his own lands either. But you know that, yes?"

"Yes. And that's why you're here?"

"It is." She wouldn't lie to him, pretend that she'd come to rescue him and his fellows, or that she'd even have given them a thought if Cathal hadn't run afoul of their lord. Now Sophia wished she could answer otherwise, honestly, but here in the yard of the smithy, she'd do Harry the courtesy of the truth. "Was your father here when he—"

"—took the title? He was. In the village, not the castle. Most of the folk who lived here then died, my da' said, or learned to hold their tongues and forget right quick. He…

pretended he did, at least enough to keep our skins on, but he spoke his mind when he was training me, once I was old enough to know when to keep *my* mouth shut."

Sophia felt as she did when she looked over a crucible and saw the mixture start to change. This was working; this had potential. All she needed was the right ingredient at the right time. "Do you know... Did he tell you where Valerius kept his... Where he did his work?"

"Dungeons," said Harry, and Sophia winced, for she'd never even been able to get close to the stairs that led down beneath the castle. Adney and his friends might be distinctly second-rate, but about certain things they knew their jobs too well. "And I wouldn't try it, lady. He'll have left more guards than human ones there, and worse. Nobody opens those doors when he's away."

Relief and regret just about balanced, or would have if relief hadn't come with shame. Sophia was a mortal woman, and she'd do the sensible thing—get away, tell Cathal and Douglas what she'd heard, and put together a plan that included probably magic and almost certainly a man who could actually fight demons. Yet, thinking of the time and effort lost, she looked down at her hands when she nodded, not wanting to meet Harry's eyes.

"You weren't sent here to kill," he said. "I never thought that. One man alone wouldn't come for that, except in the old stories. A woman never would."

"No," said Sophia, then thought of Cathal's sister and added as much of the truth as she could. "I wouldn't. I've never fought a man, and...another creature...almost killed me. I came to learn. Please, if there's anything your father told you, even if it doesn't seem very important, about Valerius—"

Harry snorted. "*Valerius* indeed. Doesn't sit well on

him, I can tell you that. He talks much about his forefathers being lords in Rome... Well, and so were half of ours, weren't they? His father never spoke that sort of nonsense. My da' said that he was a hard man, the old lord, but he was a man, and he'd no ambition to be anything more."

"Do you know his name?" Sophia asked. With the declaration of her goals, the mood had shifted. Now was the time for direct questions.

"De Percy," said Harry and scratched his chin as he thought further. "The old lord was John, as I recall, or mayhap James. It's on the gravestone, if you could get into the chapel tomorrow."

"That might help," Sophia said, "but—"

Gilleis dashed in, arms empty and face pale, and kicked the door shut behind her. As the other two turned to look at her, she spoke in a hurried half-whisper, words falling from her mouth like water from a pitcher. "You, whoever you are, you've got to get yourself gone. I overheard the guards... You've been asking too many questions, and they're coming *back*, all of them. They'll want to talk to you."

The meaning of *talk to you* was as clear as the identity of *them*. Sophia rose from the bench on legs that felt as if they didn't belong to her at all.

"When?" Harry asked.

"Tomorrow. Evening if the road's bad, morning otherwise. And Adney'll be by before very long to see that you're stuck here until they come. They think you're here. If you go out the back way, around the kitchens, you might make it. Keep your head down, and tell Peter at the gate that you're Joan from the village. She's about your build, and she comes to work the dairy and flirt with the stableboys. We'll keep them here as long as we can when they come, and the order will take some time to get around."

Standing outside herself, Sophia felt her heart speed up. She knew that her stomach was clenching and churning and that her throat was tight, but she observed all of that as another process, this one with her body as the crucible. None of those things mattered, regardless. "Harry," she said. "What was *his* name? Valerius's, before…before he changed it?"

"What? Why does it matter?" Gilleis was all action, grabbing Sophia's cloak and wrapping it around her while she stood waiting for an answer, shoving loaves of bread into a sack, and all the time looking toward the door. "*Go*, for Christ's sake."

"Alfred. Or Albert." Harry closed his eyes, and a moment passed while Sophia grasped the sack of bread. "Albert. Da' used to call him 'Little Bert' when he was in a bitter mood, when he thought his lordship wouldn't know of it. Albert de Percy."

"Thank you," said Sophia. "Thank you both so very much, and I hope…I pray you'll not suffer for this. I—"

"Window," Harry said and grabbed her by the waist, hoisting her up without any effort at all. "Closer to the way out. Luck to you, girl."

After that, there were no more words, only speed and the growing night.

THIRTY-FOUR

A SHORT TIME AFTER SUNSET, IT STARTED TO RAIN. MUD sucked at Cathal's feet as he ran, and his clothing was soaked before long. The wind picked up too; a storm was coming out of the northeast. He could only be glad that it was too early in the year for lightning.

Wind, rain, and distance meant he saw the men before anything else. Three guards on horseback, they were large enough to catch the eye even with the storm, and they were galloping fast enough to get attention. A second later Cathal saw their quarry.

The figure was wrapped in a heavy cloak and running, dodging between the trees on the side of the road with desperate speed but the clumsiness of one not at all used to fleeing.

A hood obscured the figure's face, the cloak its body, and Cathal wouldn't have put it past Valerius or his men to send out a decoy, yet he was moving half a moment after he saw the traveler, and there was no doubt in his mind. Whether it was the way she moved, the scent of her, or another factor that he couldn't shape in human form, he knew Sophia.

As Cathal recognized her, one of the guards wheeled his horse to outflank her, leaned down, and grabbed her by the arm. She screamed, clear even through the wind.

Cathal's leap was more than human legs could have managed, more even than he'd equaled on any battlefield. He struck as he landed, sweeping his sword down across the horse's haunches. The beast screamed and reared, throwing its rider clear of the saddle and breaking his grip on Sophia's arm.

Freed, she scrambled for the tree line again, wisely distancing herself from both the panicked horse and its former rider, though the man was on the ground and writhing. Cathal would have wagered he had a broken leg, if not worse. He wasn't disposed to care, not with the other two fast approaching.

A few quick steps brought him to Sophia. He grabbed the rope harness from off his shoulder and pushed it into Sophia's hands. "You'll need to be quick, after. Stay behind me." Then he stepped forward, putting himself between her and the oncoming riders, praying without words or very much faith.

Fighting mounted men from the ground went poorly for most. Mortal men needed either archers or a shield wall to manage it with any chance of success. Cathal had a few other advantages.

One was the horses' reluctance to approach him. Even though he was in human form, he could see them snort and balk, smelling his true nature. It took a good application of spurs to move them again, and by that time, Cathal was ready to use his other advantages: height and strength.

His first strike pierced through the guard's armor and the flesh of his thigh, and sank to the bone. The man screamed, a familiar sound. The spray of blood was familiar too. A major vessel was severed. The wound would likely be fatal. Cathal spun away, and the momentum as he pulled his sword back to his side half severed the leg.

The third man was turning his mount to run. Cathal had half expected as much. Valerius had taken the best part of his retinue to war. These men had thought they'd be chasing down an unarmed woman.

That woman was staring at the broken corpse of the soldier, and her full lips pressed together until they were a thin line indeed. Cathal had no time to speak because other men would arrive soon. He knew not what he might have said if he could have.

He felt no guilt over what he'd done, nor triumph. At best, he'd rid the world of a man who'd serve Valerius willingly, but there were many like him. At worst, he'd killed a man who'd done his duty for what might have been noble enough reasons in the end; feeding a family could put good men to bad work. That was often the way. It was war, and it was done.

Yet he watched Sophia's face until he changed and then again after, and was glad when she swung herself up into the harness that he might not have to see her any longer. He was glad to feel her weight on his neck, and that she put herself there without hesitation—without, as far as he could tell, fear. He could only hope that wouldn't change when she was no longer desperate, but that hope had to take a fifth or sixth place to other, more desperate wishes.

He crouched, gathered himself, and sprang, spreading his wings to launch himself with the wind.

Its strength was with him, carrying them far upward even more quickly than Cathal had managed at the castle, but this speed wasn't his own, and he had no sure way to control it. The wind twisted too, tossing him from side to side, full of updrafts and downdrafts and cross-breezes, and the rain poured down so hard that he could barely see.

He was above the trees, away from most mountains, and both of those facts likely saved him and Sophia. For a long stretch he flew onward, heading as much as he could manage in the direction of Loch Arach, but not truly knowing where he was going. Sophia's weight, and the warmth of her body, let Cathal know that she was still there, one of the few constants in the storm's rage.

When she began to shiver, Cathal knew they'd need to stop soon. He was wearying too, his wings tiring with the effort to stay both on course and level against the wind. Shaking water away from his face with a quick gesture, he peered down through the rain and saw in the distance a cluster of tiny buildings, one with still-lit windows. A village, he thought, and with luck an inn—or at least a manor with stables.

Nobody would be out in the storm most likely, but he still wanted a bit of concealment. A line of trees a few yards away would suffice, he decided. He folded his wings and dove, landing as gently as he could manage under the circumstances. He still hit the ground more roughly than he'd have liked, and there was a moment of deep alarm afterward when he didn't feel Sophia moving.

When he whipped his head around to look at her, though, she blinked back at him and slowly began to sit back. "I-if I'm not to g-get down," she said through chattering teeth, "you'd b-b-best tell me so now."

It took longer for her to get out of the harness, due to a sodden cloak and numb limbs, Cathal guessed, and cursed to see both. From what he could tell, she was in no danger, but he couldn't tell much, in truth. He knew human fragility on the battlefield. In all else, the men had been the camp surgeon's problem, or the supply captain's, or the steward's. If Sophia could move and speak, he thought she was well enough, but he only then realized how little qualified he was to gauge the certainty of any such thing.

As soon as she hit the ground, he was changing back to man's shape. It did little immediate good—he hadn't brought a cloak and had been warmer as a dragon—but he put an arm around her and started them toward what civilization there might be, wherever they'd ended up.

They spoke not at all on the way. Walking was effort enough.

The lit building did turn out to be an inn, one where a party of merchants was sleeping in the main room, and a tired man came forward without curiosity to meet them.

"A private room," said Cathal, and counted out the named price without thought. "Where are we?"

"Larkford," said the innkeeper. If he was surprised, he didn't show it. Cathal doubted the man cared about anything but the coins Cathal was handing him. "Take a wrong turn?"

"Several."

The town's name was unfamiliar, but the man's voice was Scottish, and that was reassuring. The fire was more so. Cathal didn't suffer from the cold, not the way humans did, but warmth was better, and he was glad of it for Sophia's sake. He couldn't hear her teeth chatter any more, and when he looked over at her as they followed the innkeeper up the stairs, there was a little more life in her face.

"They can't follow us here before tomorrow," he said, once they were in the room and the door had closed behind the departing innkeeper. "We can rest. Wait out the storm."

"Demons?" she asked. She pushed back the hood of her cloak, her wet hair clinging to her face and neck. Firelight played across both, and her eyes reflected it, somber save for that dancing play of flame.

"I'll handle them," Cathal said, tapping a finger against the hilt of his sword. "You should get out of your clothes."

Then the weight of what he'd said and where they were struck him, truly drawing his attention for the first time now that she was physically safe. Cathal looked away, surveying the room. In truth it was a small enough place, with only a fireplace and a canopied bed as furniture.

He turned his back on her and walked to the window, staring at the red-and-yellow pattern on the shutters. It matched the bedcovers, a nicer touch than he would have thought from the place. Mayhap it was better on less miserable nights. "Wrap up in one of the blankets, and tell me when you're done," he said, keeping his mind blank. "Hang your clothing by the fire. Doubt it'll be exactly dry in the morning, but damp's still better."

Wet wool made thumping, squishing sounds. They weren't pleasant; what they implied was far too pleasant. The softer noises were worse: lighter fabric, garments worn closer to the skin. Cathal closed his hands on the windowsill, careful not to break the wood, and breathed through his nose.

"Your clothing's wet too," Sophia said. Her voice was quiet, a touch rough. Cathal told himself that was probably the strain of their escape.

"I'll… Ah, I'll take my turn after you," he said, although just at the moment, cold and damp were both helpful qualities. Not *sufficient*, and he wouldn't want to turn around any time in the near future, but helpful.

More noises came from behind him: footsteps and a slight exhale, as if of effort. Then, sounding less sure of herself than usual, she said, "There's only the one bed."

Trust her to make observations. "Aye," said Cathal. He had a brief ridiculous notion of offering to put his sword between them. It might have worked for bloody Tristan, but he doubted it would for him, and Sophia was more alluring than he'd ever imagined Isolde to be. "I'll take one of the other blankets, lie on the floor. I've had worse quarters."

"Oh. Er," she said, and then he heard more footsteps,

slow ones, as she came toward him. He drew breath, trying to find words that would politely tell her to keep her distance, and then she put a hand on the back of his neck.

Her fingers were rough, damp, and cold, and the light touch ran through Cathal as strongly as the pain of a wound. "What I'm trying to say," Sophia said as Cathal turned helplessly to face her, "is that you…you don't have to. In truth, although it's kind of you to offer, unless you'd rather, you've no need to do either of those things."

She was naked.

Her wet hair flowed down her shoulders and almost to her waist, but it concealed nothing: not her full breasts, rosy-brown nipples drawn tight and hard, nor the flare of her hips, nor the dark triangle between her legs. Sophia's face was bare too, stripped of scholarly distance, reserve, and all concealment. Cathal saw there more than a trace of nervousness, but, overwhelmingly, desire.

"We could," she said, "spend the night differently."

THIRTY-FIVE

SOPHIA MADE HERSELF STOP SPEAKING. SHE WANTED TO keep going, clarifying and explaining, yet she knew that would in truth only be babbling. For the space of every word she said, she'd not be waiting on Cathal's answer. If he was going to deny her, he'd be less likely to interrupt her to do it, and so as long as she talked, *yes* was still a possibility even if *no* was in his mind.

You can't keep talking forever, said her common sense, *and besides, if you didn't want to give him the choice, you shouldn't have made the offer, nor be standing here undressed.*

The time for second thoughts was past.

Sophia closed her mouth and looked up at Cathal, past where his soaked tunic outlined his muscular chest and into his eyes. The bright green of them was a thin ring, the dark pupil large with surprise. She hoped for more than that, but didn't dare count on it. His neck was warm beneath her hand, the skin smooth and the pulse rapid. She thought about drawing back, but couldn't make herself move.

A gust of wind outside blew rain against the shutters, a hard percussive spatter.

Despite the speed Sophia knew he could manage, Cathal took her hand slowly, his calloused fingers light on her own. As he bent, brushing his lips across her knuckles, the moment felt dreamlike—but no, her dreams of late had been more active, and more horrible, even if this was to be only a polite refusal.

There was that. Whatever he said or did would be better than being devoured by shadow-men or turned to mist by Valerius. There were many worse fates than the worst that could happen here. Sophia wished she could make her gut know that, or her heart.

When he raised his head and smiled at her, she *felt* her heart throwing itself against her ribs like a wild bird in a cage. The smile, like his eyes, was surprised and uncertain. It was also gentle, and she fought back trepidation when she saw that. *Gentle* could mean *How do I say no without upsetting you?*

"Is it truly your wish?" he asked. "I expect nothing. You owe me nothing…and I owe you a great deal."

"No," she said, and even as she was shaking her head, she went on quickly. "Not this. You don't owe me…" She couldn't think of a term that wasn't medical, so she waved a hand, indicating her naked form. "And I wouldn't have it as a debt, but if you want to, then…then yes, it is. Very much so. I…"

While she was trying to work up the nerve to say *I desire you greatly*, which might have been even more embarrassing than standing before him naked and making the offer, Cathal's eyes flashed and his smile shifted, uncertainty fading and hunger taking its place. Sophia saw that much before he pulled her into his arms. After that, she wasn't in a position to examine his face, and she didn't need to.

The first kiss was light, teasing, a brush of his lips against hers and then a momentary retreat, only to return longer, and firmer, Cathal's tongue slipping against hers and back. One of his hands cupped the side of her face, while the other splayed across the back of her waist, easily spanning it, and his fingers moved in slow, almost reverent patterns against her bare skin. He used none of his strength; it was Sophia who wrapped her arms around his neck and leaned in to his body, pulled by the growing need in her own.

She knew that he was still dressed, yet had forgotten for the moment the condition his clothing was in. The chilly dampness against her bare skin was sudden, but not pleasant. She flinched and squeaked a little, and Cathal lifted his mouth from hers. "I'll not hurt you…" he began, sounding surprised and concerned.

"No, that is, maybe, probably, but that doesn't matter." Stories from her married friends and anatomical studies alike suggested there was likely some pain in the future, but that was the case for most worthwhile things. It had no bearing on the issue at hand anyhow. She plucked at the fabric of his tunic. "This is the problem, and I think you'll want to remove it in any case, so…perhaps now?"

"Ah, aye," he said, relieved and yet not entirely so. Sophia couldn't analyze that for long. He kissed her lightly again and then stepped back. "Sorry. I'm not used to—"

"You *must* be," she said, eyes going wide. Almost two centuries, and a man, and a soldier—and if *neither* of them knew what they were doing, this was suddenly much more intimidating.

Cathal blinked at her, then laughed, shaking his head. "No' used to rain, lass," he said, his accent stronger now than it usually was. "No' with women, or at least not when it was a problem."

"Oh," she said. Another time, that would be a fascinating discussion: what the east was like, what the women were like, how damp clothing on a hot day might actually add to an embrace, all manner of interesting facets. That curiosity would have to wait, because Cathal had been undressing while he spoke, and when he stood naked before her, she actually lost the use of words.

He was magnificent, like a statue from the ancient
world, with broad shoulders and a narrow waist and the
lines of his muscles firm on his arms. His skin was winter
white. A thick mat of blond hair covered his chest and narrowed almost to nothingness on his flat stomach, before
widening again between his legs. His *membrum virile* rose
up out of it, swollen long and thick against his stomach.
Art didn't show that, and texts could only portray so much.
Sophia realized she was staring, and her blush felt like fire
in her skin, but she couldn't look away.

"Although…" Cathal said quietly, and Sophia snapped
her gaze back up to his face. He didn't reach for her again,
but sat down on the edge of the bed and motioned to the
space next to him. "I'm not used to virgins. Unless—"

She shook her head. When she sat down, the fabric of
the coverlet beneath her was rough against her skin, but
not in an unpleasant way. She shifted her weight, testing,
and tried to keep looking into Cathal's eyes. They were
beautiful eyes, but just then the urge to look…elsewhere…
was hard to resist. "I am."

"Ah. But you know how it is? Between men and women?"

At that, there was such hidden dread in his voice that
Sophia had to laugh. "Yes," she said, and giggled again at
the relief on his face. "I don't make offers in ignorance,"
she said and then leaned over, kissing him this time.

Cathal drew her close, warm against her now as they
both fell back onto the bed. His hands slid down Sophia's
sides, stroking her hips, her thighs, the sides of her breasts.
Every contact was a pulse of sensation that lingered,
spread, and joined the others, making a net of feelings and
urges that spread all across her skin.

"Didn't want to scare you," he said, half muttering the
words against the side of her neck.

She shivered at the movement of his lips, at the heat of his breath. He lay on his side above her, their bodies still barely touching save for his hands and lips on her. "I wasn't," Sophia said and reached up to trace along his chest. "I'm not." The hair beneath her fingers was crisp, curlier than that on his head, and his skin smooth around it, the muscles tense beneath. "Only I know what happens, but I don't *entirely* know what happens, to speak in, um, in terms of experience, which I suppose is obvious, and I've never seen…oh. *Oh*."

Bending his head, Cathal had taken one of her nipples into his mouth. All the sensation flooded over Sophia then, so strongly that she had to close her eyes. She knew that she was writhing on the bed and making noises in the back of her throat, but otherwise she wasn't entirely sure of anything other than *wanting*, the feel of Cathal's tongue flicking over her nipple and the moisture flooding her sex.

"Aye?" he asked huskily, hands warm on her thighs.

At first Sophia could only whimper at the loss of contact, but the sight of her hands on his shoulders reminded her of what she'd been saying. "I…mmm…" His lips were on the other breast now, and she struggled for thought. Her legs opened under his gentle pressure, hips thrusting upward in such a blatant invitation that she'd have been embarrassed if she'd been able to think. "Never seen a man like you. In your state. Both. I wanted…ahh…wanted. To touch you."

"Ah." It was half a word and half a groan, and he'd obviously worked out that she didn't just mean her hands on his chest, because his hands were still for a second and he shook his head against her breast. "Not now."

"No?" The organ in question pulsed against her leg, hot and hard. Sophia shifted her weight slightly and felt Cathal catch his breath.

"No," he said, and stopped any more argument by kissing her again. She might have been inclined to continue the argument, but one of his hands found its way between her legs, gentle and insistent at the same time, and Sophia could only moan into Cathal's mouth.

His fingers circled her sex, found the bit that had swelled and stiffened at their first kiss, and rubbed, while his other hand stroked her open. All the aching need in her body centered on his touch, then on the strange but very welcome presence of his fingers inside her, moving slowly in a rhythm that was just a bit shy of what she needed, though she didn't know how she knew that. He kept on that way, playing with her while she squirmed on the bed, tossing her head from side to side, unable to think or hold still or do anything except make desperate noises and seek more of his touch.

"Please," she said eventually, and hoped he wouldn't make her elaborate. "Oh, please…I need…"

"God knows I do," he muttered, low in his throat, and swung his body over hers. The tip of him pressed against her sex, just where she was wet and aching, and it felt right, so she opened her legs more and pushed, taking him into herself for the first time as he groaned and thrust forward.

To Sophia's dim surprise, there was no real pain. At first, she felt stretched in a way that wasn't precisely comfortable, but the sting she'd heard about never happened, nor the tearing that some of the less pleasant stories had featured. She was merely…full in a new way, and one that was feeling better and better.

Cathal, she realized, was holding very still and watching her with great concern—expecting tears, perhaps, or reluctance, or demands to stop. She smiled and wished he weren't quite so tall. Kissing him in this position would have been impossible. "I think," she said, "perhaps I'm too old to be a proper sort of maiden."

"Thank God," he said, breathing hard.

"What do I do now?"

He showed her, rocking his hips slowly back and forth until Sophia found her body meeting his of its own accord. This was the pace she'd wanted earlier, she realized; this, with his member filling her and his body rubbing against hers with every thrust, building desire in a steady rhythm that got faster and faster as she jerked her hips upward, clutching him to her with arms and legs and sex alike. The desperation she'd felt before came back doubly strong, and she gave herself to it, crying out into his shoulder as she sought more and more sensation, more urgency, and then reached a point where every particle of wanting joined and crested in one moment of unthinking delight.

Above her, Cathal groaned and cursed, the tone of his voice holding pleasure that made a sharp contrast to two languages of blasphemy. He arched his back, driving himself even further inside her, and his whole body went still for a moment; then, with a flood of warmth, he sank down on top of her.

Even then, he kept his full weight off her, and his size was actually rather comforting, an anchor in the midst of storms and after new experiences. Sophia traced her fingers upward along his spine, into the hair at the back of his head and back down, only to repeat the process again, idle and, she realized, content. For the first time in a long time, she felt perfectly happy to stay right where she was.

THIRTY-SIX

AFTERWARD, SATED AND STRETCHED OUT ON A MODEST inn bed that felt like the peak of luxury just then, Cathal fought off the urge to fall asleep. It wasn't easy. He'd rolled onto his back and pulled Sophia against him, and the steady rhythm of her breathing could easily have lulled him into slumber, had circumstances been different.

They weren't.

"What happened?" he asked.

"Oh." Her voice was as drowsy as his at first, but sharpened to awareness quickly. She opened her eyes and sat up slightly. "I have his name," Sophia said with a small smile: triumph, tempered by wariness. She wasn't overconfident, his lady; she knew to call no man lucky until he died, or however the Norsemen had it. "That's the sum of the work before his men began to suspect me, but that much made itself obvious, yes?"

"Slightly." Gently, and with no small amount of reluctance, Cathal left her embrace and stood up, then crossed the room to the nightstand with its basin of water and the cloths lying nearby. "What's the long version?"

She told him while they cleaned themselves, blushing when it came her turn but not looking away from him the entire time. When she reached her escape, she spread her hands. "...and so you found me, fortune being with us both."

"Just enough of it," Cathal said, and shook his head. He'd seen how close her pursuit had been, but had not known how narrow her original escape—nor how certain her doom would have been had he not overheard the soldiers and acted. In that moment, he wished he knew less—or less of war, less of Valerius himself.

Sophia shrugged, and the movement of her naked breasts was a small distraction from Cathal's more troubling thoughts. "Fortune's not in such great supply, you know. If we had just enough, it's more than most people ever get." She smiled and reached out, the tips of her fingers touching his cheek. "To have had the flight out here, and this night? I would change my luck for no one's."

Cathal caught her hand in his. "Marry me."

The words came without thought, and yet, once he said them, he felt he'd been considering them for days, even weeks—like the time in a battle when years of practice let the body know what was right before the mind could even frame the question.

The smile left Sophia's face, and she stared at him accusingly. "Don't. That's a cruel sort of jest, and you know I'd never demand—"

"No." His hand tightened around hers. "I speak in earnest."

"You can't possibly," she said, staring at him with even more surprise and much more doubt than she'd had when he'd stood before her naked and rampant. "It's…generous of you, truly, to offer, but you know you couldn't. You're… Well, for one thing, you're the son of a lord."

"Aye," Cathal said, seeing the swing and the means of blocking it. "The younger son, and the youngest of four children. Agnes wed to my father's advantage, and Douglas doubtless will. Moiread still might. It's been many lifetimes since any of them thought to direct my life in that manner. For all they knew, I could have brought home a Saracen bride when I came back."

Mentioning the Holy Land brought Sophia's next

objection to the fore. "We don't share a faith, nor a people, nor yet a homeland. And I would go home, if I succeed and survive. I..." She sighed. "Everyone's been most kind, truly, most welcoming, but I've no wish to stay here. It's not my home."

"No," he said, and forced himself to patience. If he spoke too quickly, let impulse dictate his words, Sophia would think him insincere or at least foolish. "But it's not truly mine either. I stayed away for longer than you've been alive, and I'd never meant to come back for good. If I miss the place after I leave this time, in faith, I travel with a great deal of ease." He smiled. "You could too, for that matter."

"True."

She sounded intrigued. She sounded uncertain. Her face was all thoughtfulness and grave concentration, and Cathal wasn't sure whether he was more tempted to disrupt her thoughts or to have her turn such attention on him. He held himself back to putting his arm around her shoulders.

"As for faith," he went on, and shrugged, "mayhap I should care, but I don't. More than half the Church holds me damned already, or would if it knew what I am. I'll not promise to convert—I'd rather not have the, ah, physical ceremony, for one—but I'd not ask it of you."

"Oh," said Sophia, her mouth round and her eyes wide. "I... Well..." She shook her head, not in denial but with an attempt to bring herself back into reason, and her hair rippled over Cathal's arm. "It *would* be a scandal, still... but then I was never entirely respectable, and my family might not mind very much, so long as any children...but then there wouldn't be children, would there?"

"It's harder with us," he said. "There's a rite to breed with humans, and a risk to the woman."

"So I heard. That was one of the factors in…" She gestured to the bed around them. "Not that my family would know that, of course, but I'm old for childbearing, so they might think it unlikely, and they too have other children to carry on the name. My mother, I think, would be only glad to see me return safely, and I don't believe my father would disown me, though I don't know that he would be very happy either."

He waited, knowing that she spoke only half to him. Patience was difficult, particularly with her skin warm and smooth beneath his hand and her full lips only a few inches away. Repletion was beginning to fade into renewed desire. Yet he kept himself still, giving her time.

"But you wouldn't age," she said, "or you'd age slowly. I wouldn't know how to explain that without giving your nature away, although I suppose I could claim it was an accident of alchemy."

"That could be. Or I could just be well preserved."

"*Very* well preserved, thirty years on. Although, after thirty years…" Sophia looked down at the bedclothes and sighed. "After thirty years, my parents will have gone to their reward, Rachel and my brothers will have their own concerns, and we could go elsewhere. At that…after thirty years, I'll be an old woman. You may wish to leave then and only let people believe you'd died."

"No," he said again, leaning forward and gripping her hand tighter. "For one…if you bear a child, you'll age more slowly, live longer."

That brought her head up again, and sent the now-familiar look of fascination into her eyes. "Truly? How? Why? How long?"

"There are theories," he said with a laugh, "but I confess I never had reason to study them until now. You'd not have the years we do, but as I've more than a century's head start on you, we'd likely see gray hairs together."

"Ohh," she said, drawing out the word, and smiled. "I'd have much more time for reading than I expected, then, even with motherhood. And...if I didn't have children, even with the rite?"

"Then I'd stay all the same." He'd not considered watching Sophia age and die, and the prospect dismayed him, but the idea of abandoning her was worse. Morals were only part of it. He found he loathed the idea of no longer having her in his life, whatever form she might inhabit. "I'll stay until you ask me to leave."

She stared at him, firelight in her eyes and shadows wavering across her naked body. "That," she said and smiled at him, so gently that the room felt colder, "is kind, but it may be in the end as much a burden as a gift. I'd not want you lingering out of obligation...and minds do change, whatever you think now."

"You could say *that* much of any man." Cathal pulled back. He couldn't quite bring himself to stop touching her, but he left his hand only on her near shoulder and studied her face. Had he ever learned much about judging human emotion, it might have served him well. "If what you mean to say is that you don't wish to marry me, you should say that. I'll not take it badly."

Had she taken more time to reply, had her eyes not suddenly lost their darkness and flashed boldly at him, Cathal might still have doubted her answer. They were alone, he was a large man even in human form, and men had spoken falsely for passion before. To his great relief, though, there was nothing in her face or in her sudden motion toward him that seemed the least bit false. "No! Or, yes. I do...and so I *have* to object, to think of all the obstacles that I can." She smiled again, wryly, and ran her fingertips up his arm, over his shoulder, and down toward his chest. "If the wish of my heart is so great, then it almost has to blind me, doesn't it? Unless I'm careful, I'll miss a vital detail somewhere."

"I can't think how to argue with that," he said. Another time, he might have, a time when her small calloused fingers weren't sliding through the hair of his chest, their touch changing the direction of his thoughts as though it were the final ingredient in one of her potions. Cathal felt his cock stirring, thickening, and considered how little effort it would take to lean forward and bear Sophia back onto the bed.

He held still. She'd wanted to touch him; this time, he might have enough control to let her. He thought too that he should find words to answer her, even if he could think of no counter to her final argument. "You have time. You don't have to answer tomorrow. But"—he slid his fingers down her spine, then back up, tracing around the edge of her ear and down the delicate line of her jaw—"when you think of a new problem, bring it to me, aye? Give me a chance to argue my case."

"That seems only—" She caught her breath as Cathal leaned forward, kissing the base of her neck. His free hand conveniently settled on her thigh, soft and sleek and tense with desire. "—just."

"Good," said Cathal. He meant the conclusion. He also meant the taste of her sweat on his lips, the ragged sound of her breathing, the flick of her fingers over one of his nipples. "Good. Yes."

And then she shifted, turned toward him a little more, and curved her fingers around his cock. Everything in the room blurred around the edges then, and he thought he invoked God in either Latin or Arabic, but he didn't quite remember which. The ultimate destination of her curiosity hadn't been a surprise, and the caress was certainly nothing he hadn't felt before, but just then, from Sophia, the touch was a revelation.

However stunned he might have looked, he seemed to communicate *good* well enough, for she didn't pull back or ask if she should stop. Instead, as Cathal should have guessed, she experimented: pressure and angle, location and speed, always careful, always intrigued. *More* than intrigued, he realized gradually, for her nipples were hard again, and her face was flushed, and she smelled of arousal. She was enjoying this, and the knowledge made him moan and thrust into her hand.

When she released him, just for a moment, and touched the moist tip of one finger to her mouth, he swore again.

Sophia spoke then, and her voice was throaty. It was a good thing she *wasn't* touching him, or he would probably have been unable to hold himself back. "Can you…can we, er, couple again tonight? If it wouldn't be… I don't want to damage you, and I've read philosophers who say that men—"

"Not me," said Cathal. He doubted the theory in general, but didn't truly care, particularly not then. He thought of lewd stories about virgins, of songs and the occasional joke, and of the need hot and urgent between his legs. Reaching out, he pulled Sophia against him and rolled onto his back, kissing her until she was squirming against him and making little noises in her throat. Her breasts were hard to reach from this angle, he discovered, but fondling her lush backside, or slipping his hand down and cupping her sex, were more than compensatory joys.

In time, she sat up and back, giving Cathal a wonderful view, and, catching her breath, considered the situation.

Short as she was, kissing her left only her thighs to rub against his member, and now it stood hard and flushed, thrusting blindly into the air. Sophia gave it a long look, then turned her gaze down the length of her body to her sex, and finally nodded, "I think…like this?" she asked, making the necessary adjustments in position.

"Aye," he said, barely able to get the words out, fists clenched in the covers. "Slow as you like."

It was slow at first—agonizingly, amazingly, wonderfully slow—and Cathal thought he stopped breathing at several points. She was very wet—confirming what he'd thought when she was touching him, and that realization nearly drove him to the breaking point—but tight, and there was a moment when she winced, and then another when he was fully inside her and she began to move.

"Wait," he said and managed to sit up a little, enough that he could urge her forward and take one of her nipples in his mouth. With one hand, he found the spot just above their joining, as hard beneath his fingertips as he was inside her, and felt her internal shudder when he began to caress her there.

This time he couldn't wait and tease her; this time he found her pace quickly, reading her moans and the motion of her hips, the way her sex relaxed around him even as her fingers tightened on his shoulders. When he brought her over the edge, she was crying out his name, with no attempt to bury her mouth in his shoulder. Her body arched like a bow, like the figurehead of a ship, breasts jutting forward and head back, her hair falling over them like a curtain.

The image branded itself on Cathal's mind just before his eyes closed with his own climax, the sight and feel of Sophia's too much for him to stand for even a few more breaths.

He thought, at the very end, that she said a word or two

after his name. He even thought he knew what they were, but not certain, he kept, if not silence, at least incoherence. Best not to rely on anything said in passion, particularly when the passion was new, nor to trust his own hearing at such a moment.

He'd give her time. He wouldn't press the issue.

THIRTY-SEVEN

THE FIRE WAS DOWN TO GLOWING EMBERS. THAT WAS all right because the blankets were thick and Cathal was warm and solid against her. Sophia allowed herself a few moments to lie there, contented, and feel her body begin to fall away into sleep. Even knowing what came next, she didn't have the energy to stay alert for very long.

With a sigh, she lifted her head from Cathal's chest and said what she'd known was coming, what had in part driven her to proposition him, though she'd not been completely aware of it then. "I'm going to try to use the name now. I'm afraid you may need to keep watch."

One of his arms was circling her waist. Sophia felt it go rigid, and the steady breathing beneath her hand stilled briefly. But Cathal was ancient and experienced in war as well as love. All he asked was "How?"

"He's pulled me between worlds before. I think I can find the path on my own this time. And I think I'd best do it before he has a chance to put up very many defenses. Truly, I should have gone earlier, but I doubt I would've been able to sleep."

Time passed in popping hisses from the fire and gusts of wind from outside the window, in her breaths and Cathal's. Then he nodded, squeezed her briefly with one arm, and slid out of bed, only to return before she could do more than squeak in protest at the draft. He brought his sword with him, unsheathed, and laid it on his other side.

"A little misplaced for the tales," she said, smiling and

watching, setting as much of him as she could into her memory, "and a little late too."

Cathal laughed. "I'd thought it, before you offered," he said, gathering her against his body again and then sobering. "But I'll want it now. Demons."

"Oh. Yes." The thought made her shiver, but it was too late. Drained by cold and fright, exertion and unfamiliar pleasure, she was sliding rapidly down into sleep. "Good thought."

"I hope I'm wrong."

"Me too," she said, slurring her words. "You shouldn't fight demons naked."

She felt him laugh again. "Aye, true." He turned toward her, and his lips brushed across her forehead. "One day I'll not have to send you into danger, I swear it. I'll not ask you not to take chances, but…remember I'm waiting. Come back to me."

"I will."

Getting to Valerius's world, or the place between them, was bound to take concentration. Sophia held the images in her mind as best she could as she drifted off: falling in blackness, the shapes she couldn't look directly at, and the dark castle. Even so, the last things she remembered of the waking world were the strength of Cathal's arm around her shoulders and the sound of his heartbeat beneath her ear.

This time, Sophia landed in the tree. It wasn't a pleasant landing—she rather thought she'd grabbed for the branch as she'd entered the world, only half able to control her destination even after so much time, and the bark dug up under her fingernails—but no, she didn't have to bother with running and climbing and shadow creatures that wanted her dead. That was cause enough for gratitude, and she didn't have time for complaints.

Next came the bridge, building itself under her sight and the pressure of her will. This one was more unified, with only occasional patches of wood or empty space interrupting the solid chunks of masonry. She jumped no more gracefully than before, and the landing hurt no less, but that was all right: the oozing, stinging patches on her knees and under the ripped elbows of her dress served as proof that the stone was there and solid. *I've found the purpose of pain*, she thought as she walked, half drunk with fear and the use of power. *How delighted all the scholars will be.*

Still the edges didn't line up entirely, still there were sections where she had to hold her breath and grit her teeth in order to walk over nothingness, but the passage across the bridge was a thing done, and therefore possible, and so she reached the other side with almost steady hands and less urge to be sick.

The castle was different too.

It was still huge and dark, and the doors were still closed. When Sophia looked at the walls, though, there were spaces that blurred and warped, particularly places she'd seen in the castle in her waking world, and she knew that it wasn't entirely the same as the one Valerius had crafted in this aethereal realm. The great doors, for instance, were quite forbidding, but their wood in reality was splintering and warping, and the guards had stood in front of them singing drunken songs. They'd been open most of the time, at that. They'd had to be, as the doors of any real castle did when it wasn't under siege. So, at the seam where these doors met, space buckled like a badly sewn patch.

Sophia reached out gingerly. Her fingers went into the non-space, and she felt nothing. She pushed, lightly at first and then put her back behind it, and a resistance like a strong wind gave way. The doors swung open.

That was where the aether-castle gave up pretending to be much like the real thing. Beyond the doors there was no courtyard, no great hall full of surly men and tired women, no smell of cow dung or sound of restless horses. Beyond the doors was only a dark, silent staircase that led up and onward.

"I am," Sophia said to the force that pretended to be air, "getting rather tired of always *climbing* things."

Nothing responded, of course, and the staircase was still in front of her—but the complaint made it easier to start the journey upward.

At first, the staircase was pitch-black around her, only the steps beneath her feet telling Sophia that she wasn't lost in the between-worlds place again. As she ascended, she started to see flashes of light: not the unviewable, unthinkable *things* from the journey between worlds, but rather flickers and lines that she eventually realized came from under doors. The staircase wasn't all there was. Landings led off, and there were doors on those landings that could lead to rooms or entirely separate halls.

Sophia thought she could have opened those doors. She was fairly sure she didn't want to. What she sought wasn't there. Behind each door was a distraction at best, and a trap at worst. She kept climbing, one hand out in front of her for protection.

When she did reach the top, she didn't need that precaution. The light from under the final door was a sickly grayish-pink that reminded her of rotting entrails, but it was bright enough. She saw the thick wood of the door clearly, the steel of the bolts keeping it shut, and she didn't believe that it would fall to her as easily as the doors of the castle had. Discrepancy between real and aether wasn't the key here. This place had no mirror in the waking world.

The formula here was different.

Little as she wanted to approach the decaying light, Sophia walked up to the door and put her hand on the latch. "Albert de Percy," she said. It came out calm and conversational, the tone she might use to introduce one acquaintance to another.

The door didn't open this time; it crumbled suddenly and completely, revealing a tiny five-sided room lined with small chests. Each was dull gray, none was locked, and none was any longer than her hand. Albert—she would *not* think of him as Valerius here—might have been able to distinguish between them. To Sophia's eyes, they were all alike, and her intuition gave her no guidance.

It did tell her that she had little time. The hairs on the back of her neck were standing up, whether they existed or not, and the mouth she might or might not have was dry. Before long, she wouldn't be alone.

Sophia knelt and started flipping up lids.

Inside the first chest was a miniature lake, frozen to glassy green stillness—not what she sought, though it pained her to leave it without further investigation. When she opened the second, a gust of blue and silver feathers flew up into her face, scratching it with their surprisingly sharp edges. Sophia put up her hands to guard herself and by instinct grabbed onto one of the feathers as the rest dispersed, blown hither and yon on nonexistent wind. She slid the feather into her belt; when she got out, it might be useful or simply interesting.

Third came a single ember, sitting at the bottom of its

chest with no fuel and glowing steadily red regardless. As
the chest lid opened, the ember flared, and sparks flew out
to land and fizzle against whatever metal the boxes were
made of. Sophia almost felt sorry for it.

She moved onward to a single white rose that looked as
if it grew out of the chest bottom, with no bush or bramble
in sight: pretty, but nearly sad in the same way that the
ember had been, and she could spare no time for pity or
curiosity. The feeling of awful anticipation was getting
stronger. Had she been in the waking world, she might
have heard footsteps approaching.

Before she could raise the lid of the next chest more
than a hand's width, the thing inside sprang at her, snarling: a twisted ape face with the slit pupils of a goat and
razor teeth, and the impression of a body at once powerful
and sinuous, all of it far too large for the chest. Sophia
screamed and slammed the lid back down with both hands.
The jolt as the thing hit the lid would haunt her, she knew,
but not nearly as badly as the glimpse of that face—and the
malign intelligence she'd seen there.

Another element of the stories verified. Wonderful.

After that, she approached the sixth chest with even
more fear. Her hand trembled as she touched the lid, and
she opened it only a bit at a time, ready to shove it back
down in an instant—but nothing jumped out at her. The
chest opened quietly, and inside was a rust-colored object
about the size of her fist, not quite spherical but in its shape
suggestive of both an apple and a heart.

This, she thought, and it wasn't entirely her mind, nor
true thought at all. Not entirely willing to trust such instinct,
Sophia reached in and touched the sphere.

When her fingertips met its surface, Fergus's face rose
up before her eyes. She knew him in an instant, better

than his own mother could have—and only avoided more because she cringed back from the contact, wanting none of such forced intimacy with another mind. She knew too that his strength was fading; even the potions couldn't keep his body going forever.

"Cling just a little while longer, hmm?" she told him, slipping the soul-sphere into the bodice of her gown. The proximity was embarrassing, but the location more secure than anything else she could manage.

She turned, and the space in front of her parted with a shriek: not the sound of the passage, but of what charged through it.

The figure was a man—more or less. In the world of flesh and bone, he might have looked entirely like one, but this world didn't only reflect the physical. Like Cathal and his family, Albert de Percy hadn't been entirely human for longer than Sophia had been alive. Unlike them, he'd made the changes himself, not seamlessly, and now, whether because of the place where they stood or because of Sophia's intrusions, he was falling apart.

One arm was too long, started too low, and ended in a withered hand whose yellow fingernails were claws. His body was otherwise that of a man in his prime, but his face was ancient, with skin like parchment and sunken cheeks. One eye was clouded and blue, the other huge and red, with the goat pupil of the thing in the box.

He came through screaming—no words, only shocked anger. Sophia might have sympathized—this place was the core of his power, her presence an outrage—had he been less vile, and if she'd had time. But he was grabbing for her at once. His normal hand fell far short of her, but the claw swiped through the air only a hairbreadth from her shoulder.

Sophia hurled the feather at him.

She'd had no thought save that there was little within her reach except that and the heart. If she'd hoped for anything, it was that the feather would cut his face as it had scratched hers. She certainly hadn't expected it to blast them both away from it, but it did, the wind stronger than those that had pulled at her when she'd ridden Cathal through the storm. It flung her backward, onto the floor. The stone still hurt to land on, but as she scrambled to her feet, she saw that Albert was lying against the far wall.

Her path to the stairs was clear.

She ran, holding her skirts in both hands, heeding the stairs only that she might not trip. However Albert's strength might be failing him, however breaching his defenses and freeing the elements might have hurt him, she feared to fight him at the center of his power.

In truth, she feared to fight him regardless, but she was no longer certain she'd be able to escape that.

On the first landing, hearing the footsteps running after her, she nonetheless took Fergus's soul into one hand and tried to wake herself up as she'd done before.

The world wavered around her, shimmered—but stayed.

Sophia wished she could even feel surprised.

THIRTY-EIGHT

WAITING WAS FAR FROM NEW FOR CATHAL, YET SO MUCH of it in quick succession scraped at even his patience.

As Sophia fell asleep, he switched to the vision of the otherworld. The room looked much the same as it had before, but the woman at his side lay in a nimbus of sunset pink, with shades of gold closer to her face. Unlike the time in Fergus's room, a small ribbon of silver wound its way out of the space just above her head, only to vanish—not broken, he didn't think, but stretching off beyond his sight.

Did that mean she'd reached her destination? Cathal wished his vision extended that far, or that he'd taken more of an interest in magic. Nothing to do about it now, though, but watch where he could and thank God no demons were coming out of the walls yet.

He wasn't sure how much time passed. The wind and rain outside gradually quieted. He heard an owl once after that. Those were the only things that changed for what felt like hours. Cathal stood on occasion, paced the room to keep himself awake, then sat back down and watched Sophia.

The fourth time he did so, the aura around her looked different: not dramatically, but the furthest end he could see of the silver ribbon looked darker than the rest, more like lead. Unless he imagined it, the room was colder too.

Yet he hesitated. The fire had died down—he knew not what the change in shade meant—and Sophia might not have another such opportunity. She'd not thank him for pulling her away before she had a chance to accomplish her task. Cathal's hand tightened around the hilt of his sword, but he waited and watched.

Darkness and dullness advanced. Sophia's chest rose and fell as calmly as ever, and she showed no signs of distress. Even when shallow cuts drew themselves across her face and hands, she made no sound, moved not at all.

Cathal, on the other hand, swore in three languages and stopped himself at the last instant, his outstretched hand above her face, poised in a long moment of indecision.

A wind from nowhere blew through the room, and the smell of open graves filled his nose. He snarled.

Enough.

"Enough," he said aloud, more gently but clearly. He knelt by Sophia's side and spoke into her ear. "Wake up, lass."

She didn't respond. Blood oozed from the scratches on her face, that and the motion of her breasts the only signs that she still lived.

Right: sounds might not reach her. He should have expected that. It was no reason to be alarmed. Cathal told himself that as firmly as he'd ever calmed a nervous beast or a new squire. He felt not much more in control than one, nor of much more use.

When a gentle shaking of her shoulders, then a harder one, got no result, alarm looked more justified. When bathing her face in cold water brought no result, Cathal knew he was right to fear.

At the final extremity, holding back as much of his strength as he could and hating himself nonetheless, he slapped the side of her face once, briskly. The mark of his hand turned red, but that silent reproach was the only change. She didn't even wince in her sleep.

Her aura itself was darker now, and the silver ribbon

had gone completely dull. Where it reached Sophia's face, bands of gray were beginning to ripple out of it.

Cathal swore again, regularly and viciously under his breath in every language he knew. To the tune of the profanity, he picked Sophia's damp kirtle off its drying place by the fire and wrestled her limp body into it. He thought he managed not to hurt her, though he heard the cloth rip twice; the cloak was easier, yet still a clumsy job. It didn't matter. They would be enough decency—and enough protection—for the journey ahead, and anything else be damned.

Downstairs, the inn was dark. A few men in the common room snored regularly, but none seemed to wake as Cathal carried Sophia to the door.

Outside, it had stopped raining. That would make his task a shade easier. He hurried away from the building, toward the nearest open space, and only noticed the boy when he spoke.

"What are you *doing*?"

The lad was fourteen or fifteen, his eyes huge. A village boy, Cathal thought, probably come to earn a few coins caring for horses, maybe to hear a few stories. He'd have one after this.

Cathal didn't care. "Enough, please God," he said, not breaking his stride. In his arms, Sophia weighed nothing at all; a few yards more and he'd be in the trees, and the clearing wasn't far from that. "Don't get in my way."

Of course the boy tried to tackle him. Cathal would have, in his place. It was a valiant effort, and when Cathal flung him off, he hoped the lad didn't break anything.

He yelled too loudly to be badly hurt, at any rate.

That did it. Everyone in the damned village would be out shortly. There was no time. Cathal set Sophia on the ground in front of him, braced himself, and transformed.

The boy stopped yelling and started screaming.

Dragon form didn't swear well. The mouth wasn't shaped for human speech, and the words slipped away from the mind itself. The best Cathal could do, as he carefully picked up Sophia in one claw, was an ongoing hiss. Steam curled from between his teeth and into the night air, and the man who'd come to the door with a lantern almost dropped it.

Cathal leapt into the sky and away, hearing the panic spreading in his wake. It was nothing, he was certain, to his own fear. He knew what he faced, and what he could lose.

When Cathal landed at Loch Arach, the sky was beginning to lighten in the east, the wind was warm, and he was weary through every scale on his body. The flight had been more peaceful than fleeing through the storm and shorter than he'd feared, and yet it had been too long, as he strained every other muscle to go faster while keeping his forelegs relaxed and his talons away from Sophia's body. He'd watched her aura keep darkening and her breathing continue, steady and slow, just as Fergus's had done.

No distance would have been short enough to suit him.

He didn't bother to hide his return. Douglas was waiting in the clearing and took Sophia into his arms with a startled look but no hesitation. Practically, it was a relief to let her go. Douglas had far more strength just then and was far less likely to hurt her by accident. Cathal squelched any urge to cling.

They headed to the tower as soon as he'd transformed. Cathal gave his brother the story in short sentences, paring it down to the most important parts. He hoped he'd not left anything out; he didn't entirely trust his mind.

"What can we do?" he asked finally.

"I don't know." Douglas entered the tower room, passing Cathal as the younger man held the door, but not looking into his face. "If she was going to the aether on her own, I would say she found trouble there."

"And?"

Carefully, they placed Sophia down on the table. Douglas took off his cloak and folded it, then slid it under her head. "The cord is still attached to her. If I'm right, that means her soul is yet her own."

Cathal nodded. He'd seen no silver ribbon coming from Fergus's head, not even in the few moments when he'd come back to himself. "Can I go there with her?"

"Not you," Douglas said too slowly and after too long a pause. "Not yourself. It *may* be, here, that we can send her your strength, but—"

"Do it."

Their eyes met over Sophia's face. Cathal read caution in Douglas's, all of the warnings and objections that his brother wanted to state, but none of them passed his lips, and in time he dropped his gaze and shook his head. "Aye. Go find a page. Send for dry clothes for the both of you, and food. It'll take me time to prepare. And send for Madoc."

Cathal paused on his way to the door. "The Welsh boy? Why?"

"He's half decent with magic. We'll need two, and you'll be in no condition to assist."

Had Cathal had the energy to take that as a slight, he would have soon found himself proved wrong. Before the spell began, Douglas and Madoc propped Sophia upright and bade Cathal sit before her, then bound each of his hands to hers, winding the ropes from fingertips to elbows and back again. He knelt with his legs beneath him and struggled to keep his balance, in no condition for the pacing they did as they chanted, nor for bending and drawing shapes on the floor in chalk.

He might have spoken or joined the chanting, but the incense was strong and touched with poppies. Cathal wavered, balanced, breathed deeply, and tried to fall into the rhythm of the chanting. He felt her heartbeat through their joined wrists, steady but quick.

Then the force of the spell tipped over and the effect began. Cathal felt energy draining away from him, slowly at first, seeping from his palms into Sophia's. At the same time, her aura brightened. He could see no other difference, nor feel any in her body, but he began to hope.

He kept hoping still as the chanting continued and the flow of energy quickened. Now it was like water running downhill, like snow melt in the spring, and his legs wavered beneath him. The room grew blurry.

The chanting slowed and stopped. Cathal heard footsteps, then Douglas. "Shall we unbind you? It won't stop otherwise."

"No," he managed, though his voice was hazy. "No." He repeated it stronger, with a glare, though he didn't take his eyes from Sophia.

Until she freed herself and woke, he would be with her, the cost be damned.

THIRTY-NINE

SOPHIA RAN.

She raced downstairs in the darkness, and this time she didn't bother to look at the doors or the light that came from beneath them. She cared only that she kept her footing and that she outran the shape that ran behind her, his feet heavy and his breathing as twisted as the rest of him. Betimes he stopped to scream threats at her. They were ugly things, but she let them pass over her mind.

The more breath he used to shout, the less he'd have to run. Sophia wasn't sure if that was entirely true in this world, but she let it comfort her.

She flung herself out the castle doors just out of Albert's reach. The courtyard felt larger than it had before—mayhap it was, the way things were in the aether—but she ran across that too, ignoring the pain in her side and the burning in her lungs, and then stopped short.

The bridge had vanished.

She had no time for surprise, despair, or even thought. Bending down, she wrenched off one of her shoes and tossed it across the gap. Sophia sent her will along with it, and so she wasn't wholly startled when the shoe landed upside down and grew in a flash, such that the sole stretched from the edge of the forest and upward into a tree. She was profoundly grateful, or as grateful as she could manage the attention to be. As soon as the bridge looked stable, she was lunging at the edge.

At that, she was just in time. The claws of Albert's long

arm scraped down her back, tearing her gown open in four wide strips and scratching the skin beneath. Sophia yelped, more in fright than pain, and jerked away onto the bridge.

There was no railing this time, nor even ropes. For all that, she couldn't afford caution. She kept to the middle, fixed her eyes on the tree ahead, and went as fast as she could drive her body. The chill of her exposed back—real air or not, it was cold enough—and the stinging pain were spurs. When she wanted to hold back out of fright, she told herself that a fall from the bridge was probably better than what the monster behind her would do if he caught her.

Even so, when she reached the tree and pulled herself onto the branch, it was with the last of her strength. Sophia's legs and arms were shaking and boneless. Every breath was an ordeal, and the view before her eyes was misty. She could see Albert clearly enough, climbing across the bridge toward her with dreadful persistence. The effort, or the screaming, had taken its toll on him. The skin on his face had cracked, and a ghastly red line ripped its way from the bottom of his chin to just beneath his left eye.

She shuddered, swayed, and clung to the tree for support.

Damaged he might be, but he was still master of this place, and she doubted that she could sway it very much against his will. The shoe had most likely worked because it had mirrored a real object and its use in the context was plain, but she had few of those left, and she could think of few ways to turn them against Albert.

Calcination. Dissolution. Go back to the source.

Sophia looked upward. The tree kept going, and at the very top, tiny in the red-gray sky, she saw a shifting spot of pure black.

That was where she needed to go, if for no other reason than that it was the only place open to her. She doubted

she'd find a pleasant reception on the ground. Sophia gritted her teeth, grabbed a branch, and pulled.

Her body barely moved. She tried again, and felt tears
start running down her face with the effort—exhaustion,
frustration, fear, or the shrieking pain of her muscles—but
nothing happened, and Albert was almost to the tree. His lips
drew back from his teeth, the smile splitting his skin further,
and Sophia screamed with all the breath she had left.

Out of nowhere, fresh energy poured into her body.
It started at her palms and spread down, burning along
her arms but in a pleasant fashion, or at least a useful
one. Sophia thought of Cathal's kisses, of the way he'd
touched her and of feeling him deep inside her when she
climaxed. The power she felt now wasn't quite the same,
but it was close.

She pulled herself upward a third time, and this time
hauled herself onto the next branch. Albert turned his face
up to her and hissed. "Bitch," he said, "you'll know your
place before I finish with you."

Sophia didn't respond. Talking was a waste of climbing
time and of energy, even though she was feeling stronger
with every moment. She hugged the tree trunk now and
pulled herself upward, a feat she could never have accomplished in the real world. She was making changes again,
even if they were small ones. If Albert realized that, or if
he didn't have to make his own changes to follow her…

Don't think of if. *Go.*

The voice in her head was her own, but the words might
have been Cathal's. As she took in more and more energy,
she kept thinking of him, and no longer just in terms of their
physical coupling. The force giving her strength had in it
the peace and warmth of falling asleep in his embrace, the
triumph of that moment when the first potion had seemed as

if it would work, and the freedom of flying through the night with him, with all the stars above her and the wind in her hair.

He was with her. She couldn't have explained how, but a part of him had reached her even across the way between worlds, and that aspect was giving her the means to go onward.

Beneath her, the tree fell away. She could see Albert climbing after her, but not much below. The view didn't diminish as it would have in the waking world, or as it had before, but dissolved into red-gray. Was the world itself disintegrating around them?

All the more reason to climb fast.

Albert had stopped screaming. Sophia could hear him scrabbling up the tree behind her, and his labored breaths echoed in the silence just as hers did, but otherwise he made no sound. She would have felt encouraged, but she knew she wouldn't have had the breath to scream either, nor yet to speak, even with Cathal giving her strength.

Up and up they went. The tree started to thin. The branches were no longer thick enough for Sophia to even try reaching them. Before very long, the trunk might not support her weight either. Albert would break it before she did, most likely, but that would be small comfort as she fell.

She could do nothing about that, save think *hold together* at the tree as firmly as she could manage. Either it worked, or it didn't need to work, or Albert was doing his own reinforcements—he might not be wild about the idea of falling to earth either—for the trunk swayed as she climbed but didn't break.

The entrance to the world-between came closer. It wasn't properly a hole in the sky that Sophia could see, or a passage like a doorway. The treetops and the sky drained away into it, if things could drain upward. They blurred and distorted as they went. High in the tree, Sophia saw the stretching and stopped. She knew that the world-between was her best hope. Her body knew that this was *not* the way the world was supposed to work, that even looking at the passage too long made her eyes hurt, and she froze in atavistic terror, far worse than the first sight of Cathal's dragon form had provoked.

Albert had more knowledge of other worlds. He'd long ago decided that the rules of this one, moral and even elemental, didn't govern him. He hesitated not a moment, but found from some hellish corner of his soul an extra burst of strength.

His clawed hand sank deep into the flesh of Sophia's waist, yanking her away from the tree trunk.

Naturally she screamed. Even without the claws, his touch was vile. Through her gown, she felt his arm almost *squirming*, as if it were many small insects and not part of one singular body. He smelled like the demon that had attacked her in her laboratory, and his laugh of triumph was high and bubbling.

Her first impulse was to pull away. Albert would be expecting that, and so Sophia bridled that reaction, forced her body to stillness, and made herself look beyond her disgust. She saw that the world-between was very close, not even really *up* as much as *around*, and that the branches were reaching toward it. She saw that Albert was holding on to the tree with his human arm. His knuckles were white.

Sophia let herself go limp—the other reaction Albert would have expected from a lady. Then she turned toward him. With all her strength and Cathal's combined, she flung both arms around the monstrosity, pushing off the branch with both feet at the same time. As she'd intended, one of her arms hit the one Albert was using to hold the branch, and she put her weight as much behind that arm as she could.

As they toppled, Albert grabbed for the branches again.

Sophia had hit him with too much force, though. His claws scored three lines in one branch, but skidded off without a firm hold.

Together they hung for a moment, weightless; then together plummeted toward the void.

She began to pray.

Then claws clasped her shoulders, larger and yet far gentler than Albert's were, and she heard the beat of great wings above her. Sophia looked up, hope suspended and aching in her chest.

Cathal, shimmering and faint but present, bent his scaled neck around so that his eyes could meet hers. He still couldn't talk in dragon form, but Sophia understood all he would have said: that he didn't have the power to fight Albert directly in this world, but that he would hold her up while she did what she could.

He was *there*. He wouldn't let her fall.

The three of them flew suspended through the place between. The red-gray world was nearly gone, swallowed in black and unseeable shapes of light. It was very small, and she doubted that it answered as much to Albert's will now that he was out in the blackness.

He still clung to her, and she to him. Sophia didn't want to turn him loose into the void, there to perhaps find heaven knew what resources. If she'd had a weapon—

She thought of the boxes, and how they trapped powerful souls within their enchanted walls. She'd touched them; she knew them; in theory, she could command them. Sophia closed her eyes, let go of Albert with one hand—he showed no inclination to try to escape, with the void all around them—and *willed*.

The box in her hand was heavy and cold. She hoped she had the right one: she dared not open it to make sure.

"Albert de Percy," she said, and he snapped his head up to glare at her. Sophia stared back at him, right into the eye with the goat's pupil.

"Like calls to like," she said in Greek. "Be one with your master, and one with his bonds."

Before he could look away, she faced the box toward him and opened the lid.

The ape-thing lunged forward, shrieking. Albert had no time to get away—and indeed, Sophia didn't think he could have. In a whirlwind moment, she saw him pulled toward the box, eye first, such that his whole body distorted and melted. For the moment, either the spell held both demon and magician, or the creature was too distracted by its prey to think of escape.

That wouldn't last long.

Holding her breath, Sophia waited until the last of Albert's trailing robes had come within the box's rim, then slammed the lid—none too soon. A crashing blow made the box shudder against her hand, far too forcefully for an object of its size.

"Be gone," she said, and flung it as far as she could into the blackness.

She and Cathal both watched it go, and both let out their breath at almost the same time. Sophia giggled, a touch hysterically.

"We should go too," she said, "though with luck not to the same place he did." Quickly, she reached into her bodice and drew out the rust-colored sphere she'd taken from the chest, holding it tight in both hands.

Now. Wake up.

FORTY

Silence reigned in the tower room. Douglas and Madoc had finished their chanting, Cathal feared to disrupt the spell, and Sophia neither spoke nor moved except to breathe. The time might have weighed more lightly on Cathal if she had. Little as he liked the thought of her in distress, it was even more unsettling to see scratches appear on her arms while she sat as placidly as a nun at prayers.

It was fortunate that Cathal's energy was draining away, fortunate too that the process clouded his mind. He was a patient man, but he knew not how he might have acted, waiting at such a time in the fullness of his strength. Even his willpower wasn't infinite. Weakness made the minutes easier to endure.

The floor swayed beneath him, but he stayed sitting upright. His feet went numb, and then his hands, but he didn't move. Dimly he knew that his mouth was dry and that his body ached in muscle and bone, as well as on a deeper level that he couldn't have named. Cathal let all such knowledge enter his mind and then depart. None of it could make any difference.

Lost in hazy vision and the struggle to hold on, he wasn't the one who noticed the change. Madoc's quick inhalation and Douglas's low curse alerted him. He blinked, forcing his eyes to clear briefly, and then saw a dark red-brown glow, the color of rust or autumn leaves, surrounded Sophia's hands down to her elbows.

Fergus, he thought. *Then…?*

He couldn't begin to guess. Neither profanity nor prayer came to his mind. He couldn't think of a word that would have sufficed for that interlude, when he saw the change and knew not what it meant nor what came after. Hope would have tempted fate.

All at once the silver ribbon coming from Sophia's head blazed, sunlight bright. Cathal's eyes closed instantly, the body's mindless protection coming to the fore. When he opened them again, her hands looked the same, but the cord was gone.

He no longer felt the outflow of strength. What little reserves he had were his; the connection between them had no pull any longer.

Balanced between fear and hope, with no idea which way to turn, he seized Sophia's hands in his. The russet glow surrounded Cathal's fingers as he interlaced them with hers, and briefly he felt Fergus's presence as well, as it had been during a hundred nights sitting by campfires.

Good man.

"Oh."

By himself, Cathal would have thought he'd imagined her voice. It was faint, no more than a whisper, but Madoc met his eyes and nodded, and Douglas, off to the side and dispassionate, was the one who managed to reply.

"Madam, we welcome you back. We'll have you free shortly, and your wounds tended."

"Am I back?" She blinked. Her eyes, staring up into Cathal's, were dark and liquid and lovely, the awareness in them perhaps the most beautiful thing he'd seen in more than a century of life. "I—"

Embracing her was not possible in their position. Cathal settled for squeezing her hands. "You're here. You're with us." He remembered then that she hadn't been conscious for any of their journey and added, "At Loch Arach."

She smiled. "You were with me," she said. "I saw you."

"I'd never have it otherwise," said Cathal.

Douglas cleared his throat. "Perhaps we might stop the bleeding before we converse more?"

"Ah!" Sophia said, and looked down at her hands. "My wounds are not the important matter here, though of course I thank you for your kindness. I'll need to get to my laboratory quickly." As Madoc and Douglas untied her bonds, Sophia was already trying to get to her feet, stumbling upward while she held her hands in front of her.

"Then I would carry you there, lady, if I may," said Madoc, bowing quickly. "For our host—who would much prefer the honors—will need assistance himself, and I'll not manage him as well as his brother might."

"Yes, of course," Sophia said abstractly. Even as Madoc picked her up, she was staring at Cathal. "But...are you well? What happened?"

"We'd ask you much the same question." Douglas, much less courtly, draped one of Cathal's arms over his shoulders and hauled him to his feet. "He'll live, and probably live well, once he's had a few weeks' sleep and about ten dinners."

"Thank you kindly," Cathal said, and smiled at Sophia. "But he's right in the essentials. I didn't want to leave you without reinforcements, aye?"

"You were just in time... I don't know how much you saw or felt, but..." She could not have been a comfortable armful, for she was sitting upright to talk and keeping her glowing hands well away from Madoc. Nonetheless, Cathal envied the Welshman and cursed his own weakened state. "And Albert is dead. Valerius, that is, and I'm not entirely certain that *dead* is a sufficient word for his state, but I know none better."

"Then you've done great work already," said Douglas.

"Not enough of it, my lord. Not yet."

Douglas's shoulder bruised Cathal's sternum, and the uneven way of climbing stairs was far too slow for his liking, but he didn't try to walk on his own. His legs still felt unsteady, and the walls had a tendency to swim. Besides, the tower room wasn't very far from Sophia's laboratory. Cathal wanted to take credit for wisdom in that regard, but knew it was only good fortune.

A comical bit of rearrangement happened at the door. Douglas left Cathal leaning against a wall while he ducked in front of Madoc and Sophia, opened the latch for them, and then came back to retrieve his brother. "I feel like a side of venison," Cathal said.

Douglas snorted. "You're not half so appealing."

They stayed against the far wall of the laboratory, out of the way. Cathal watched Sophia as she cast her eyes about the place, looking over vials empty and full, cold braziers and unused mortars. She bit her lip in thought, then nodded, as if in response to words only she could hear.

"I'll need the gold chalice," she said. "It should be in my trunk, near the top. If you'll put me down in front of the table—" She broke off and frowned down at her hands.

"No." Cathal nudged Douglas in the side. "I'll hold it for you." That felt right, though he couldn't have said why: a half-remembered lesson of his youth, perhaps. "Get me over there."

Douglas started to object, then fell silent. His eyes sharpened, reminding Cathal of their father's. "Aye, that might help. Considering."

He didn't say what he was considering. Cathal didn't

have the energy to ask. His hands were clumsy with the trunk's simple latch, and raising the lid left him pale and sweating. Thank Christ, the goblet in its white silk wrappings was at the top. If he'd had to dig through the trunk's contents, he might have lost consciousness. The trip back across the room felt as though it took an age.

"Are you *certain* he's well?" Sophia asked, giving Douglas a stern, searching look. "My lord" was clearly an afterthought, and not a very heartfelt one.

"Nothing's certain, madam, as I imagine you know well. But I'm sure that the danger has passed."

"I only need rest," Cathal said, not because he had any way to be certain, but because the worried look on Sophia's face was a blight in itself.

Both wounded, each supported by another, they held each other's gaze across the table. That wasn't enough, but it was sufficient. Sophia was the first to smile, Cathal not far behind.

He pulled off the wrapping and twined his hands around the stem of the goblet. Already the metal was warmer than it should have been. Cathal had the sense of a presence, the idea of a hum or a breeze, as he held the goblet out and up so that Sophia could reach it.

For just a few breaths, he saw her lips move, forming words in a language he didn't think he knew. Then she put one glowing hand on each side of the chalice's bowl, and the rust-colored aura began to vanish.

The metal itself looked the same. Even when Sophia's hands only looked mortal again, illuminated by nothing other than the pallid morning sunlight, there was no change in the goblet itself. It shone a little, but only the light of sun on metal, and Cathal knew alarm. Had they failed at the last? Had they done the wrong thing?

Sophia smiled again, and her whole face lit with the expression. "Look," she said, and lowered the goblet.

The bowl, which had been both empty and dry, was half-full. The contents reminded Cathal of wine, somewhat faded, or of November leaves, except that they still glowed. He could see the sides of the bowl clearly.

With immense care, aware of every motion of his hands, he put the goblet back down on the table. "Do we take it to Fergus now?"

Sophia shook her head. "We have his soul... He'll need that which lets it settle back into the body. The first potion I made for him, I believe, or a version of it, and that I fear, will take a few days longer." She looked down at herself and made a face. "Nor can I do it with such a recent wound. The influences would be entirely wrong."

"You'll have your few days," Douglas said. "Now that Albert is gone, it's only Fergus's body we need to worry about. That's lasted until now."

"And I'll see to it that he endures long enough." Madoc smiled and shrugged, as much as one could shrug with an armful of woman. "The ways of my people are older even than this castle. Mastery of most is beyond me, but what I do know will, I think, suffice to be a safeguard in this case."

"Good," said Cathal. It was one of a few words that remained within his grasp. His head was drooping, his eyelids lowering.

"*Cathal*," said Sophia, checking herself in a forward motion that would likely have upset Madoc's balance entirely.

He smiled at her again and brought forth the other word that came to him. "Bed."

FORTY-ONE

THREE DAYS LATER, SOPHIA SAW CATHAL AGAIN FOR THE first time.

After they'd both been carried away to separate beds, Sophia had slept, *truly* slept, for a day and a half, then woke to Donnag's wondering ministrations, Alice's brusque relief, and her weight in bread, butter, and honey, with a fish stew afterward.

Alice's ankle was recovering, but she still could do no more than hobble a few feet on crutches. It hadn't improved her temper at all—"I'm glad you didn't *gravely injure yourself* while you were gone," was the first thing she'd said after she'd embraced Sophia and they'd both wept a little—but she'd occupied herself with writing down the songs and legends she'd learned at the castle. "I'm thinking I'll become a wandering scribe," she said. "It can't possibly be any worse."

When Sophia reached the part in her story about staying in the inn with Cathal and skipped straight from there to her decision to hunt Albert in dreams, she knew she blushed, and she knew Alice could read her face. That hadn't changed. But Alice looked at her silently, smiled, and asked, "What happened then?"

Sophia told her. Alice shivered over the description of the castle, made properly repulsed noises at Albert's appearance, and shook her head at the end of it all. "Vile excuse for a man. I agree with Lord MacAlasdair. The world's better for not having him in it."

"Yes," Sophia said sincerely. She felt the weight of

her deeds on her and suspected she ever would, that she would carry the memory of his screaming dissolution to her dying day. That was right. Albert had been a person once, and even good deeds shouldn't happen lightly when they involved human life. But she meant what she'd said, and it was a comfort to her in itself.

She'd discovered a potion, and she'd pared away a bad part of the world. In doing so, she hoped, she'd made life better for Gilleis, Harry, and the frightened people of their lands as well. Whoever inherited could be no worse than Albert. Plenty of people had accomplished less in their lives.

Yet what she'd told Douglas was still true. Whatever came later, Sophia still had one great task immediately in front of her, and it was no trifle.

When she could leave her bed, she went to the laboratory. There, at the proper hours, she distilled and recalcified, measured and ground. There, at the proper hours, she prayed. There, in her brief free time, she ate and slept. Except for servants with trays of food, none disturbed her. "Douglas gave orders," Alice said when she intercepted a servant and brought food. "And I wouldn't defy that man for all the riches of the Orient."

"I don't *need* the riches of the Orient," said Sophia, who was beginning to think of a few matters on which she'd risk Douglas's displeasure.

Douglas's orders were one of the reasons she was surprised to come out of her laboratory and find him standing there, calm and still. "Are you finished for the moment?" he asked. "I would speak with you."

"Yes, of course," she said, "though not inside... The mixture's at a sensitive stage. Is Cathal all right? I know his method of coming to my aid was an unfamiliar one, and if there's anything I can do—"

Douglas held up a hand. "No. That is, he's hale enough to plague those nearby. He's not a man for idleness, my brother. Though not a man for the wars these days either, I'm suspecting."

The direction he was going was obvious. Sophia considered saying that Cathal hadn't told her of a decision one way or the other, then thought that his proposal likely counted, *then* wondered if he'd expect her to come on Crusade with him. All the while, remembering both the proposal and the circumstances surrounding it had her blushing fiercely, and she settled for just asking, "My lord?"

"Ach, for heaven's sake. Marry the man."

"I—"

"If he's not asked yet, tell me and I'll beat him until he finds the courage. I know damned well he wants to. The entire *castle* knows it."

Sophia bit her lip. "He has, my lord. I told him I wanted to, but I wished to give us both time to think. Him especially. It was…a situation in which I didn't know that we were thinking clearly," she said, feeling quite able to boil water on her face, "and I know that he has many duties."

"Ha," said Douglas, rolling his eyes. "He's done more of his duty in the last five years than the rest of his life combined. If he marries a girl with a sound head and a good spirit, I'd call it a damned miracle. The castle will be in good hands, should he leave," he added, and went on before Sophia could speak in Cathal's defense, "and I'll talk Artair around. Not that I'd imagine it'll take much. The youngest child's hand in marriage *is* generally the prize for services like yours in tales…but you're not getting half our lands. They're small enough as it is."

He turned then, a man who'd discharged one duty on a list of fifty that day, and left Sophia stunned and blinking.

The next day she woke at dawn to the bath she'd requested, then to a white linen gown that was doubtless another of Agnes's castoffs. Sophia didn't bother taking this one in, simply rolling up the sleeves and kilting the skirt before she went back to the laboratory. She stopped a page on the way.

"Tell Sir Cathal he can expect me a little after noon," she said, barely noticing how the Gaelic came from her lips now. "Assuming, of course, that nothing goes amiss."

Sophia knew that he stared at her, and that he kept staring after she left, but the knowledge was remote and immaterial. The possibility of *amiss* worried her a good deal more, but she didn't dare dwell on that either. She focused on the details instead: each breath and footstep, then the weight of mortar and pestle or the circulation of steam.

This time she was more careful of the angle when she poured the topaz into the potion, but it turned out that she didn't need to be. The flame stayed low and spread out, covering the mouth of the goblet from edge to edge, and its heat wasn't as fierce as the other had been.

This is right, she thought, knowing it as she'd known that this potion, altered *so* and *thus*, was the way to reintroduce Fergus's soul to his body. Such knowing had been easier ever since she'd come back from the aether—no mysterious certainty, but rather as if she were a seamstress considering a dress, knowing that the line she wanted required such a set of the sleeves.

She wondered if that was how Cathal felt about battle. She wanted to ask him. There was, Sophia was finding, no end to the things she wanted to ask him.

When she carried the potion into Fergus's room, Cathal's face was briefly the only thing she saw.

Soon enough her mind recalled itself to her purpose. She looked to Fergus, pale and unconscious on the bed, and she thought of Douglas and Sithaeg waiting a few yards outside the door, just far enough for probable safety. Sithaeg had darted one look upward as Sophia passed. Her eyes had been frozen rivers, torrents forcibly held in abeyance.

Sithaeg's expression was enough to damp the giddiness uncurling within Sophia's chest, but only barely. Had she doubted, it might have hit harder, but she came to Fergus's side with the cup in her hands and the craftsman's certainty of his masterpiece.

It didn't make her careless. She knelt slowly and smoothly. The potion rippled with her movements, and little waves hit the sides of the goblet, but not a drop spilled over. On the other side of the bed, Cathal propped Fergus up with equal concentration. Their movements took on a rhythm, a call-and-response. The narrow bed and the man within it became the center of a ritual no less formal than any official rite.

A wedding, for instance.

Sophia didn't blush to think about it any longer, nor did she instantly reject the notion as impossible. The thought was there, and there it sat, while she tipped the goblet carefully forward, felt the potion's weight shift within it, and watched Fergus's throat to see that he swallowed and didn't choke.

Halfway through, that all became much more difficult.

The warmth Sophia remembered from the first potion bloomed in the air around Fergus then, and the chord without a source filled the room. Neither ended this time, but grew until the heat was almost unpleasant and the beauty of the sound nigh unbearable. Mortal frames were no more meant for such joy than fragile glass was meant to hold hot liquid. There would come a moment of breaking, regardless of goodness or courage on either part.

Sophia held on. She saw Cathal's hands, tight around his friend's shoulders. The sight helped her will steadiness into her own arms, and she had the sense that it went both ways, each of them giving strength to the other.

A glow like sunrise unfurled itself just over Fergus's heart. It swept over him, giving radiance to every inch of his wasted body and all the pale skin that showed over the bedclothes. Where his arms and legs had been solid but withered from disuse, they gained flesh, until he looked no worse than a winter of idleness might have left him. The light moved upward, giving substance to his neck and face, settled in pools onto his closed eyes, and finally covered the top of his head.

All the room was still. Stillness was all. Either word or act was unthinkable, though Sophia yet retained enough idle curiosity to wonder if the whole world had gone quiet. It felt possible, and if it were so, fitting.

The chord swelled and faded. The glow died. Both were swift, yet gradual, not the abrupt end of an unfinished process but a due conclusion to all that had come before.

Fergus opened ruddy-brown eyes, more than a trifle dazed but as full of life as Sophia's own. He blinked up at Sophia, then at Cathal. "Christ's wounds," he said, his voice little more than a whisper. "You did it."

"*She* did it," said Cathal. "I helped a bit."

He sprinted to the door, and Fergus turned to Sophia, moving slowly and awkwardly, yet not with the impediments she would have expected from a man so long inactive. "I saw you. Here, once, but also…wherever he had me."

"Yes," Sophia said. She put the empty goblet down on the nearby table. Soon, she'd clean it with all due reverence...or as much as one mostly ignorant human woman knew how to provide. She was beaming; she didn't think she could stop. "He's gone."

"I'd bloody think. Who are you?"

"Sophia Metzger. I came here from France, while you were—" She gestured. "I'm an alchemist. And a sort of magician now, perhaps."

Fergus shook his head, but never got to say what was on his mind. Sithaeg rushed through the door then, moving like a woman half her age, and threw her arms around her son.

The time for explanations was past, or yet to come. Sophia slipped through the crowd and out of the room, making her way to the small door that led outside.

Winter's chill yet lingered, and the rising sun hadn't had much time to warm the air, but Sophia stood on the battlements and could feel spring approaching. The breeze that ruffled her wimple was gentler, lacking the knife-edge of winter days, and she could see a few brave leaves unfurling on the trees below her.

Come spring, Loch Arach might actually be rather beautiful.

Fergus would live to see it. In time, Sophia would tell him how, or Cathal would. For the moment, she was minded to let him *have* the moment: the reunion with his loved ones, the simple joy of living once more.

The landscape in front of her blurred, and she wiped her eyes—on her sleeve, as she'd not had the foresight to bring a handkerchief, but nobody was there to see.

A strong arm sliding around her waist proved her wrong, and so did a kiss on the back of her neck. "My love," Cathal said, "just say the word, and I'll take you home."

She turned and laid her head against his shoulder, welcoming the shelter of both his body and his cloak. Spring was coming, but her gown was thin. "Would it be home for you too, if you did?" She was bold enough to ask it on that morning of triumph. "I do love you…but, or perhaps so, I'd not bind you to one place if you'd rather wander again."

Cathal rested his head on top of hers. "Lass," he said, "the place where you are is home enough for me. And being with you is journey enough as well."

Light filled her until she could have floated with it, or sung songs of praise to the four corners of the earth. To avoid alarming the guards, who stood a fair distance away but probably would have still heard her, she settled for practicality. "My parents' home, then, for a start," she said, thinking that—if all went well—they'd have many years to travel too. More than any human would have been gifted. "When the roads and the seas are better. It would alarm the city to have you fly in, you know, and I don't know how Alice would feel about such a journey."

He laughed, joyous as a youth. "We travel the mortal way, then."

"Well…" Sophia remembered the night clear and blue around her and the stars almost in her reach. "This time."

Cathal pulled back just enough to let her see his smile. He leaned down and kissed her then. Breathless, she put her arms around his neck, and they stood there for a long time, with the spring morning rose and golden behind them.

Keep reading for a sneak peek of

HIGHLAND DRAGON REBEL

*Available November 2017
from Sourcebooks Casablanca*

1320

MOST MEN CALLED FOR SOMEONE AT THE END.
Mother was popular. God, Christ, the Virgin, and various
saints all received their share of pleas. Occasionally, dying lips
shaped themselves to a specific name: a lover, a child, a sibling.

Moiread had never heard a man ask for the one who'd led
him into battle.

In the minds of the dying, she'd done enough.

The field far below her was sodden red, good growing land churned into dirt by hundreds of desperate feet.
It would recover eventually and bear all the richer for the
day's work. Blood improved the earth—her grandfather had
made sacrifices along those lines in his day—and most of
this blood came from Englishmen, which lessened any loss
she might have felt.

Fee, fau, fum, she thought as she flew high above the
carnage, remembering giants in children's tales. Giants
and monsters: all took a great deal of effort to kill, and the
English hadn't had a Jack with them that day.

For her, the battle had gone well. Oh, she'd taken a slash to her belly that stung like the devil, and an arrow had nicked the tip of her right wing, but both wounds had come from normal steel. A good night's sleep would heal them. She'd dodged the few glowing crossbow bolts that would have done her more lasting damage, and her fiery breaths had hit the English armies hard in return. It was rarely practical for the MacAlasdairs to take dragon shape in battle, but when they could manage it, they generally left a mark.

She folded her wings and dropped, landing near the back of the army. In the second before she changed back to human form, with its less acute senses, the stench of burnt flesh was almost overpowering.

Then she was herself. The smell wasn't so bad. The screaming was worse. When she was human, it was easier to understand the words.

"M'lady," said Angus, her second-in-command, meeting her as she walked out into the camp proper, "'tis good to have you back."

"Our count?"

"Ten dead, six as good as, twelve injured." That was only among the hundred or so of Loch Arach's men-at-arms. Two other lords and their men had fought with Moiread against the English, there by a stream whose name she couldn't call to mind right then. "Young Lord Murray got a poleax to the back of the head. His priest's with him. He'll last a few hours yet."

A man was crying nearby. His sobbing sounded faint and twisted, but not wet the way it would have been from an arrow to the lungs. *Gut wound*, Moiread thought. "The English?"

"Mostly fled. Fifty hale prisoners, twice that wounded. Lord Fraser's for killing them all...says the English aren't likely to pay any ransom, considering."

"That they aren't," said Moiread slowly.

Slaughtering prisoners was poor form. It wouldn't be the first battle since Berwick where it had been done, nor other acts that Moiread preferred not to think about. Men drunk on victory and rage were unpleasant creatures, and hard to rule. The MacAlasdairs, not being entirely mortal, had an easier time keeping their soldiers in line, but there was always a struggle.

She flexed her hands. "I'd rather not spill more blood today. I'll see what I can do. First, I'll see Murray."

The young lord had been a pleasant companion, decent at dice and fair of voice. He'd taken both her feminine nature and her draconic one in stride after the first shock. Even if none of that had been true, he was a lord. Rank meant standing at each other's deathbed.

He was likely the lone dying man, out of the hundreds on the field—out of the thousands over the course of the whole bloody war—for whom Moiread's presence would make any difference at all.

ONE

Scotland, 1328

HOME.

"Praise God!" said Angus, and although Moiread didn't share his vocal devotion, her silent thanks were equally heartfelt. She could have kissed the dark walls of MacAlasdair Castle like a sailor returning to land. She settled for an ear-to-ear grin and a yell that made the guards at the gate straighten up in alarm before they saw her face.

It wasn't just that she'd been away for more than twenty years. It wasn't just that she was coming home victorious. The damn sky had opened for the last two days of her journey back. Her cloak had struggled valiantly before giving up and now hung like a giant sponge across her shoulders and down her back. Her mail would need hours of polishing, and the damp leather beneath the chain had been chafing her for the last ten miles. Her boots were squashy, and the fat, elderly plow horse she rode was up to her fat, elderly hocks in mud.

Even if Moiread wanted to abandon her men, she couldn't have flown in that weather. Between the gusts of wind and not being able to see more than a foot in front of her face, she'd probably have ended up in Rome. And while dragon blood meant that cold and wet wouldn't harm her like they would mortals, it didn't make them more pleasant.

But up ahead were stone walls to keep out the rain, a roast turning on a roaring fire, and her room, full of clean, dry clothing, another fire, and—praise Christ and all the saints in heaven—a *bed*.

She grinned at the bowing guards as she passed them—too slowly for her tastes, but the horse had served her well and she didn't want to strain it—waved to the servants in the great courtyard, and practically jumped out of the saddle with more spirit than she'd had since midway through Yorkshire.

"Have her rubbed down well and give her a hot mash," she told the stableboy, a lanky redhead who'd probably been toddling when she left. "We've been a long time traveling."

"Aye, Lady...Moiread?"

Clearly he'd picked up the name from the older grooms talking around him. Or he'd seen the soggy banner her men carried and realized there was only one MacAlasdair woman likely to ride in at the head of a company. Moiread laughed. "That's the one, lad," she said, and extracted a coin from her belt pouch. "Don't worry... You'll have a chance to get used to me this time."

Now free of the horse, she made good speed to the inner door. A number of smells filled the staircase beyond, but the castle was clean, and food odors were the strongest: bread and meat. It was just past lambing season, Moiread remembered, and her stomach growled at the notion, sounding nearly as loud as her own roar could be in her other shape.

"Lady Moiread!"

One of the maids rushed up to her and dipped into a curtsy, the top of her blond head coming briefly to Moiread's waist. It didn't rise above her chest when the girl stood either. She was a short one, and Moiread was taller than most men.

"Aye," she said, trying to remember how to talk to servants who weren't also fighting men. The maid was a few years older than the stableboy, Moiread thought, but nonetheless young—nobody she'd have known ten years ago, and that visit had been a short one. "I'll want a fire in my room and a bath."

God's wounds, but it was a relief to make such requests freely, knowing that she wasn't condemning a brace of footmen to sudden and intense labor. At most of the places where she'd been quartered, from farmhouse to castle, baths meant dragging tin tubs up a flight or two of stairs, then heating buckets of water and carrying them as well. For the MacAlasdairs, sorcery made those matters considerably easier.

"Yes, m'lady. Your father's given orders for both already."

"Did he? Good man." Her scouts would have given Artair warning, even without divination, but Moiread's father was always busy and not always prompt about passing his knowledge on to the housekeeper. This time the dice seemed to have come up in Moiread's favor.

The maid nodded. "Only he says to tell you, m'lady, that you're to dine in the hall tonight."

"Oh."

Moiread shoved a splotch of wet hair off her forehead and thought less charitable, less filial things. *I just got home!* was one, and *I hope he doesn't expect three coherent words out of me* another.

"There are guests, m'lady, from Wales."

"And Artair doesn't think he can entertain them by himself? The world may be ending." The maid kept tactful silence on that. Moiread couldn't blame her. "Very well. Tell the laird my father that I am, of course, at his service. I'll even try to look civilized for the occasion, though I can't promise not to fall asleep in my soup if it goes too late."

"My lady," the maid said and curtsied again before

nipping off to tell Lord Artair a most likely *heavily* altered version of Moiread's sentiments.

Artair would probably translate them back into the original adeptly enough. Being family for more than two centuries provided them with a private master language of their own.

Dripping her way up two flights of stairs, Moiread wondered idly what Welshmen were so important that Artair had demanded her company for the occasion. Her mother's people had ties to the country, but Wales had been under English rule for decades, having lost to the same bastard excuse for a king who'd tried to take Moiread's own country.

Longshanks must have spun in his grave when his stripling grandson signed the treaty with Scotland. The idea still made Moiread smile, the better part of a year later.

No, the prospect of a formal dinner couldn't lower her mood, not with that memory fresh to take out and polish. She'd have that story to dine on, and she'd eat better than she had in months. Meanwhile, the fire in her hearth already warmed the room, a metal tub of water stood steaming in front of it, and two maids were waiting nearby.

Quickly, they plucked Moiread clean of cloak, belt, and boots. The mail gave them a moment of trouble—they were used to waiting on ladies, not soldiers—but they took instruction well and Moiread wore her hair short to some purpose. In little time, she was naked, ignoring the way the girls stared at her scars, and easing herself into the hot water.

"Welcome back, lady," said one of the maids.

Moiread sighed with pleasure. Odd how being surrounded by water was so vile when it was cold and near bliss when it was hot. She flexed her toes against the end of the tub and leaned her head back on the other rim. "I am never leaving again."

MacAlasdair Castle hadn't changed a great deal in twenty years.

A few of the tapestries in the great hall had been replaced; a hunting scene now hung where Madoc remembered the martyrdom of Saint Sebastian. Outside was rainy late spring rather than snowy early spring, with brave buds beginning to show themselves on the trees, but that was due to the time of year rather than the years gone past.

The long, dark-walled hall with its high ceiling was the same, of course, as were the heavy tables lining it. Those probably hadn't changed in generations, let alone mere decades. A fire roared in the hearth, necessary for most of Scotland's year. The people also looked the same: mostly small and dark, a few outliers, brisk and busy and talking quickly in Gaelic the whole time.

Most dressed in the *léine*, the long shirt, and trews, with plaid cloaks pinned around their necks. Except for the reds and blues of the plaids themselves, their clothing was dark or undyed wool. On the dais beside Madoc, Artair and Douglas were brighter figures, their layers of robes and the fur at the neck and wrists proclaiming their wealth, but their clothing was as it might have been for half a century, without the changes Madoc had heard about from the French court.

Well that might be. The MacAlasdairs' blood had mingled with that of a dragon's far in the past, and fifty years could be a blink of an eye even to Douglas. It certainly was to his sire. Madoc didn't remember a time when he hadn't heard of Artair and his brood, and he himself aged slower than most men, though without the MacAlasdairs' other gifts.

Artair—immense, gaunt, and white-topped, like a

mountain taken human shape—was a change. He'd not been present in person on Madoc's last visit and now sat at the head of the table, rarely speaking but nonetheless holding all eyes either on him or ready to glance his way at a moment's notice. His younger son, Cathal, and the woman Cathal had taken to wife were absent, off in France, as was the lady Douglas had taken hostage during the first and least successful bout of their war with England.

In almost all other respects, the castle was as it had been, and Madoc was glad of it. Change was as inevitable and as obvious as a spring flood almost everywhere else, and while he bent to it, he welcomed the chance to linger in a steadier place.

"Oh yes," he replied to Douglas, drawing himself back from memory and picking up their conversation again. "It's been that wet the last few summers. We've had a struggle getting any sort of stores in, and the crops themselves have been poorly. My father's for clearing more of the forest. He says that way we can maybe sell the wood, and the land opened up may be richer."

"Could be," said Douglas, "but forest land is a tricky sort, even without the trees. Here it's half rocks, best kept for pigs and deer."

Neither he nor Artair said so, but Madoc suspected it also gave them concealment. Men like Artair wouldn't want their villeins seeing all they did—or all they were.

Even without those considerations, he'd have preferred to believe Douglas. Lord Rhys, Madoc's father, was probably right. Opening the forest to more fields was the practical thing to do and best for their people…and yet Madoc had too many memories of playing in the forest as a child or hunting in it as a young man. He loved its twisting pathways, the shadows beneath the trees, and he could never quite be easy with the idea of diminishing them, however slightly.

But this is no easy world, is it?

He sighed and distracted himself by spearing a slice of pork as the platter came by. The MacAlasdairs hadn't stinted on their hospitality during his last visit, in the middle of war and soon after winter, and the changes since had been for the better.

Madoc was about to say as much, phrased more diplomatically, when movement from the lower tables caught his eye. Those seated were turning, a few nudging their neighbors to take their attention from food or conversation, all looking toward a tall, slim figure striding up the hall toward the dais. Thus alerted, his companions on the dais turned as well, and Artair smiled. "Ah, good."

Paternal affection suited his predator's face oddly, but it was also unmistakable.

Just as unmistakably, the woman approaching was of his line. She almost had Madoc's height. He thought they would see eye to eye, or nearly, and he was a tall man for any people but the MacAlasdairs. For a woman, she was broad-shouldered, with full breasts and slim hips, and she carried herself like one used to bearing the weight of armor. Just then, she wore only linen and wool: a blue-gray kirtle and a rich, blue overgown embroidered with white flowers. Above the fabric, her skin was winter pale but with shades of olive, her hair glossy dark brown and short as a page's, curling slightly below her ears.

"My younger daughter," said Artair, rising as the woman reached the dais and curtsied. "Moiread, lass, 'tis well to have you back home."

He gave her a quick embrace, kissing each cheek. Douglas, farther away, stood and bowed, smiling warmly.

"It's good to be back, Father." She had a pleasant, smooth soprano voice. She also had Artair's ice-blue eyes, but her gaze was both amused and weary. "Douglas, you're looking well. And my lord"—she curtsied to Madoc—"I take it you're the reason I'm keeping myself awake for a few hours."

"Madoc, heir to Avondos," said Artair, while Madoc was trying to decide whether Moiread had meant to be suggestive. If she hadn't spoken so straightforwardly, and if her father and her brother hadn't been so close at hand, his thoughts could well have gone along those lines in a more decided fashion.

Later, he told himself firmly. *Think on that later*.

ABOUT THE AUTHOR

Isabel Cooper lives in Boston in an apartment with two houseplants, an inordinate number of stairs, a silver sword, and a basket of sequined fruit. By day, she works as a theoretically mild-mannered legal editor; by night, she tries to sleep. She has a house in the country, but hopes she doesn't encounter mysterious and handsome strangers nearby, as vacation generally involves a lot of fuzzy bathrobes.

ALSO BY ISABEL COOPER

Dark Powers
No Proper Lady
Lessons After Dark

Highland Dragons
Legend of the Highland Dragon
The Highland Dragon's Lady
Night of the Highland Dragon

Dawn of the Highland Dragon
Highland Dragon Warrior